THE WINTER KEY

BLOOD LEGACY SERIES BOOK 2

ELISE HENNESSY

Flutterbye Trail Press
797 Sam Bass Road #2541
Round Rock, TX 78681

First edition

Editing by Red Loop Editing
Cover Design by FrostAlexis Arts
E-book Chapter Art by Real Life Design
Published by Flutterbye Trail Press

ISBN: 978-1-7345137-4-5 (E-book)
ISBN: 978-1-7345137-5-2 (Print)
LCCN: 2020912340

Feedback: Encounter a problem with this book? Let us know at
elisehennessyauthor@gmail.com

Books by Elise Hennessy

Books in the Altare World

GRYPHON RIDER ACADEMY
Second Chance
Chosen
Storm Front
Wild Flight

ROYAL SPY INSTITUTE
The Crown Heist
Five & Chance

Also by Elise Hennessy

BLOOD LEGACY SERIES
Dream Walker
The Winter Key
Queen's Return
Court of Illusions
Shadow Dance
Rule the Night
Dhampir's Wish

Blood Curse
Blood Legacy: The Complete Series

The Winter Key

Blood Legacy Series Book 2

Elise Hennessy

Chapter 1
Julian

Julian Fairfax planned to break more laws in one night than he had in over three centuries of straitlaced existence. To vampires, laws were more akin to polite suggestions unless backed up by force. Until Julian found himself in an abandoned subway tunnel, strapped from head-to-toe with enough weaponry to take down an army, he'd always toed the line. He followed the Deveaux Accords for fear of the wrath of the largest and eldest coven in New York City coming not only for him but also for the men and women he'd served and protected for so long.

No longer. He'd left his coven out of necessity, saying goodbye to his friends so his actions would not be traced back to them. If anyone were to be punished for what he was about to do, it would be him and only him.

He passed by a wall tagged with faded, teal spray paint. Edging around a corner, he found another tunnel full of rubble on ancient, rusted tracks. He picked his way around the worst of it, his focus farther in. Dubbed "Bloodhound" for his supernatural ability, Julian could sense the location of anyone whose blood he'd tasted.

Tonight, he focused on the woman Kimberly Cox, an unpleasant vampiress he'd managed to bite a couple months prior. Married to the equally vile man who led the coven living underground like a horde of sewer rats, Cox still resided in the place Julian needed to find most.

Haven headquarters. So named after the giant media company, Haven, long cultivated by Bryant Collins, Haven's coven master.

Collins and Cox rarely left their underground fortress hidden deep within a warren of old subway tunnels. And why should they? Referencing the Deveaux Accords, attacking a vampire in the safe space of their main headquarters was subject to equal and opposite force being used against the attacker's coven. Harsh but necessary to prevent all-out coven warfare and the risk it would bring in exposing vampires to the mortal world.

Within the vault of Haven's central home was someone Julian dearly wished to meet. He didn't know her name, only her face, which hovered in the back of his mind like a fever dream. A woman in her late twenties with curly brown hair and a constellation of freckles over a button nose. She was in danger because of him, and they didn't know each other yet.

He shook his thoughts away, focusing on putting one leg in front of the other. He was about as quiet as a knight in full armor, each step heavy with the stiffness in his limbs. With his teeth clenched tightly to prevent shivers, he was freezing down in this tunnel despite the lingering summer heat.

The cold, he recognized, somehow came from himself. Some parting gift from his run-in with a Sorceress determined to punish him for the sins of his past. He soldiered through, sure it would thaw and melt away given enough time. The kind of time he couldn't spare away from the mission at hand.

Julian drew a dagger from his side as he heard a dull thud echo from up ahead. He'd come to rely on this weapon for stealth, gunshots too loud and noticeable to fellow vampires' preternatural hearing. Shuffling to another bend in the path, he peered around as he picked up the sound of a fist smacking flesh.

A woman's silhouette pinned a man to a wall scribbled with graffiti. Twin streams of blood leaked from his nostrils as he shot her a baleful look. He choked out a curse, his face shading to an unflattering purple. "You gonna talk now, tough guy?" the woman asked, her voice low and full of menace.

"I told you...I ain't squealing..."

"Wrong answer." Without lifting a finger, she had his lips parting in silent agony as his hands flew from her iron grip on his neck to pulling locks of hair from his scalp.

Julian stepped out into the open, having seen enough. He had a good idea of who she was, even though he hadn't seen her in nearly two decades. "Phantom," he said, recognizing her face as she whipped toward him in surprise. She was someone who used to walk the outskirts of his coven's territory as an agent and body-guard of a rival coven master.

What was she doing here? He recalled she used to serve Coven Rosas, who had no strife with Haven. She bared twin fangs at him, half the length of an adult vampire's. By virtue of being a dhampir, a half-human, half-vampire, she wielded one blood ability with terrifying effectiveness. He'd been on the receiving end of a couple psychic shrieks from her, powerful enough to bring him to his knees. He approached her warily.

"Bloodhound," the Havener sputtered, trembling as he caught sight of Julian as well.

"Don't suppose a Lion like you wouldn't mind softening a guy up for me?" She shot the Havener a look of disgust. Referencing the lion insignia Julian used to wear for his old coven was a way of pinning his classification.

If he were to call her out the same way, he'd reference her as a Rose...a symbol she was not wearing. So, they were both rogues, chancing upon each other by sheer luck. "Out of curiosity, what did he do to you?" he asked. His Italian accent rolled the words off his tongue.

"This particular idiot belongs to an organization that kidnapped my best friend, and I intend to get her back." She propped a fist on her hip. This close, Julian could make out her dark leather against skin a shade of brown that was perfect for blending into the shadows of the night. Chocolate-brown eyes flashed with determination.

"Your best friend," he echoed, wondering if she was the very same woman he sought to save.

Phantom turned back to her quarry with a scoff. "Where is she?" She leaned into his face with the demand, open mouth suggesting another shriek would be coming if he didn't tell her what he wanted.

"What does your friend look like?" Julian asked. Both looked his way, the Havener mid-answer just to gape at him instead. His mouth snapped shut.

She bristled with annoyance. "Do you mind?"

He kept going despite how it looked like he would soon be on the receiving end of her painful ability. "Is she of above average height, brunette...curly hair? A little like yours?" Phantom had pinned her curls into a ponytail, which bobbed from side to side as she narrowed her eyes at him.

"You sound like a creep right now, Bloodhound," she said.

"You answer my question, and I'll get this guy to sing." He gestured to the Havener, who shook his head rapidly.

He had heard that Collins fired anyone Julian managed to bite to prevent the very thing he sought to do. Tracking them back to their headquarters, to finally locate it after so many long years. Maybe that wouldn't happen to this man now that Cox was amongst those bitten, but it was obvious that his status as Bloodhound preceded him. "Then yeah, that's what she looks like," Phantom said after a few moments.

They *were* looking for the same person, then. He took a few steps closer, looked into the bloodshot eyes of the man she'd been interrogating, and reached forward with his mental influence. Vampires had a way to briefly control or charm mortals by using mind control, a psychic ability they all shared. It grew stronger over time. Usually, it was used to make someone forget they'd had a chance encounter with someone with teeth like hypodermic needles. It could also be used to turn a younger vampire into a thrall.

The victim would be forced to do the bidding of his master until dismissed. He knew from experience that being a puppet for another person was straight from a horror show. It was the only way to get this man to talk anytime soon if he'd already taken a couple shrieks from the Phantom without breaking. That didn't mean Julian didn't second-guess everything about his decision to pry into this unfortunate man's mind.

The other vampire's will broke to Julian's with ease. He was a young vampire, then. The spark of conscious thought in his gaze faded to blank obedience as he awaited his first order. "Where is she?" Julian asked.

"N-not here." The last vestiges of the other man's self-control faded with a twitch. "The boss moved her to Haven Tower."

Julian cursed under his breath. He'd wasted hours trekking this far into the tunnels for nothing. "Where's Haven Tower?" Phantom asked.

The only response she got from the other vampire was a little smile. As Julian's unwilling thrall, he would only be forced to answer anything Julian asked, and he at least knew that much. "Is she unharmed?" he asked instead, considering he already knew where the landmark was.

"Yes. She...she's supposed to be bait."

"For me," he said, because he knew how Haven worked. The other man bobbed his head with a heavy swallow.

"The boss was sure you would come storming straight at us. We're ready for you down here." Meaning they were quite willing to turn these tunnels into a death warren while Julian chased the memory of a face and a feeling.

He kept picking the Havener's mind, finding he didn't know much more. Stationed down here to scout, he'd been found by Phantom before he could relay any information to his fellows. If it weren't for her, Julian would've been spotted and forced to fight his way through Haven in futility.

"Thanks," he muttered, knocking the other man unconscious with a well-placed punch.

Turning around, he started climbing back toward where he started. Quiet footsteps followed. "I'm coming with you," Phantom said.

He grunted, not attempting to outpace her. He needed to

keep his strength up for storming Haven Tower. "You will be a liability," he said.

"I almost forgot how much I hated full-blood vamps like you." Her voice rose angrily. "Look, just because I'm only half a vamp doesn't mean I'll slow you down. I was good enough for Rosas for nearly—"

He whirled around, fangs bared. "You keep yelling and they'll find out we've been here. You want that?" he hissed.

"I'm just saying," she muttered.

He waited until the echoes of their voices faded. It was unlikely he'd be able to shake her, much as he wanted to continue his mission alone. He searched for the words to explain that he was willing to do just about anything to ensure her friend's safety, including killing several Haveners on the way or laying down his own life, an extreme he didn't expect her to match. Feeling like rubber in his mouth, his tongue slipped around the words. He'd never been one for talk rather than action, leaving the eloquent explanations to his friends gifted with such things.

He felt her gaze burning on his back as he led the way without clarifying a thing. "Why do you care about my friend anyway?" she eventually asked, keeping her voice hushed.

He did the same as he responded. "You would not believe me if I told you." He kept his gaze roving over every mound of rubble and wandering the ceiling and walls, searching for any hint of a hidden camera he'd missed on the way down.

"Try me." He imagined her squaring her chest, defiance painting both words.

How could she believe what he'd been through? He hardly trusted his own memories. His silence must've bothered her, because she spoke up again before he did. "Because I've lived with her for two years, and not once did she get a visit from the Bloodhound or receive any sign that she might have some sort of secret admirer."

"That's because we haven't met yet. I'm on a mission to save her." Even as he said it, he knew how it sounded.

"Yet you don't know her name," she pointed out.

"Would you like to fill that gap in my knowledge? Considering I may be taking you to Haven Tower."

As he took a bend in the path, he caught a glimpse of her crossing her arms. "Tell me why you're on a mission to save someone you don't know first."

He took a deep breath, blowing it out his nose. "She's my life-mate." Someone he'd searched the world for many times in his long years. The perfect match to him, the woman destined to be his soul mate.

He scowled as she muffled a hail of mocking laughter. "Yeah, okay. Sure. What's your proof?"

"You wouldn't believe it," he repeated. "And no, I'm not going to 'try you' on this one. You'll just have to see for yourself." His experiences were too raw. And besides, if she knew the truth, she'd think he was truly insane. He set his teeth against the cold and told himself he'd see, too, when he beheld this mystery woman for the first time.

Chapter 2
Olivia

Olivia Cooper had gotten far in the past by feigning an interested expression and great enthusiasm. She figured in the midst of a kidnapping, she would need to pull out all her tricks. At first, she didn't know why she'd been placed in the back of a car like a sack of potatoes, hog-tied and beaten, but she made sure to use the fact that they'd ripped the tape off of her mouth once she was safely contained. Anything she could do for herself from then on out, she would. She didn't want to be another statistic.

Even with a shiner threatening to seal her right eye shut, she'd made small talk with the driver, a lonely vampire named Ron who'd been tasked with the job of moving her on his own. They were going to New York City, he confided, along with far too many embarrassing details about his anime addiction. Ron eventually stopped at a rest area and apologized about the rough treatment. He sat her up front and fed her a granola bar before off they went, racing against the clock of the oncoming dawn.

"So why are we going to NYC? I've always wanted to see it," she said, getting as comfortable as she could with rope chafing her ankles. Despite knowing she'd gotten a last-minute message to the one person who could help her, she hid a writhing bud of panic behind a smiling mask.

Her roommate and best friend had taught her more about self-defense than anyone else, always saying Olivia was too gullible for her own good. She heard Charlotte's voice in the back of her head even now. *"Why are you trusting this guy just because he gave you food and apologized?"*

If you have any other ideas, I'm all ears, she thought to herself.

Ron emulated a leaky faucet as he told her all about vampires. Information she already knew, courtesy of living with a half-vampire who loved to tell stories of her glory days in the very city they were going to. She pretended to be interested, knowing he was building up to something. "And I'm a Havener, dedicated to purging the wicked from the night," he said, flashing her an expectant look.

"So, you're a vampire," she said as if she hadn't noticed the otherworldly, flawless looks he had. She'd studiously *not* looked at him, not wanting to get taken by any mind tricks if their eyes met.

"Yes. Please don't be scared, though."

Her forced smile shaded to a grimace. Why shouldn't she be scared? He was still part of the group that busted into her home and kidnapped her. She might've been placed with the rougher guys if it weren't for the one good hit she got on the meanest-looking one when he first came at her. They'd separated her from that aggressive man. At least Ron was talking to her.

"And...you kill other vampires," she continued.

"That's right. But only those that deserve it." He nodded, his expression full of the kind of zeal she thought was reserved for a fanatic. "My boss sent a task force down to get you because we need your help."

Well, this boss of his was officially on her lump of coal list. As much as she poked and prodded Ron on the drive north, he had no answers as to *why* she was important and could possibly help his organization.

She hoped Charlotte would be able to help her, even with the limited scope of the message she'd been able to send. Her cell phone was lying on the ground of their apartment some hundreds of miles away now, with a panicked message chain and a shaky video. She'd managed to get a shot of one of the thugs and the shoulder badges they all wore, a lighthouse in white thread on a brown background. Knowing this guy was from Haven, she figured it was an identifying symbol.

Hopefully, that was enough. If it weren't for her faith in her friend, she would've melted into a puddle of panic by this point. Especially once New York City's skyline came across the horizon, backlit by the sky as deep midnight shaded to the first hints of morning.

"Hey, look over here," Ron said, their eyes meeting for a moment.

A rookie mistake, Charlotte would say. He used his mental influence to put her to sleep.

OLIVIA WOKE WITH A GROAN, SEVERAL POINTS ON HER BODY aching with the reminder of bruises. Her eyes flew open a moment later. She'd been untied and placed on a plush office seat somewhere dark and quiet. Moonlight seeped in from a window open to the elements, illuminating the edges of office furniture and computer monitors.

She dove for a keyboard, her gaze darting around for signs of Ron or any other thugs. The hair on the back of her neck lifted as she confirmed that she was alone. *This is really weird,* she thought as she shook a mouse to wake up the screen. Haven's beacon lit up the top of the screen, and it asked for a login and password.

Quirking her lips, she pawed at the pens and notepads covered the desk, hoping to find some sort of credentials she could use. She repeated the process at three more desks, checking every drawer. Lots of notes, handwritten and typed, and a few scripts, but nothing she could use.

"Well, I can't be that lucky," she muttered under her breath. Maybe her captors had forgotten about her or gone home. She could try walking out the door to see what happened.

Before she tried that, though, she poked her head out the window. She white-knuckled the window ledge as a wave of vertigo hit upon seeing just how far down the ground was. Distant streetlamps and the honking of car horns told her that life went on without her. That wasn't a way out, so she pushed herself backward onto solid tile.

Her heart leapt straight to her throat as a door slammed somewhere close and footsteps followed. A woman's voice drifted in from the window, haughty and smooth. She sounded like the kind of woman Olivia's parents liked to rub elbows with, rich and vain. Pressing closer to the window, she peered upward, catching a glimpse of a balcony overlooking the city. Maybe there was a penthouse suite above her, occupied by the aristocrat who tapped her fingers on the metal railing, causing a *clink clink clink* from an undoubtedly expensive manicure.

Olivia listened closely, wondering if this woman knew she had a captive only a few stories down. "Of course I'm sure..." The wind masked the rest of what she said, whipping the words away on a growing howl.

"This seems like an elaborate gamble, that's all," replied a man's voice. He, too, seemed like someone from her past, but not in the same flattering way. There was a note of desperation in his tone when he addressed the woman. He sounded like a starving artist or failing businessman, desperately grasping for a handout.

"Do you question my methods, Elandros?" There was a note of danger there, a viper in the leaves waiting to strike.

"Of course not. It's just...your last plan was nearly foolproof. Yet, somehow—"

She scoffed, dismissing his concerns quickly. "There's always a margin of error." Olivia imagined a regal hand wave to go with her tone. "I'm not playing around anymore."

"Yes, Your Majesty." She leaned forward to catch the muttered words. "So, you do not want me to take care of the Sorceress or the Ancient you empowered?"

"No, you moron. How is she going to share her blood if you go kill her?" Scorn for her companion oozed from her. Olivia blinked in shock at how casually they spoke of murder.

"I just don't think we can trust—"

She interrupted again with a snap. "When I want your opinion, I'll ask for it!"

In the silence that followed, Olivia got to her feet again,

rolling her shoulders. It was time for her to stop sitting on her rear and try to get out of here. These two weren't talking about her or anything that could possibly help her. "Our new guest is about to run. How about you go show her some hospitality?" the aristocrat continued.

Oh crap.

Cold sweat coated her back as she leapt forward, trying the closest door out of the room. Another dark area lay on the other side, this time a cubicle farm. She latched the knob behind her and crept along the wall like a spy in one of her favorite movies, channeling her muse to the task. *You are a spy, silent and quick. Think like a spy.*

Anyone could still be in one of the cubicles, considering how she assumed vampires liked to occupy dark spaces. If the aristocrat and her desperate companion were a level or two above this floor, she knew she didn't have long before one of them came to check on her. She decided that her best bet would be to pick an empty cubicle and hunker down rather than to paw around in the dark in search of a fire escape or elevator. Her normal, human legs would not be able to outpace a vampire's speed.

She tiptoed her way into a cubicle at random, relieved to find each abandoned. Rolling aside a chair behind a cramped desk covered in knick-knacks, she wheeled it back once she'd pulled herself in a tight ball. Her heartbeat thundered in her ears as moments shaded to minutes.

Her best bet would be for the man to take a cursory look around and give up. Or be even lazier, waiting for her at the elevators and giving up when it was obvious she wasn't trying to escape so blindly.

How long would he wait? She couldn't stay here forever. Eventually, whomever actually owned and used this cubicle would return, and she needed to be long gone by then.

She startled when a voice rose somewhere close. "Come out, little mouse. I promise I won't bite." It was the man from before, somehow entering the cubicle farm silently.

"I admit, you had me for a moment." A set of knuckles rapped on the plastic separating her cubicle from the next. "Why don't you come out? That looks uncomfortable."

"Oh no, very comfortable. You should try it," she said, proud that her voice didn't shake.

"I know of better places." The chair wheeled away from her. A white-gloved hand came out of the gloom to help her up. She considered biting it, but then this vampire would consider her some rabid dog rather than a lady. She took his help grudgingly.

Chapter 3
Olivia

Elandros, the vampire with a voice like a desperate businessman, took her to a boardroom complete with a television and coffee maker. She made coffee. This was already shaping up to be the second-longest night of her life, just after the previous night when she was kidnapped and bound just to be abandoned here.

Wherever *here* was.

"Coffee?" she asked, glancing over her shoulder at the vampire who sat casually beside the only door out. His appearance hadn't discredited any of her assumptions so far. He was dressed like an entrepreneur of old in a fine tuxedo and cravat, his dark hair slicked back. By virtue of avoiding eye contact, she'd only seen the profile of his aquiline features and a hint of unnatural red in his gaze.

"Yes. I take it black." He sounded bored, and she debated whether or not to make herself the interest of the hour for someone she guessed to be pretty old.

Heart in her throat, she made that decision. *Feign interest and enthusiasm,* she told herself, turning around with two paper cups in hand. Hers was the color of someone who liked a little coffee with her milk. "How can you stand it without cream?" she asked, placing his cup down.

"I am averse to milk," he said, barely sparing her a glance as she sat across from him. He held a cell phone and a set of instructions. The tiny booklet looked comical in his long fingers.

She watched him glance from a diagram to the phone before him, programming it more slowly than an elder picking up their first device. His eyes weren't the red she'd first thought but a maroon the same shade of dried blood. Questions filled her head, but she thought most of them would be too unflattering. "You're lactose intolerant, then. Do you have troubles if you drink the blood of someone who's drunk milk recently?"

"Why are you questioning my dieting habits?" His brows drew tighter together.

"Consider me curious. I figure I'm stuck in this room with you, so we might as well get to know one another."

When he finally looked her way, he seemed so unamused that she wished she could grab her words and shove them right back in her mouth. He breathed out his own tension with a sigh. "Help me make this infernal device do my bidding, and then I'll answer your questions."

She got up and gingerly perched on a seat next to him, aware of some palpable pressure haloing him. It made her arm prickle with goosebumps as she reached across to take the phone and help him with setup. The "infernal device," as he called it, was asking for an email address, something he didn't understand at all.

"I'm getting the feeling you've never used a phone before," she said.

"That is correct. Yet mortals all seem to be using them constantly. What is the allure?" The hairs on the back of her neck stood on end as he turned his full attention on her.

"Plenty of fun stuff to do on a phone. There's games." Even as she said it, she thought he didn't seem the type to be entertained by bright flashing colors. "And you can talk to anyone in the world through it. If they have a phone and you have a phone, you can send messages to each other."

His attention turned back to the device. She rubbed her arms to ward off a chill. "That is quite useful to my purposes. Teach me how to use it." As he spoke, he tossed the instruction booklet aside.

Not very helpful for old technophobe vampires, she thought.

"It's not that hard," she said. Marking the time she said that—1:23 a.m.—she proceeded to learn just how hard it was with no foundation of technology. He made a user-friendly system seem downright hostile.

Throughout, she considering sending a message out for help. Would this old man really understand what she did? He watched her closely, like he was expecting her to try something. But her first slip-up wasn't getting caught sending out an SOS. It was referring to him by name. Elandros. Just like the aristocrat upstairs had.

"How did you know my name?" Any progress of goodwill she'd made with him vanished as his expression shuttered.

"Uh..." she couldn't call it a lucky guess. She hadn't heard of anyone else with a name like his. "I heard you talking to someone earlier."

"More mind games." He grunted and lifted his phone closer to his face. "You heard her tell me to find you, thus prompting you to run."

"Yeah, it kinda went like that," she admitted.

"You've helped me with this device. Allow me to help you." His gaze seemed to pierce right through her. "Nothing here is as it seems. You are here because my queen desired your presence."

"Oh, well, why doesn't she come meet me then?" That woman was also going on her lump of coal list, right next to... "What happened to the leader of Haven needing my help for something?"

His lips twisted in amusement. He looked ready to call her a silly child for believing that. "Allow me to amend my statement. My queen required you to be present here. She manipulates the future to her liking based off her visions. Something will happen because you're here instead of wherever you came from."

"Uh-huh," she said dubiously.

"I will tell you of one decree that should set you at ease. She required that you not be harmed. The one who punched your face has been dealt with."

The way he said "dealt with" with casual finality didn't reassure her at all. "So, how long am I supposed to be present, then? What's the name of your queen so I can sue her for my kidnapping?"

He chuckled without humor, prompting her to remember how rudely the woman had spoken to him. "It would behoove us both if I didn't say her name. Thus, she will not see this conversation happening with her future sight."

"You're pretty good at dodging that, huh?" She pushed onward before she could lose her nerve. "She sounded like she didn't respect you. You don't deserve that."

Elandros leaned back in his chair, sipping his coffee and staring out the window. If she'd struck a nerve, he didn't make it apparent at first. She didn't think he would respond. But when he did, his voice was hushed. "I think I like you, girl. For the rest of your stay, mind your tongue when it comes to her."

She took a moment to really look at him, at the stiffness in his shoulders and jaw. A glimmer of something in his eyes. Fists poised on the table. He was afraid of whomever he was referring to as his queen. And if he was, she thought it might be prudent to share a healthy dose of caution and change the subject. "So...how long was I supposed to be here again?" she repeated without her earlier fire. With only embers to hold onto, her hands began to tremble in her lap.

Someone else held the cards to her fate. This mysterious woman with enough pull to call herself a queen. Did vampires even have royalty? Or was this vampiress some sort of self-appointed noblewoman?

"A couple more hours at most." Elandros cut through her musing as he shrugged. "My queen informed me that Haven will relocate their forces here. I have my orders for what to do when that happens."

She licked suddenly dry lips. "What does she want you to do?"

"You'll see." He knocked back the last of his coffee, inspecting the empty paper cup before pushing it back toward her. "Brew me another."

Chapter 4
Julian

"Do you want me to leave you by the side of the road?"

Julian felt frost forming on the steering wheel as he drove downtown amidst late-night traffic. The buildings around them grew taller and grander in time with Phantom's wheedling from the passenger's seat.

"You want to know her name, right?" she pestered, just as she'd been pressing for more information ever since he tried giving her only the pertinent facts in the subway tunnel.

"She can tell me her name herself," he muttered.

She tossed an errant curl over her shoulder. "Okay, how about my name then? Tit for tat. I'm Charlotte, retired bodyguard. Your apparent lifemate is my best friend."

"I'm Julian." He grimaced as he thought this dhampir might be his key to understanding the woman whose face haunted him. "You would not believe the rest."

"You keep sayin' that, but I really think you should—"

"Try you. Yes, I heard."

She looked at him expectantly. "Well? How about now?"

The edges of his reason started to fray. Why not tell her all the details and see for himself how insane she thought he was? "You remember how an island came from the bottom of the sea recently?" he began. This, at least, was broadcasted everywhere on the nightly news. Violently detaching itself from the sea floor, it caused a cataclysm of earthquakes and other natural disasters to rock the globe. Charlotte raised a brow and nodded.

"The island is not Atlantis. It's called Nyixa, and when it rose, several Ancient sleeping vampires woke with it." He glanced her way to see if he'd lost her, but she now wore a self-satisfied and curious expression, motioning for him to go on. "I had a run-in with one of them. Lucia. She calls herself Queen of Vampires, but since emerging from her sleep, she's only acted against most of us. Especially me."

"Well, what makes you all that special?" she asked with a chuckle.

"I look like my father."

Charlotte's attention turned back to traffic, lips quirked to the side. "You're right, I do find this all hard to believe."

He could've left it at that, feeding her just enough truth to satisfy her. But he wanted her to have another kernel of knowledge. "Lucia showed me your friend and tipped off Haven as to where to find her."

"Now why would she do that, Bloodhound?" she frowned. "How would she *know* to do that?"

"Magic. She has magic." He stopped the car as close to Haven Tower as possible and slammed the car door, head tilted back to take in the skyscraper that housed Haven as well as several other telecommunications companies on its various floors. Dread wormed its way in the pit of his stomach, because if Lucia could have his potential lifemate captured and brought to New York on a whim...

Well, she would be expecting him. And the last time he'd been alone with her, she'd turned him into a puppet to do the dirtiest of deeds she required. He stood paralyzed at the thought that Lucia could be somewhere in the tower, waiting with a knife to his lifemate's throat. Or worse, having her corpse strung up as an example to him.

Someone snapped their fingers before him. "Earth to Bloodhound. Wake up."

Charlotte propped a fist on her hip as he took hold of himself again. He wondered if he should warn her what—and who—they might be up against here. "Let's go," he said, shaking off the film of icy fear threatening to engulf him. Moving one leg after the other, he followed Charlotte up to the sliding glass doors that separated them from the entry foyer.

They opened, releasing a gust of air-conditioned wind. Exchanging a glance with her, he entered and drew a small knife made for throwing. She took out a dagger from her side, having borrowed some of his arsenal for her own use to provide him better backup. To make their entrance as quiet as possible, he reached out to establish mental speech with Charlotte. All vampires could speak to each other with the power of their minds, but he figured it was more difficult for dhampirs, especially to begin the connection. *"There's a directory over here. Haven only rents a few floors from this establishment."*

They crossed a lavish, marble-inlaid floor to where a bank of elevators rested for the night. Haven Entertainment was listed as the top four floors. *"So, do we take the elevator, or do we hoof it?"* It didn't sound like Charlotte had a problem with mental communication, coming through clearly even without making eye contact with him.

"The stairs. It'd be too easy to pin us in an elevator car," he said. He'd spotted the corridor that held the stairs close by and went there next to creep upward. Charlotte snuck ahead of him, her more graceful form and dark leather blending in with the shadows. If anyone checked the cameras, they'd definitely be able to see him. But she might evade notice. He let her go ahead to scout as they climbed flight after flight of stairs. There was no sound save for the grinding of grit under his boots and the muffled thump of his steps. His heart throbbed in his ears to fill the gap, full of breathless certainty that things weren't as easy as they seemed.

Charlotte waited for him in the shadows, stopping before a door marked with a plastic sleeve that protected the Haven emblem. *"Voices on the other side,"* she said.

He took a deep breath, looking her in the eye so she knew how serious he was. *"If you meet any Ancients, run."*

"I'm not a coward, Bloodhound," she scoffed.

"I mean it. You see a veiled woman or anyone with red eyes— you run." He asked himself if he, too, would run upon seeing Lucia or Elandros again, something he'd pondered ever since going on this mission. What would he do to have the innocent woman they'd stolen freed from their influence?

He steeled himself, knowing he was about to find out one way or another. Charlotte didn't reply, instead unlatching the door and letting it drift open a few inches. Booted feet approached from the other side. She slipped around like a snake, and a few moments later, someone's bulk dropped to the ground with a *thud.*

Julian followed her, seeing an unfortunate Havener passed out, blood dribbling from both nostrils. Withstanding her shriek was a better fate than if Julian had gotten to him first—Julian was aiming to kill tonight.

They were in the back of an office area with papers thrown haphazardly across the ground. Julian saw why a few moments later; the desks were upturned. He let his throwing knife fly with enough force to strike a man rushing to take cover. A pained groan followed.

He used a corner to shield himself as a hail of gunfire unleashed from the remaining Haveners. Sweat froze all along his back as he shivered. *"Ah, Julian. I knew you'd come."* The new voice was smooth and womanly, more chilling than whatever was making him permanently cold within. She was here, just as he'd expected.

"Lucia," he snarled.

"Your service to me was at an end. You didn't need to return." He didn't allow her voice to distract him. He drew a gun of his own and traded fire with the men pinning him and Charlotte down.

"Well, I suppose I do have something that belongs to you." As she continued, his fingers curled to fists. He made to embrace the anger in him as it rose to a boil, just to find it colder than the frost that formed on his skin. She'd caught him just as he was firing another volley. Ice crystals crept up the barrel of his weapon,

catching his attention for the split second it took for a bullet to skim his forearm in a burning line of agony. He dropped the gun, flexing his hand.

It happened between one misty exhale and the next. The cold rushed up his arm, extinguishing the pain of his wound to numbness as that foreign feeling pushed itself from his palm. The man who'd struck him started clawing at his neck, an icicle protruding a few inches from his jugular. Two more of the deadly projectiles were stuck, quivering, in the wood of their makeshift blockade.

Charlotte stared at him in astonishment as he took advantage of the moment, drawing a few throwing knives and finishing the Haveners that went to help the first. "How did you do that?" she hissed at him while he picked up his dropped weapon and began to sweep the room.

The man he'd struck with magic would live. He'd withdrawn the icicle, the wound closing itself rapidly with vampire healing. "Where is she?" Julian demanded, standing over him with his gun pointed straight at his forehead. Out of the corner of his eye, he saw that his own damaged arm was repaired, but not in the same way.

Instead of mending closed, his flesh now bore a line of ice like a frozen river. It was so surreal he nearly dropped his weapon again. He turned his demands on Lucia. "*What have you done to me?*"

The Havener before him stammered nonsense as Julian had a head full of Lucia's mocking laughter for reply. He shouldn't have expected anything else. "Collins holds a woman prisoner. Where is she?" he repeated, nudging the man with the frozen nose of his gun. With how cold the weapon had grown in his hand, he wondered if it would fire.

The Havener shivered, hitching his thumb upward. "T-top floor."

Julian nodded, delivering a swift blow with the butt of his weapon to render him unconscious. He turned to Charlotte, who was still staring.

"Did you know your eyes are glowing?" she asked.

Chapter 5
Julian

HE DIDN'T BOTHER BEING STEALTHY, STORMING HIS WAY UP the three flights to the top floor of the Haven operation. "No one will bother us," he told Charlotte, and he was right.

She was spooked, not that he could blame her. He didn't know what to make of himself either. The aura around him was starting to relent from a flurry of snowflakes back into his usual chill. He'd always had a cold aura—it ran in his family—but every other vampire manifested the power of their mind as a hot, pins-and-needles sensation to quickly communicate how old their mind was.

However, he'd never been so cold as to freeze water vapor into his own personal storm. Lucia had done something to him while he was enthralled to her and Elandros, and were he an older vampire able to stand toe-to-toe with them, he'd be demanding answers more directly. His heart beat with dread, knowing he would probably have to face one or both of them the moment they arrived at the top floor.

He kicked the door in, and it hit the opposite wall with a bang. The fluorescents were off on this floor, leaving the world shrouded in grayscale to his enhanced vision. He swept the area by panning with his gun, stopping with it pointed at the heart of a shadowy figure.

Standing in the middle of the corridor was the only man who'd bested him in a real fight. Julian bared his teeth in a sneer to keep from trembling. The cold wasn't the only reason he was wracked with sudden chills. Before him, with eyes like smoldering coals, was one of the Blood Princes, a vampire Ancient who'd been released from magical slumber the moment Nyixa had breached the ocean waves. Despite being asleep for the better part of a thousand years, he was amongst a select group of vampires who had grown to incredible vampiric ability from the passage of time.

Prince Elandros, the Legion, was dressed in his usual finery, looking more prepared for a ball than a fight. "Hello, Julian. I've been expecting you." He spoke with a measure of boredom, inspecting and buffing his nails.

Charlotte spoke up loudly. "You know, you make a terrible villain if you deliver your lines that way. Know who taught me that? My best friend. Where is she?"

His otherworldly red eyes turned toward her standing just behind Julian's shoulder. "I was not talking to you."

Before she could open her mouth, Julian interceded. "You're right, I'm here. Lucia wanted us to cross paths again."

"Indeed she did," Elandros said, gesturing an elegant hand behind him. "She could not see to you personally, so she sent me. You can put the weapon away. I'm only here to deliver a message."

Julian didn't so much as twitch. He already knew this man fought dirty.

"Very well." Elandros paced forward despite the threat of Julian's weapon, either calling his bluff or knowing that Julian's numb fingers would hamper his reflexes. When dealing with an Ancient, even a split second of hesitation was enough to miss a shot or lose a life. "She's here, mostly unharmed. And yes...it is too easy." With one last smirk Julian's way, he was gone in a blur of speed. The doorway to the stairwell banged closed.

"Mostly unharmed!" Charlotte exclaimed, pushing past him to rush through the rest of the floor.

Julian stood rooted in place, focusing on a different statement. "Too easy," he agreed. Haven had barely put up a fight for a group that was dead set on killing him. Neither had Lucia and her lapdog, Elandros, who could've easily ended him here.

Familiar disquiet twisted in his stomach as he followed the sounds of women squealing. In the hallway, Charlotte had her arms around someone else and hugged her tightly. Over Charlotte's shoulder, he got his first glimpse of her in person, the woman whose face haunted him. Haloed by a head of brunette curls, she had a generous pattern of freckles over her cheeks and elfin nose. Her lips like twin rose petals uttered her friend's name and the words he longed to have spoken to himself. "You have no idea how good it is to see you."

Then she opened her eyes. Well, one of them. The other was sealed shut with a swollen purple bruise. She met his gaze, her lips parting in a surprised 'o' that was an understatement to how the sight of her hit him. Like a punch to the gut, he knew her like any vampire knew their lifemate. A sense of rightness seized him. Even with a black eye, she catapulted to amongst the most beautiful of women he'd lain eyes on.

He wanted to make sure she was never hurt in such a way again. To be her shield and protector, the true match to her. Kindred souls matched together by the hands of fate.

Her expression shaded to uncertainty as she parted from Charlotte. "There's a guy," she whispered, pointing at him.

Charlotte looked over her shoulder and sighed. "Yeah, he's a friend. I guess."

Taking this as his cue, he stepped forward, offering his hand. "Julian Fairfax. I'm also here to help." Without her seeing his contributions to get to this moment, the words felt lame on his tongue.

She shook his hand anyway. "Cold hands, warm heart, right? I'm Olivia," she said with a bashful smile that melted its way straight through him. For the first time in days, he was immune to the cold within himself.

"That's right." He knew this was his moment to say something witty or charming to catch her attention. So, of course, his tongue slipped on anything he could've said for a prolonged pause. She let him go, turning back to the friend she'd known for longer than him.

"Do you know where we are?" she asked.

"Downtown New York City. We can get a hotel room and be on the road when you're up to it," Charlotte said.

"I have a place you can stay," he blurted, catching them both off guard. "For free," he added. After working with him this evening, he wondered if Charlotte had mustered up enough trust to agree to an evening visit in his house.

Charlotte considered, drawing the other woman away from him. That didn't prevent his vampire senses from overhearing what they discussed. "It's not a bad idea. He's from one of the three biggest covens," she said.

He watched his lifemate's profile. She stood straighter, listening with more confidence than she'd projected to him. "Will we be safe if we go with him?"

"Safer than if we stay here, for sure."

"I'll take anywhere that's safer than here," Olivia admitted. They lingered together, dropping their voices further. When she chanced a glance back at him, he realized they must be talking about him more directly. He turned his gaze to the wall, where a generic motivation poster hung with a picture of a bald eagle and American flag.

After what felt like an eternity, even though it must've only been a few minutes, the two women turned back to him fully. "We'll go with you," Charlotte said.

JULIAN KEPT GLANCING IN THE REAR-VIEW MIRROR TO CATCH a glimpse of Olivia in the backseat. She rested in a limp sprawl on the upholstery as he took both her and Charlotte out of downtown New York City. They left the lights behind in relative silence other than the accompaniment of the radio as a comforting hum of voices and music.

Charlotte kept her gaze out the window, her lips pressed in a troubled line. He was glad she was willing to see past old coven ties and didn't immediately suggest to her friend that they run far away from New York—and him. Her thoughts must've drifted the same way as his, as she spoke to him privately. *"When will you tell her?"*

He didn't consider the woman in his backseat but the creeping frost taking over his steering wheel. Much as he loathed to admit it, he knew his problem was growing worse. While Olivia's safety was now his biggest concern, making sure he didn't freeze into a block of ice took a close second.

"When the time is right," he said.

"So, she really is your lifemate?" she prompted, a frown creasing her face.

"My one and only," he confirmed with a nod.

She pinched the bridge of her nose. *"Something's wrong here, and I don't like it."*

Spoken just like his inner voice, which hadn't let him forget what Elandros had said for a moment. It went against everything he knew about vampire nature, to give a gift like uniting him with his lifemate without there being some sort of catch.

"I told you before. It's magic," he said with vehemence. He hated whatever Lucia had done to him, poisoning his body with cold. And that feeling extended to her power of future sight, capable of planting threads and weaving together events until the end result was a masterwork of an unpredictable twist to Lucia's favor.

She'd used him before for such an event, only thwarted at the last minute. He knew it was happening again. Just the barest net laid out to ensnare him. If he didn't figure out the bait and switch soon, he'd face another conclusion with more than just his life at stake.

Charlotte made an unimpressed scoff, earning a shrug from him. It wasn't his job to prove what he'd been through, but she needed to be wary of what was coming.

They arrived at his home not much later, a quaint postage stamp of a place he spent little time at. His nerves jangled when he went to pull into his driveway to find another car already parked there. He recognized it as one of the unremarkable cars his former coven used when travelling discretely.

Parking alongside it like nothing was wrong, he opened the garage from a button on the dash. "Head inside and get comfortable. I'll be right behind you," he told the ladies, shutting off the engine.

He helped Olivia from the car and watched her and Charlotte go inside, hands in his pockets. Waiting. Wind whistled through the trees, curling covetous fingers through his short blond hair. Insects sang to one another like an evening choir.

After a few minutes, he realized his friend wasn't going to make this easy on him. He sighed and went to his garage, taking out a ladder. He propped it on the side of the house and scaled it, alert for any signs of movement above him. Someone was indeed waiting for him behind his chimney stack, legs kicking off the side of the house as he overlooked Julian's backyard.

"Let's get one thing straight. I don't accept your resignation," the other vampire said the moment Julian spotted him. His coven master, Alexander Rehnquist, was wearing all black, except for a pair of lion insignia at his shoulders. A few straps over his person indicated weapons, both hidden and not.

"I resigned so you and the coven won't be held responsible for what I just did." Though Julian had broken fewer rules than he'd expected, he'd still attacked a rival coven and killed a few of its members. Retribution would come for him specifically as a rogue instead of for his coven.

Alex's evergreen eyes narrowed. They'd known each other for over two hundred years, and during that time, Julian had learned every sign of his friend's moods. To see a shapeshifting vampire like Alex have his pupils reduce to slits meant that his instincts were close, and usually, that meant to take cover from his anger.

"That's rubbish, and you know it," he snapped.

"I did what I had to for the sake of the coven," Julian said. He didn't have it in him to argue further, some distinct part of him numb from the cold within. He was just...tired. The whole rescue didn't go as he'd planned, and troubled thoughts swirled just below the surface.

"What, exactly, happened?" Alex asked, taking a deep breath to calm down. He patted the space next to him.

Despite himself, Julian sat. He watched the other man shiver with a detached sense of wonder. His coven master was the strongest vampire he was willingly subservient to, and to see him affected by his cold aura brought validation to how surreal his sudden chill was.

He licked dry lips and told Alex nearly everything, save for the icicles he'd managed to summon. Trying to track Kim Cox to Haven Headquarters just to meet the Phantom, Charlotte, right before he stepped into a trap. How easy it ended up being to rescue his lifemate, like picking up a friend for coffee. And finally, Elandros's damning words spoken for Lucia.

"Is the girl really your lifemate?" He clapped Julian on the back once he nodded. "You've been looking for her forever, and now you've got her in your house. How are you even sitting here right now?"

Julian's hunt for his lifemate was nearly legendary amongst his friends and the few women who'd ever shown interest in him. Very few knew why he was so focused on finding his perfect match, a search that'd taken nearly two centuries. But instead of echoing Alex's enthusiasm, he kept a somber expression as he glanced at the sky and the setting moon. Daytime would be coming soon.

"It's too easy," he said quietly. "Can't you see Lucia's fingers in this?"

Alex's cheer faded as he stroked his jaw thoughtfully. "You're right. I don't like that part at all. By the way—we don't say her name anymore. It helps prevent her from seeing this moment with her future sight."

That made sense, so he made a note of it. "All right. Neither do I. But I accept that I've broken the Deveaux Accords and will need to leave for a while at least—"

"No, you're not leaving," he said firmly. "When it comes to Haven and Coven Rockefeller, the Accords are off. If you'd only talked to me before you left..." He shook his head, lips pressed together.

Julian didn't say that his friend had been in an infirmary bed, recovering from heavy trauma relating to what Lucia had done to him, too. They both bore scars from the woman's grab for power. "So, we're at war," he said.

"We are. And even if we weren't, you would still be coming back to the coven. I don't care how many Haveners you killed. Bloody hell, go kill the lot of them." Alex bared his teeth as he spoke, as if wanting to sink them into some of the action as well. He turned to give Julian a stern look, punctuating his words with the press of his finger to Julian's chest. "I stand behind you, like I always have." He laid his palm flat, pressing something there.

Reaching up, Julian caught a pair of shoulder badges before they could tumble away. They showed the familiar insignia of a lion head, something he'd worn proudly ever since Alex had established a proper coven. "I'm sorry," he murmured. The backs of each badge still had severed threads from where he'd cut them off.

Dipping his head, Alex said, "I have a new job for you. It's urgent. You're starting tomorrow."

"What's the job?" Knowing Alex, it would be unpleasant, so Julian could show true contrition by doing it well.

"You'll get the full debrief tomorrow, but we are fighting a war of two covens verses ten. We need a logistics man to coordinate ten covens worth of fighters. Prince Sirius wanted the job, but he doesn't know the streets or any of the men. I proposed that he work with someone in the know...my legendary head enforcer, the Bloodhound." He made it sound so reasonable, but the reality was he'd just placed a giant, messy wad on Julian's plate and told him to untangle it.

Julian knew the twelve covens of New York intimately as someone who acted as an enforcer, another word for Coven Rehnquist's vampiric police force. Not every coven was old and established enough to have enforcers, but Alex had said *fighters*, implying people without a hint of training.

He forced a smile. "Great. Thanks."

Alex clapped him on the shoulder as he stood. "Think of it

this way. I'm putting you as close as possible to a Blood Prince so that no foul Sorceress can try to target you again."

As he followed suit, Julian released his tension in a sigh. He knew he was a target for Lucia, and he had a good idea of why, but he would sleep easy using this to extend protection to his newly found lifemate. The duty would be challenging, but at least he knew his coven master was still looking out for him.

"Oh—and do you mind if Violet and I crash at your place for the day?"

"Violet's here?" Julian asked, surprised that Alex was parted from her.

"Sure. I let her into your house earlier." He flashed a roguish smile. "Someone has to entertain your guests after all."

Chapter 6
Olivia

Olivia took in the house with a cautious eye. The eye she could see out of. She and Charlotte had agreed to this because they needed somewhere safe to stay, and this man's house was bound to be more protection than the apartment Olivia had easily been stolen from. The two of them were in desperate need of new housing anyway.

Yet there was a light on in the kitchen and the smell of sizzling eggs and bacon in the air. "Does this guy have a wife or something?" Olivia whispered.

The house was plain in a Spartan, manly way. If someone wasn't cooking breakfast, she would've automatically assumed her would-be savior was a bachelor. "Pretty sure he doesn't," Charlotte said.

Together, they peered into the kitchen to find a petite blonde woman tossing an omelet as she hummed a jaunty tune. She turned and cried out in alarm, nearly missing her flip. When she startled, so did Olivia, clutching her chest.

"You're not Julian," she said. Her eyes glinted metallic in the overhead light. Olivia nearly scrubbed hers as she realized the other woman really did have shiny, silver irises like twin coins. The rest of her was understated in comfortable street clothes and slippers. She definitely seemed quite at home.

"He let us in," Charlotte said. "You got enough to share?"

Laughing with relief, she nodded. "Yeah, sure! I brought my own stuff since Julian's a classic vamp and doesn't have any food in the house..." Her gaze found Olivia's and she frowned in concern. "Pardon my manners, I'm Violet. I'm kind of crashing this place."

They made their introductions with her as well. Olivia smiled wide since Violet seemed embarrassed to be caught out like this. "You seem like a really nice home crasher," she offered.

"Well, Julian's a friend, and my mate's known him for a long time." She shrugged. "It was his idea. You look like you've been through some stuff, though. Want me to try to heal your eye?"

"Oh, are you Gifted?" Olivia asked, proud to remember something about vampire culture. The Gifted were a unique subsect of vampires who only inherited one ability, independent of who turned them—the power to accelerate healing for other vampires to the point they could bring someone back from the brink of death.

Violet's lips quirked. "Well, not exactly. I have magic. I'll show you after we have a bite to eat." She neatly plated her omelet and whipped up some eggs for the next.

Olivia and Charlotte exchanged a glance. "Julian was muttering about magic, too," Charlotte said.

"Whatever," Olivia sighed. She didn't have enough energy to play along. Instead, she circled around the kitchen to discover Julian had bar stools where she could sit and watch Violet bustle around.

She was glad to get her bacon and eggs once Violet was done. It felt like her bruise was throbbing in time to her heartbeat now that another person had brought her attention to it. Chewing just made that side of her face hurt, but she gobbled down the first real food she'd had in days regardless.

Violet left the room and returned with a dusty tome as they ate. "Very wizardly," Charlotte commented while the silver-eyed woman flipped thin old pages marked with the fine penmanship of a scribe.

"Just need a magic wand, right?" Violet smiled, stopping somewhere in the middle and murmuring a few words as her fingers flashed through some sort of sign language. She clucked her tongue and repeated the gestures more slowly with one hand, holding the other behind her back.

Charlotte sat back, her eyebrow raise saying what she didn't speak aloud. *This will be good.*

"Okay, are you ready?" Violet asked Olivia cheerfully.

"For magic?" Olivia tilted her head back and forth. "So-so. I'm willing to try anything once, though."

"Time to *eye* our luck," Violet said with a giggle at her own joke as she came up to Olivia's stool. "Hold really still."

"Call the pun police. Eee-oh, eee-oh." Charlotte chuckled, turning to watch. Biting her lip, Olivia clasped her hands and tried to make herself still.

She felt warm fingertips on her face. Violet leaned in, flashing her sign language and intoning foreign-sounding words. There was a jerk as her bruise throbbed hard, and after a spike of pain, she could feel the swelling recede. Her lid lifted, blinking as she saw how close a pair of glowing fingertips were to poking the epicenter of her old wound.

"See? Magic isn't so bad," Violet said cheerfully a few moments later. "Quick, easy results. No need to sleep off the healing."

Olivia probed around her eye socket, her mouth hanging open. "So, if you're not Gifted, how...?"

"Long story," she admitted. "But I'm a Sorceress. You probably want to get to bed—"

"No—wait," Olivia protested. All semblance of tired doldrums was gone the moment she realized her face was completely repaired. "Thank you! You're now my favorite person. Please tell me everything about you and how you can do magic and what a Sorceress is..." She paused for a breath.

"Oh, she's your favorite person, huh?" Charlotte griped.

Olivia propped a fist on her cheek. "Okay, you both are. Concurrently."

All three of them tensed up when a door slammed and heavy footsteps came their way. Julian took one glance at them and scratched the back of his head self-consciously. "Hi, Violet. Look, I'm sorry for—"

"One hundred percent not your fault. We were both victims." She interrupted before he could finish forming his apology, leaving him to sigh in relief.

A second man came out of his shadow, moving with fluid grace as he threw open his arms. "Ah, ladies! Nice to see you." He flashed a charming half-smile to them while Violet came to his side. They embraced with a brief kiss. The two of them looked like a dedicated couple, fitting together like two pieces stamped from the same puzzle. Violet introduced him as Alex, her mate.

"Before we retire, I wanted to extend an offer of protection to you both until you get back on your feet," Alex said to her and Charlotte. "I've heard what happened to get you in this situation. Let my coven shelter you at our headquarters until we figure out why Haven wanted Olivia so badly."

Charlotte had a calculating gleam to her eye as she considered. "That's a generous offer for a mortal and a dhampir rogue."

Olivia elbowed her with a big, forced smile. "We would love some extra help, thank you."

"Then we'll get you settled there tomorrow," Alex promised.

Charlotte leaned over and murmured in her ear. "I think I know what this is about. Julian has something to tell you." Despite her low tone, both men flinched like they'd overheard. Olivia sat up straighter. Why would they do that, unless Charlotte had the right of it?

"Why don't I show you to a guest room?" Julian offered Charlotte through gritted teeth. With Alex and Violet bidding her a good day—Olivia imagined that was the vampire way of telling someone to sleep well—she was left alone with a cluster of dirty plates.

She felt awkward, like everyone else was privy to some secret that directly concerned her. As much as she liked Charlotte, her friend was something of a rabble-rouser, and something about "Julian has something to tell you" felt like throwing a lit match at tinder rather than an innocent secret.

Deciding to wait for Julian to tell her whatever secret she missed, she sat back and patted her face. That silver-eyed woman had magic, and next on her agenda, after secrets and sleep, was asking her how to get some too. Raised on a solid diet of movies featuring princesses and magic, Olivia often tried to align her boring, square life into the round peg that was the world of fantasy and magic she wished existed. She could pretend—and often did, to her parents' chagrin—that she was a part of that world, but ultimately, it was just acting.

And she hadn't made it as an actress. No matter who your folks were, without a lucky break, many aspiring actresses ended up like Olivia...pursuing more concrete occupations with an acting degree gathering dust on the wall.

She heard Julian before he came back into the kitchen. He walked loudly, like a marching knight. With how big a man he was, she imagined he'd gained the confidence and swagger of someone who went straight into fights and always emerged the victor. If she were somewhere north of six feet, with the muscle to match, maybe she'd feel the same way.

He came in wordlessly and cleared the plates, placing them in the sink before he drew a stool and sat across from her with a sigh. He seemed like a tired military member returning home, with his buzzed-short blond hair and fatigue lines creasing his otherwise handsome face. He was completely clean-shaven, with a strong jaw and generous lips. A solid brow gave his wintery-blue eyes a hooded look.

He looked to be deep in thought. She gave him time, her curiosity rising when it seemed like this was a more delicate subject to tell her about than she'd originally thought. "Olivia," Julian said finally. His accent caressed her name like *Oh-leev-ia*, and she smiled from that exotic touch.

"I wanted to wait to tell you this," he continued, measuring each word. "But it is important you understand what's going on. I think you were kidnapped because of me."

"Okay. But how? I don't really know who you are," she pointed out.

He scratched the back of his head, which she figured was some nervous tic. "In this case, that does not matter..." As she gazed at him expectantly, he finally spoke the truth he was struggling with. "You're my lifemate. I felt it the moment I saw you. You'd feel it too, if you were a vampire."

She sat back, blinking in surprise.

"It seems like you know a bit about vampires, so maybe you know that every vampire has a perfect match," he continued. It seemed once he'd cleared the block on his words, they continued to flow more evenly. "Like a soul mate. Someone just like them or, in some cases, their exact opposite. Two folks cut from the same cloth. That's...that's what you are to me."

He eyed her with obvious nerves, but she was starting to smile. She covered her growing excitement with two clasped hands. "I understand if this is really sudden—I'm not going to make any moves or anything. Not until you're ready—"

"Really?" she asked, bouncing with delight.

"Of course. I want to be respectful and—"

She smothering a handful of giggles as she interrupted. "No, I mean, really? We're lifemates? Love at first sight?" She could feel her eyes twinkling.

"Yes, really." His shoulders sagged with relief as he took in her expression.

"Oh, how romantic!" It was something straight from her fantasies, a gift toward a more magical, interesting life. "You know what this means, right?"

"Hmm?" A smile threatened the corner of his mouth.

"Why, we need to go on a date soon. Just you and me."

Now he really was smiling, the first positive emotion she'd seen from him in their limited time together. "I would like that."

"Me too. Know what else I'd like? Sleep. I have a lot of questions for you, but they can wait until after my face gets acquainted with a pillow." If she thought about it too hard, she'd start asking questions now and open a can of worms that would worry her all through the night—well, day. She was on vampire time now.

"That's fair. Why don't I show you to a room?" He offered a hand up, and she took it absently, surprised at a flick of static between them.

Chapter 7
Julian

Julian didn't sleep well. He attributed it to the cold, though part of him worried that more sinister forces were at work in his dreams. Lucia had attacked his dreams before, using dream walking, twisting his sleep into fragmented nightmares for a solid week before she made her move against him. He hadn't been aware of it consciously.

Lying in cold sheets, he couldn't say now if it was shivers or nightmares that kept him from the rest he desired. Either way, he made a conscious decision to mention his affliction to someone who understood magic at the first possible convenience. He couldn't keep telling himself nothing was wrong when he could barely move his stiff joints upon finally getting out of bed. He'd never made a snowstorm from his aura before, and he'd certainly never shot icicles from his palms like deadly projectiles.

Something was seriously wrong. He drank his coffee piping hot from the coffee maker that evening to feel some semblance of warmth after packing his things for an extended stay at Coven Rehnquist's headquarters, which doubled as Alex's mansion home. He imagined there was not much room left there after recent events.

If he had to share a room with a Blood Prince, he'd do it just to get a semblance of safety from the oppressive idea of Lucia lingering over his shoulder.

Alex was up first, joining him with a cup of tea. They sat in companionable silence. Just like Alex kept a perfunctory amount of coffee in his mansion for Julian and his nephew, Julian had a handful of tea sachets hidden in some dusty corner of a cupboard. He couldn't stand the stuff, comparing it to medicine.

"I'm surprised you're not with Violet right now," Julian remarked once he'd gotten a good dose of caffeine.

"She needs her rest," he said. "She hides it well, but she's exhausted. All this magic being thrown around and she still barely understands it and how to use it."

Julian nodded, a frown tugging at his lips. Violet had been exposed to some vile magic, with Lucia having made a failed gambit to switch her old, twisted body with Violet's. He'd had a front-row seat to that horror show and was humbled the woman was already on her feet at all.

He didn't want to linger on the past, even though his mind's eye showed him Violet's face with Lucia's too-wide smile as a reminder of what they were up against. Chaotic, vain evil. "Congratulations, by the way." He cleared his throat, which felt distinctly strained. Alex raised a brow. "On your mating, I mean. Finding a second lifemate. You're proof lightning can strike the same place twice."

Alex's face softened. "Thank you. She makes me very happy. I hope you feel the same way soon with the woman you've saved." Julian nodded in agreement, wanting the level of "stable and happy" Alex wore so well.

"Say, why don't you take her out after we debrief?" Alex suggested. "It's a lot of information, and you'll need time to process it. You could go spoil her in the meantime."

Julian was immediately torn, because that idea sounded far more appealing than how he thought his day would go. He was imagining poking and prodding by those who understood magic to figure out where his cold was coming from. That was the kind of thing he should invite today and push getting to know Olivia back until he could master the cold he struggled with.

"I could give you some dating pointers," Alex said lightly, clearly misinterpreting Julian's silence.

Rather than revealing his personal burden, Julian decided to play along. "Why not? You are successful, obviously."

They bantered about possible dates until the ladies emerged one by one, looking as ready to go as possible when two of them didn't even have a change of clothes. Julian knew they would be fixed up with new clothing and supplies quickly by Petra Jolovic, their coven's resident provider, who took special joy in decking out new members to vampire life.

With that in mind, Julian considered that Olivia might not even be ready to go on a date. Maybe they should get the help they needed before he asked her out. He still admired her as she walked by, her curls bouncing with each step.

"Well, ladies, it's a good time to get going," Alex said, ushering out Violet and Charlotte with a wink to him.

"Are you ready?" he asked Olivia, taking in her face. Now that her bruises were healed, she had a cute charm that made it hard for him to look away. Her hair was pulled back into a messy ponytail with individual strands trying to stick out in their own way.

"Yeah, sure," she said. Her rosebud lips were pursed in thought as they got into his car. "So, I have questions."

She'd warned him as much yesterday, and it sounded like she'd only saved them for the sake of his answers not getting in the way of her rest. Which meant the reality of their situation was about to encroach. He would need to explain himself better than he had upon revealing that they were lifemates. He'd gotten lucky that she thought it romantic rather than crazy. "And I have answers, hopefully," he said.

"Okay. First, I have to admit that Charlotte is a little wigged out about you. Like, she wants to drop this whole situation and run." She was watching their surroundings as she said this, hiding her expression.

"What do you think?" Hopefully, she wouldn't let her friend continue to lead her around as if she couldn't decide for herself.

In the reflection off the window, he saw her bite her lip. "I don't know what to think. The guy who was holding me captive warned that everything wasn't as it seemed, and I think he might be right about that."

"Who? Elandros?" His voice was low and cold with revulsion.

"Yeah."

His fingers tightened on the steering wheel. Frost crystals formed at the edges of his grip. "What else did he say to you?"

She shot a glance toward him. "Not too much. You know, small talk. I helped him get a cell phone set up, which he was hopelessly bad at. He said something about how his queen wanted me to be in that place, not the guy who'd given the green light to my capture." It was like she'd casually placed him in an ice water bath. He shivered, clenching his jaw to stop shivers.

"That's a really bad thing, isn't it? You look like you've seen a ghost," she continued.

"Did he mention that she can see the future?" he asked once the worst of the chills were past.

She considered for a few moments before nodding. "Something about that, yeah. Manipulating variables. I didn't really understand. It sounded like crazy-person or really old vampire talk."

His dread was a living thing, tangling in his throat and strangling off any reasonable explanation. All of what she'd just said continued to lay the path where Elandros and his "it is too easy" left off.

His pretty lifemate was still in danger because of him. It might come for her now, or it might wait for a vulnerable moment when they were least expecting it.

"You're right. This is bad," he confirmed with a sigh. "He didn't say anything else?"

"Well..." she leaned her head back, brow pinched as she focused. "I overheard him talking to someone else about murder. She called him an idiot because he wanted to go kill someone she'd made a mistake with."

His thoughts immediately went to Violet, but the inverted puzzle that was Lucia's logic continued to baffle him. "All right. Thank you for telling me."

"So, what does that all mean? Why did they kidnap me just to let me go?" It was hard to look into her earnest expression and not spill everything he knew in one ugly lump of truth.

"It's a long story," he said instead. "The woman he serves is a piece of work. She only has her best interests at heart despite how innocent things seem now."

She crossed her arms. "Kidnapping me wasn't innocent. And we have time. Tell me your long story?"

By the landmarks, she was right. They'd be in this car together for another fifteen minutes, and she needed to understand what was going on and how she possibly related to it. So, he started from the top, as he had with Charlotte, explaining what Nyixa rising from the ocean really meant. Ancient vampires bringing their ages-old strife back to the surface of their world.

She surprised him again once he finished explaining that nine Ancients had risen and most were in New York City, clasping her hands under her chin. "That's so cool," she gushed. "This is straight from a fantasy movie, you know that?"

"It's reality," he deadpanned.

"Well, what exciting times we live in, then. Think about it." She gasped. He quietly admired her enthusiasm, even if it was misplaced by the seriousness of their situation. "How often does an entire island rise from the ocean? Releasing someone with real *magic* into the world."

"It's too bad she's pure evil." And he had been a firsthand witness to that. "The only good thing she did was share her magic with Violet, but that was a ruse to trade bodies with someone who was young, beautiful, and a Sorceress."

Her dreamy smile vanished. "For real?"

"Pure evil," he repeated. "So..." He took a deep breath, knowing he couldn't control how she reacted to this but needed to hear it for herself. "You may be the starting point of a new plot for her to gain what she wants. A new body, or something else."

"Something else. Why would I want the face of someone you seek to love?"

He nearly drove off the road, the car wavering as he got it under control. "What's wrong?" Olivia asked, nearly as nervous as he felt.

"What have you done to me?" he demanded of Lucia now that he knew she was listening in on him somehow.

"Nothing you don't deserve, kinslayer," she responded in a velvety purr. He imagined her smooth words coming from her fanged maw and shuddered as cold swirled through the whole car. He rolled the window down to let in the humid summer air, flashing Olivia a look of apology.

He expected his mental connection to Lucia disappear now that she'd gotten in her quips. However, she didn't fade out, lingering at the back of his mind like a dark cloud. *"The time for games is nearly at an end. I promised that you would be the one to dismantle your life, one person at a time. Your nephew lies near death in the hospital... I wonder who's next?"*

She left him with that message, and his gaze immediately went to Olivia.

Chapter 8
Olivia

They arrived at Alex's mansion home without any more outbursts of freezing cold. Olivia felt quite official when she was invited to the informational meeting alongside Julian. She could tell that Charlotte was chagrined to be left out of whatever was going on, but she was pulled aside by someone by the name of Petra who was apparently buying them both clothes and other supplies for their stay in New York.

The only thing Julian had convinced her of was that her new situation wasn't nearly as exciting as she'd originally thought. So they were lifemates. To think she was the perfect match to an ice king made her nervous, no matter how attractive the strong and silent type was to her. And she was definitely interested based off his vampire-handsome looks while at the same time wondering how she would crack the shell of someone so reserved.

She found herself longing for her apartment and her mundane evening job waiting tables but then gave herself a mental shake. So soon into something interesting, she wanted to go back to boring? No way! Every story had its call to action, and she refused to deny hers despite the fear and doubt threatening to crowd out her interest and enthusiasm.

So, she sat alongside Julian in a big meeting room without looking back or asking to leave. Alex was at the head of the table, with Violet at his right hand. Around the room were less familiar faces, and the presence of some of them made her feel less at ease. Charlotte had taught her about auras a while back, how some vampires couldn't help leaking a bit of their power. Other vampires would know how old the offending person was by the amount of power in their aura, but humans would just feel discomfited.

Her gaze kept going to the man who'd introduced himself as Adrius, King of Vampires. Maybe he was the one with a broken aura barometer, just letting a power leak go. He was the biggest man she'd ever met, yet he'd kissed her fingertips like an old gentleman. His eyes were dark and watchful, set in a face creased not with age, but instead a lifetime of burdens. It was hard to tell on first glance when he also sported a bushy black beard braided and knotted intricately.

His younger brother was beside him, Prince Sirius, the Dawn. She'd known they were related upon sight, as they had nearly the same features. But while Adrius seemed quiet and detached, Sirius's maroon eyes gleamed with a fanatic's light, and his lips curled as if waiting eagerly for someone to say something he could argue with.

At the other end of the table sat a small blonde woman by the name of Sorsha, dressed like someone coming straight off a Victorian era set. Her dress was made of aquamarine satin, with intricate, dark lace down the front. Her sleeves were belled, a tail of satin moving with every gesture she made. Olivia admired the dress, imagining the woman to be a vampire from another time who couldn't quite let go of old memories.

Sorsha had promised as they came together for this meeting that her presence brought a dampening spell, so they could fling Lucia's name around like a curse word without the woman being able to see the moment with her future sight.

Alex had introduced her and the two people on their feet flanking her as "special guests," which was a distinction not even the King of Vampires and his brother received. She wondered about that as she also noticed Sorsha's companions, Keegan and

Ash, weren't at ease. Both had visible weapons from another time. Keegan had a sword on his hip, and Ash had a bandolier over her shoulder, which glinted with knife hilts.

Olivia was dying to ask about what was up with them, but she recognized that she was blessed to even be invited to this meeting with such a motley assortment of people. "A thousand years ago, I was beholden to your father and his men," Sirius said, looking to Julian as he spoke.

Julian stiffened at the mention of his father. *Sore spot,* she thought.

"And now, so much later, his son and spitting image is in the same place of power. Alexander recommended you to teach me of your lands and ways," Sirius continued. He didn't seem too pleased either.

"I would be honored to take up the mantle of such a task," Julian said. The formal courtesy made him seem flat.

Alex cleared his throat. "That's not why we're here today. Julian has been absent for a few days and has missed all the plans we put together. And our newcomer, Olivia, needs to understand just what kind of cluster we're dealing with."

Chuckling humorlessly, Adrius turned to her. "It would behoove you to keep an open mind."

"It's a lot at once," Violet said in agreement.

Olivia's curiosity burned brighter as they danced around the subject, glancing to her almost apologetically. "It's fine. I saw magic last night for my own self. I won't think you're crazy or anything."

Alex flashed a grin, showing a hint of pearlescent fang. "Well, we are all a little crazy, love. If you're not too, we'll teach you."

Julian held up a hand. "Where is the Curator?"

Immediately, Olivia felt a shift in the air. Sirius's eyes seemed to glow as his hands clenched to fists. "Resting. I've taken up her duties for the time being," answered Sorsha before Sirius could open his mouth. Her voice was like music—soft, sweet, and soothing.

"Let us begin," Adrius said, placing a hand on Sirius's

shoulder with a warning glance. "We have a problem a thousand years in the making."

"Lucia," Julian said, his voice dipped in vitriol.

"An instigator." Sorsha glanced around the room before lifting her hand. An orb the size of a small bowling ball rose over her shoulder, glowing from within with its own light. Olivia suppressed a gasp at how beautiful the foreign thing was, glimmering with gold dust under its glass surface. A pair of clockwork wings rose from behind it, the metal shaped like delicate feathers. Each bore a symbol on the fringes of the primaries. "For the uninitiated amongst us, this is an occultarus. An item that magnifies magic."

Sorsha made a gesture with one hand then the other. The first shot a stream of clear light at the occultarus, the second, a splash of water. Upon contact with the beautiful tool, shards of glass appeared and connected like a puzzle, turning into a wide-lipped glass that gently landed on the table just in time to receive a stream of water as the occultarus magnified the splash of water into a tall drink, complete with the *clink clink* of two ice cubes splashing in afterward.

"Showoff," whispered Ash behind her hand.

Olivia took the glass and inspected its dewing surface for any imperfections. "How...?"

"Magic," Sorsha said with a wink. "It's safe to drink."

Shrugging to herself, she tasted the water, finding it crisp and ordinary. "I'm sold. You have magic and a special crystal ball."

"What you probably don't know is that my special crystal ball, as you call it, is powered by a donation of magical energy from a much, much larger version called an Eye of Worlds. There's two. Well..." Sorsha's delicate features tightened. "There were two. Not only did they give us the energy to make occultari, they also served as grounding points for the veil between worlds."

Olivia glanced around at everyone else. Other than Julian raising a brow, no one else seemed surprised that this woman was suddenly talking about other worlds. Sorsha looked Olivia dead in the eye and said, "I'm a fae, from the land of Faerie."

She couldn't help it; she started to laugh. "No way!" When no one else laughed with her, her tittering faded to unease.

In reply, Sorsha snapped her fingers. Between one blink and the next, her true nature became apparent and left the room in slack-jawed awe. Except for Violet, who elbowed Alex and said, "I told you, didn't I?"

Sorsha's fae appearance kept her old-fashioned clothing but forewent everything else familiar about her. It looked like someone had superimposed the night sky upon her skin, leaving the imprint of midnight velvet sprinkled with winking stars. Her hair stayed up in a messy bun, but it was like someone had spilled glitter over her stark white hair. Some had gotten into her eyes, which were so wide and full they'd make a makeup artist weep with envy.

Curiously, her eyes were absent of pupil and sclera, instead showing a solid glow of golden stars that shifted like the surface of her occultarus. The rest of her features remained delicate and familiar, except her ears, which rose to points. A set of butterfly-like wings rose from her back, pinned awkwardly against a seat not made for such features. Like the rest of her, they glimmered with random pinpricks of light.

Behind her, Keegan and Ash remained in their human forms. Sorsha's light reflected from Keegan's eyes, making them sparkle as well. "Like I was saying, I'm a fae, from Faerie," she smiled. "I'm an astral fae, to be more specific. A fair Seelie fae, which means I cannot tell a lie."

Olivia reached up and pushed her jaw back into place. "You're the most gorgeous woman I've ever seen," she said, her hands flying up to frame her face. "This is, like, my childhood dream. To meet a real-life fairy!" Though she had to admit not being able to tell a lie must be quite a handicap.

"Glad to give you the experience." She flashed a starry wink before turning back into her human form. Clearing her throat, she added, "My identity and what I'm about to tell you cannot leave the room. All right?" It was obvious she was talking to Julian and Olivia, though everyone around the table nodded.

"Defeating Lucia needs to take a backseat to a new task,"

Sorsha said. Julian stiffened immediately, and Olivia hoped that he would at least hear out what the pretty fae had to say. "Most of you were on Nyixa when the Eye of Worlds there was destroyed. That's a *huge* deal on the scale of supernatural events. To the point where a new one needs to be constructed before midwinter or we have some serious problems." Her starry gaze landed on Julian. "Do you believe in demons?"

Chapter 9
Julian

Julian wasn't as impressed with the fae woman as Olivia, who seemed quite enamored by the flash of a pretty glamor. The only woman he had any attraction to was his life-mate, and even then, he knew he wasn't man-of-the-year in expressing that to her. He needed more time with just the two of them to tell her properly.

But Sorsha's question hung in the air between them. He figured he was going to be educated on this whether he believed or not. "Yes, I believe in demons. There is enough evil in human and vampire kind alike as proof."

Adrius shook his head. "I'm so glad Gwendolyn isn't here right now. Just mention the demon-word, and she rants."

While he might be relieved, Julian wanted the Curator, Gwendolyn Firetree, there at this meeting. She had helped him in the past and continued to do so for his friends. When Violet turned up with silver blood and no understanding of her powers, it was Gwendolyn who'd taken her and Alex to a safe place and taught Violet what she needed to know to be a successful Sorceress.

But he could see how talk of demons would get her fired up. Gwendolyn was a former nephilim, a half-angel, half-human, turned vampire to continue serving her faith while keeping the world orderly. She was the shadowy Curator for the longer time, "curating" or removing the oldest and most corrupt vampires through extraordinary means. He saw her secret weapon right in front of him, three fae with unknown and obviously powerful magic at their fingertips.

"Well, let me take a page from her book for a minute," Sorsha said, clearing her throat. "Demons are the worst, most vile creatures to inhabit this world and the next. You may think you know evil, but most have never met evil to this degree. A true demon has no goodness within them, only a desire to see mankind and the world destroyed in the most painful, drawn-out way possible."

With a gesture, her occultarus started to project a model of Earth with a thick gray circle around it. It divided into quarters, marked "Angels" at the top and "Demons" at the bottom, with "Unseelie" to one side and "Seelie" to the other.

"I'm going to try to make this as simple as possible," Sorsha said, pointing to the junction where demons and Unseelie met. A glass ball appeared there, obviously cracked in half. She did the same where angels and Seelie met with a ball of golden light, much like the occultarus she wielded.

"Violet saved us from a second wave of Fell attacking the world. Thank you for that," she said, inclining her head to the Sorceress. Julian murmured to Olivia an explanation of what a Fell was, the grotesque cursed fae that were the predecessors to vampires. Known for their insatiable hunger and jaws lined with fangs, they'd nearly consumed the world a thousand years ago before Adrius and an army of like-minded vampires slaughtered them and claimed the island nation of Nyixa for themselves.

Olivia looked quite overwhelmed, her face paling. "Right, okay," she muttered.

"But in saving us from that wave, the Eye of Worlds on Nyixa was destroyed," Sorsha sighed, pointing to her diagram. "It was the Dark Eye, the one that keeps the veil opaque for demons and Unseelie fae. Without it, by midwinter..." The diagram's thick gray veil blew away like clouds to a breeze. "On the darkest day of the year, the Light Eye that remains intact in Faerie will be unable to keep these bad actors from breaching the veil and causing havoc on Earth."

Julian felt his body chill to the bone with the implications. What was worse, an invasion of demons or of Fell?

"How do we repair it?" he asked. She was right. In the scheme of things, Lucia would still need to be dealt with, but this took precedence. Yet they were still at war with her and the mega-coven she'd assembled from her supporters in New York City. In all likelihood, his job would be to end this war as soon as possible while the more magically-inclined helped Sorsha with the Eye of Worlds.

All three fae looked grim as Sorsha waved away the model of Earth. "We have to do what's never been done before. This goes all the way back to the origins of the fae."

The occultarus made a new image for them. This time, it was of a man's tall crown, jewels glimmering within its gold minarets. "Our first king was named Oberon, and this was his crown, fashioned with long-lost magics in the heart of the forging world," Sorsha said. "There are thirteen gems in it, each holding an immense amount of power from one of the thirteen schools of fae magic. Oberon was the greatest Sorcerer of our kind, and it was he who created both Eyes of Worlds, sealing concentrated angel magic in one and demon magic in the other to keep Earth safe from the never-ending conflict between both sides. He gave his life to do it, but the crown lived on and graced the head of every Seelie King that followed."

"Well, that's cool," Olivia said. "Some fantasy stuff for sure. The all-powerful crown for the strong king."

"Except it nearly fell into the wrong hands. The man who created the Fell curse wanted it for himself," Sorsha said.

Olivia snapped her fingers. "Of course. There's always a bad guy scheming to have the MacGuffin."

The fae blinked owlishly. "I'm sorry, a what?"

"A MacGuffin! You know, an important item that moves the plot of a story forward? There's always a MacGuffin in a good story," she said with a smile. "Especially movies."

"Something tells me there aren't many movies in Faerie, love," Alex said dryly.

Sorsha shook her head. "Anyway. An Astral Archfae of the

time, Izell Firebrand, saw the catastrophe that would follow if he got his hands on Oberon's crown. So, she shattered the enchantment keeping the gems linked to one another and melted down the gold to make rings for each individual gemstone. From there, she sent them to Earth and laughed in the face of the man who wanted to use them for his own purposes. Izell famously told him that the greed of mortals would ensure the gems would never be reunited in full again. And so far...she was right."

Julian rubbed at a dry patch of skin between his thumb and forefinger, lost in his own thoughts. If she was implying what he thought she was, their only hope lay in reuniting all thirteen of those gemstones and using them to repair the damaged Eye of Worlds. "Is it...possible?" he asked quietly.

"To find them all again? It will have to be," Sorsha sighed. "Vampires of Adrius and Sirius's time called the gemstones the Fell Keys, as in the keys to victory. At one point, I think they had eleven of thirteen. That's the current record."

"But two of them are lost in the Fell Lands permanently," Adrius put in, his dark gaze elsewhere with a cresting of pain across his features. "My wife Nyah died there with them on her fingers." Now it was Sirius's turn to put a hand on his shoulder, murmuring private words of comfort.

Violet opened her mouth as if to say something before closing it with a shake of her head. She and Alex glanced to one another to share mental words.

"We will have to repair it with what we can salvage." Sorsha gazed at the crown's image with her lips pressed tight in determination. "We already have two Keys."

"Oh yeah? Who has them?" Olivia asked curiously, leaning around Julian. "How can we help?"

Adrius answered for the fae, holding out a meaty hand. On his ring finger was a masculine band marked with a tiger's eye stone. "I have the Shield Key. And Gwendolyn has the Portal Key."

"What does it let you do?" she asked, her fingers twitching like she wanted to touch the piece of ancient fae history.

He adjusted the band with a sigh. "A long time ago, I had it magically attached to me as a sign of devotion to my wife. It can only be removed if I die. And in my many years, I have died many times, but the Shield Key's magic is unique in that it always brings me back."

Julian sat straighter to know he was in the presence of an item *that* powerful, even though Adrius made it sound more like a burden than a blessing as he swept his thumb over its stone face. If a simple gemstone could bring back the dead, what could the rest do?

"That's intense," Olivia said, shifting uncomfortably under Adrius's dark gaze.

"As for how you can help, I asked that you attend for a specific reason," Sorsha continued, her attention back on Olivia. "My fellows and I are temporarily cut off from Faerie. Due to Lucia's meddling with the Dark Eye before its destruction, we are the only three that were able to make the crossing at midsummer a few days ago. When we left, the Seelie King was shoring up the Light Eye's magic and our defenses against possible Unseelie assault. Things are in a state of panic there."

It made sense to Julian that the destruction of something so important would send shockwaves through a magical community. "What I mean is..." Sorsha sighed, scrubbing at her face in a less-than-graceful manner. "Ash, Keegan, and I are all you get on the magic front. We can do a lot. I'm an Archfae myself. But...it's still only three of us against a possible invasion from Hell and the Unseelie if we aren't successful. We need help. We need to start turning and training more Sorcerers and Sorceresses with the unwitting gift Lucia gave to us." She gestured to Violet, who seemed to know this twist was coming. She nodded, lifting her chin with a determined expression.

"Are you asking if I want to be a Sorceress?" Olivia gasped, a hand over her chest. "I would *love* that." Julian's attention snapped to her in shock at her quick offering.

"Wait—no," he interjected. Despite how radiant her excited smile was, he quashed it with a quick denial.

"What do you mean, no?" Her gaze flicked between him and Sorsha.

"You've just gotten here, and this is the unknown." Magic had ruined his quiet life, and he'd be damned if he didn't give her a dose of reality. "There are only two vampires with magic, and it's incredibly dangerous."

Her brow drew together. "Yes, and I intend to be the third."

"Why don't you sleep on it?" he suggested. Over her shoulder, Alex was making an exaggerated face of distress and shaking his head as Julian pressed and Olivia's face flushed.

There was an edge to her tone, a leery look in her eyes that reminded him they were near strangers. "I know what I want, and that's what I'm volunteering for."

"So there you have it, old chap. Our plan, such as it is," Alex put in loudly, with Julian reluctantly allowing the segue. "You and Prince Sirius are going to be leading our men in taking on Lucia's coven. Things have been suspiciously quiet in that regard. While you do that, we're mounting a search for the remaining Fell Keys." From how he spoke, it was apparent he thought that was like finding a set of needles in the massive haystack that was the world and, as such, impossible. "And our magical friends are going to do everything in their power to both repair the Eye of Worlds and train as many Sorcerers as possible in the eventuality we have to hold off a supernatural assault until help comes in the form of nice fairies or angels or whatever's coming next. Bloody hell." He rubbed at his forehead.

"I see you're taking this well," Julian murmured.

"We have one more hurdle," Alex said, putting his arm around Violet. "How do we turn a human into a Sorceress? Traditional vampires have a ritual and the tools for the job." He unsheathed his fangs in meaning.

"We'll just have to experiment. It'll be fine." Violet leaned into his side.

Olivia was starting to smile again. "Experimenting is fine. I'm down to experiment." The sort of words Julian dreaded hearing. The lifemate he'd just found, experimenting with her life.

"Well then, let's not dally," Sorsha said, rising from her chair at last. Her occultarus returned to her, floating around her like a moon to its planet.

Everyone made to stand, except for Adrius and his brother, who both motioned to Julian. "I need to pick your brain, Marcuson," Sirius said.

Julian knew he was being referred to by his father's name as a traditional surname that he should still have—Julian, son of Marcus, or Marcuson for short—and it made him flinch. "I'll be right back," he muttered, accompanying Olivia as she left the room. "You don't have to do this, you know that, right?" he said.

She turned back to him, her lips pressed together in what would soon be ire if he kept pushing the subject. "I'm doing it."

"I mean...this is unknown territory for us. You might be at risk trying to become a Sorceress yourself," he warned, searching for what might make her second-guess this snap decision. "They'll make you drink blood."

She seemed to consider that and him, her eyes dancing over his face. Taking a deep breath, she said, "I appreciate that you're concerned for me. Just remember that that magic fairy woman just promised me magic. Real magic. Who would say no to that, even if it involves some risk?"

She backed away from him, shrugging like she'd already proven her point. He didn't realize Sorsha was listening in until he glanced up to find her flashing him a reassuring smile. The fae mouthed the words, "I'll take care of her."

He figured that was the best he would get for now. He nodded and returned to the meeting room, his heart heavy with cold and conflicting emotions. At least the two vampire royals gave him little time to worry, grilling him on numbers and other specifics as they mapped out the war to come.

Chapter 10
Olivia

Olivia couldn't get Julian's disappointed face out of her head as she followed the group through the mansion. She knew she was making a too-quick decision she might regret later. But *magic*. The promise of being able to emulate what she'd seen from Violet and Sorsha had her motivated. She wanted to make her own tall glasses of water, to heal, to make projections, and do whatever else they were capable of.

The world may depend on it.

She wasn't just Olivia Cooper, washed-up actress and daughter of two very disappointed businesspeople. She was one of the only people who knew just what was at stake and could take it upon herself to become Olivia, the Sorceress. This was her true call to action, the moment she'd waited all her life for.

Sorsha took her into what looked like a medical wing, where a man with Blood Prince maroon eyes was sorting supplies and talking to a vampiress with sharp features. They both wore scrubs, fresh off a shift at a hospital, their hands waving in an animated debate. "Hi, Jaromir. Hi, Melanie," Sorsha said, reaching for a refrigeration unit marked with a biohazard warning. Both medical professionals turned and smiled.

The man, Jaromir, then stared intently at Olivia. Hard enough that she felt like he would burrow a hole right through her.

"Um, hello," she said, feeling her shoulders draw in. *Interest and enthusiasm,* she reminded herself, taking a breath and shaking off those nerves with the best smile she could offer.

"This is Olivia. She's going to be our first trial patient," Sorsha said. She removed a plastic vial, like the type used in blood donations, from the fridge. This one was full to the brim with silver liquid.

"No." Jaromir hadn't taken his gaze from Olivia. "Let me turn her instead. I can sense she will be Gifted."

Olivia felt the room shift as everyone turned to look at her, including Violet and Alex, who'd settled in a corner to watch this happen. She felt a blush creeping from her neck all the way to her ears.

"Do you think..." She cleared her throat, not accustomed to how nervous she was to have the speculative attention of all these people. "...that will keep me from becoming a Sorceress?"

Jaromir's expression softened. "It's just...the Gift is so rare. Let others try to gain the silver blood. You're already special."

She felt like she was about to become a petulant child stamping the ground. *But I want magic,* she imagined herself whining.

No, that wouldn't impress a Blood Prince at all. "What if having the Gift and Sorceress magic would make me *extra* special?" she reasoned.

Sorsha motioned her over with a shake of her head. "Jaromir, I just spent the better part of an hour explaining why this is so important. At least let me try to change her."

He looked ready to argue but clasped his hands instead with a sigh. "I suppose Sorceresses also have healing magic."

"That's right," Sorsha said with a hint of cheer. "All right, my two Gifted. Have you thought through how best this would work?"

"Well, we've certainly argued about it," the sharp-featured woman, Melanie, said. "Traditional vampire turnings involve a swapping of blood between sire and fledgling. But there's an inherent mix of blood because the sire bites his intended fledgling first and then feeds blood back to them."

"Yet that's not how Lucia, Nyah, or Violet were turned." Jaromir went from disappointed to professional in a blink, pulling out a couple of diagrams to show Sorsha. "They got their blood directly from a Sorcerer Fell. Lucia drank cursed blood from the source, and we all know how well that turned out. Nyah and Violet drank a more purified version combed free of its magic. One became an Alchemyst, the other a Sorceress, so the purification process did not end with the same results."

"Have you considered it was a difference in body composition between both women?" Sorsha asked, engaging with him on a discussion of humors.

Olivia shot Violet a bemused look, hoping for a friend amongst these strangers talking about her like a clinical subject. The Sorceress came over to her side. "They've been going on about this for a while," she confided. "Like, before we found you to do the first test. If this works, you're going to be the first Sorceress that wasn't turned into one from some ancient guy's blood. But since there's been so few, they don't know how this is going to go."

"I can tell the uncertainty is killing them. Especially the Blood Prince," Olivia said.

"Personally, I think you should just plug your nose, drink my blood, and be done with it," she said with a shrug. "It's really gross, I know, but at least you didn't have to taste what a thousand years in a vial does to blood."

Olivia felt her face pucker with distaste. "You did that willingly?"

"Well...not quite. But I don't really remember it, so that helps?" Violet said with what levity she could muster.

"So, what's the holdup, then? If I get fancy magic, I can get over the whole blood thing." Though the more everyone hesitated, the more grossed out she became by the reality of that idea.

"They're comparing regular vampirism to magical vampirism," she said. "Which is like apples and oranges, by the way. I'm going to be so glad when you're a Sorceress so I'm not the only one around here that needs human food. Maybe my *generous, thoughtful* mate will buy more of a variety."

Alex glanced their way. He was standing a polite distance away from their conversation. "I feel a disturbance in the force."

"So, you eat regular food? Not blood?" Olivia was too relieved to acknowledge they were engaging in some couple-y humor.

Probably an inside joke anyway. She thought to Julian for a moment, wondering if they'd have a moment to get to know each other better. Maybe make some inside jokes of their own.

"Yup! It was a relief to me too." Violet smiled. Her teeth were noticeably not sharp where vampires usually had overdeveloped canines.

They both startled when Melanie slapped her palm against a desk in frustration. "Look, I know you two are still in the Middle Ages, but I want to run some tests on her with *modern* equipment first," she snapped.

Olivia hadn't realized they'd been arguing that heatedly but was also glad when the other two agreed and turned to her. Seemed they had a plan at last. They started with a blood draw from her. Melanie headed back to the desk and its equipment to run a complicated battery of tests.

While she did, Olivia passed the time chit-chatting with Violet more. She was glad to know the other woman didn't just look it—they were the same age, unlike everyone else in this room, who were well over three digits. As a fresh Sorceress, Violet didn't know much more than her about magic. Sorsha was apparently in the process of building her a new occultarus. Her first one, Violet confided, was made from the energy of the Dark Eye, so its loss wasn't so bad in the scheme of things when an occultarus aligned with the Light Eye would be more responsive to her.

"There's a lot more to magic than you can learn in a week, like I've tried to. I'm glad Sorsha is around, because she's used it for a really long time," Violet said.

"How long is a long time?" With Sorsha's exotic features, it was difficult to put any sort of age to her.

"I'm not sure. But probably as long as the Blood Princes have been around. One of them raised her and Keegan," she confided.

"So, a thousand?"

"That's just too old," Olivia said, whistling low.

"Time moves differently in Faerie. I'm much older, technically," Sorsha said, apparently overhearing them. She was shaking the vial of Violet's blood as she listened in on a new hail of medical jargon from Melanie reading out bloodwork results.

"Like, how old?" Olivia asked tentatively as the fae approached with the vial outstretched.

"I wouldn't let it concern you. I stopped counting a long time ago," Sorsha said. She pressed the vial into Olivia's waiting palm. "Your doctor has the results she needs. And it sounds like Olivia is perfectly healthy?" She directed this over to Melanie and Jaromir, whose heads were nearly touching as they reviewed a few printed sheets of paper.

"Green light." Melanie nodded.

"The transformation may induce her to sleep. I recall it took a day for Nyah," Jaromir said.

Violet glanced to Alex, who looked pensive. "The circumstances where much different, but Violet slept for a long time as well."

"Right. Good thing I'm sitting on a bed," Olivia said, holding up the vial. "So, just drink this? Or did you decide you needed to do something fancy with it?"

The two Gifted doctors exchanged a glance. "Just drink it," Sorsha said before they could speak up.

"Right on." She popped the top like it was a bottle cap and looked anywhere but downward as she tipped into her mouth. Even with her nose pinched, she nearly wretched as she swallowed the silver blood. But she was a performer through and through, and under so many pairs of watchful eyes, she muscled through it.

She glanced at the vial once she was done, seeing a silver residue at the bottom and feeling no different. Other than grossed out, that was, unpleasant goosebumps prickling her arm.

"I drank it all. When does this stuff start work—?"

Shouts of alarm sounded around her as the world pitched sideways. Someone caught her before she could hit the ground, placing her on her back. *The ceiling tiles are spinning,* she thought with wonder, reaching a hand up toward them. It crumpled back to her chest as her eyes shut. *Just a little nap...*

Chapter 11
Julian

Julian had plenty to keep him occupied for the next day. It turned out that Alex's offered plan to give him the rest of the evening off wasn't in the cards. Not when Olivia lay asleep as her body either accepted or fought the transformation induced by a drink of Violet's blood.

Instead, she remained in his thoughts as he studied the numbers and a traditional map of New York City. Someone had already taken colored highlighters to it, sectioning out the territory that belonged to each individual coven. The biggest section, belonging to Coven Deveaux, was cut off from the rest by enemy territory, which was circled in red. Their best strategy was surrounding enemy Coven Rockefeller's land and forcing them to retreat. That would leave them with only one place to go.

The subway tunnels. He had a separate map for that, one he updated by hand with known chokepoints and possible trap locations. It was incomplete knowledge—most of the area that Haven inhabited underground belonged to a different coven aboveground. One of the first things his new fighters would need to do was help him fill in the gaps on this map.

It was possible that, at last, he and his friends could be rid of Haven, who'd declared for Lucia against the majority opinion.

He would be glad of it, but he could barely concentrate on the lines before him and the numbers of men and women each coven was willing to spare toward making a joint army. His mind kept wavering back to Olivia. What if Violet's blood wasn't pure enough to facilitate a transformation? She could've drunk the equivalent of poison in the name of getting the precious magic she desired.

Sirius eventually dismissed him, seeing his distraction, so Julian went to the medical wing to find it abuzz with activity. Melanie, Jaromir, and the three fae were all discussing Olivia. The curtains were drawn around the first bed.

Seated in a wheeled chair right beside the folds of white cloth was Charlotte, scrolling on her phone. She was dressed in street clothes now, looking much more comfortable except for a scowl that twisted her expression. "Bloodhound," she acknowledged upon glancing up.

"Phantom," he returned.

"How am I supposed to keep my friend safe if she rushes headlong into the next danger with arms wide open? For *magic* of all things?" she asked matter-of-factly.

He found another chair to roll over and sit with her. "This was her choice. And there's enough medical personnel and magic-wielders in here that I imagine she'll be fine."

She raised a brow, looking him over. "If you think that, why are you here looking like you're full of worry?"

"Because she's still my lifemate." But she was here out of worry too, he thought. "Did you know that you're the first dhampir I've met?" he asked out of nowhere. Half-vampires were so incredibly rare for several reasons, namely that vampires strug-gled to conceive in their advanced ages, no matter their partner. But a half-vampire was also an unstable sort, more likely than not to mutate to full vampire status and lose the unique ability to have a foothold in both the worlds of day and night.

"I'm so very honored," Charlotte said dryly.

"Is it true that dhampirs feel an extra sense of loyalty to those they feed from?" He knew his answer when she stopped the casual inspection of her nails to shoot him an uncomfortable look. "You've fed from Olivia."

"Look, I'm not here to get in your way or anything. It's an

instinct thing that a lot of older vamps take advantage of." She crossed her arms, looking anywhere but at him. "I served Rosas for so long because he would only let me feed from him. He finally dismissed me because hired pure-vampire muscle is still better against other vampires. It was a relief to drink someone else's blood, because I finally got to forget about him."

"No wonder you left New York," he said, hoping Rosas had paid her handsomely for her service. Though he figured that wasn't the case, not when it was easier to let her dhampir instincts keep her tethered in place.

"And now I'm back, because of her," she sighed. "I know why you're asking. I ain't here to step on your toes. I'll get another blood host as soon as I see that she's happy with you."

"Have you ever tried tracking the vampire side of your family?" While he appreciated the promise, he could sympathize with her plight. She had to pick the right person, or people, because she'd be compelled to stay with and protect them. As far as he knew, a dhampir only fed once a month, leaving him or her stuck with their choices for a while.

"Oh, sure. My dad skipped out on my mom, but she's long gone." She affected a shrug. "I probably won't ever find him."

"Give me what you know, and I'll try to help you find him," he offered.

Her eyes narrowed, and her arms crossed harder, like the press of steel bars. "Why?"

Hooking a thumb to himself, he said, "Bloodhound."

"No, I know your claim to fame." She gave off an unladylike snort. "Why offer to help me?"

"Because I can't imagine being beholden to anyone just for a taste of their blood," he admitted. She might have a mental scream harsh enough to incapacitate even a Master vampire such as himself, but what was that worth when she could be so easily manipulated? He'd recently been played like a puppet to the strings of someone far more unpleasant than Coven Rosas's leader and hoped such a thing would never happen to her.

"Hmm." It seemed she wouldn't accept his offer, as her stance remained unchanged.

Well, I tried, he thought.

"I'll tell you everything once you do something for yourself first," she said finally, rubbing her arms. "Your aura is still cold as heck. Don't think I've forgotten your glowing eyes or anything else I saw in Haven Tower."

His lips twisted as he realized he hadn't asked anyone for help, so caught up in Olivia and everything else going on all at once. He could endure a little cold. Though with her reminding him, a *little* cold crept under his skin, drawing shivers down his spine.

"You got someone you can talk to about it?" she asked.

He nodded slowly. "I've been meaning to."

She made a shooing gesture. "So, do it. Take care of yourself first."

With a sigh, he stood, not realizing Charlotte was inspecting the chair until he turned to see frost evaporating from the back-rest. She gave him a pointed look, and all he could do was shrug and go to Sorsha. The fae sounded like she was wrapping up her time in the medical wing, turning to him like he was expected.

Perhaps he was. Who knew if she had the same magic capabilities of Lucia, who saw the future and lined up chance meetings?

As if his thoughts summoned her, Lucia's voice came into his head like the brush of poisoned silk. *"So this is the fae. I have scried so hard, but my mind's eye always looks away before seeing her face."*

He felt ice water drip down his spine as Sorsha turned and offered a brief smile. "Hello, Julian. Do you have a question?"

"Could I speak with you? Privately?" he asked, eyeing her two companions standing against the wall, looking bored yet alert.

Keegan and Ash exchanged a glance. "Not fully private," Sorsha said with an apologetic smile. "Let's step out into the hall, though."

"Pretty and blonde, just like Violet. I wonder what her blood will taste like," Lucia continued to whisper despite his best attempts to block her out.

Out in the hall, a different woman's voice spoke up, husky

and low. "A presence hangs overhead. Good or bad, who could say?" It was Ash, and despite her vague words, she stared directly at him.

"Can you do something about it?" he asked, hoping, for all their talk of magic, one of them had a counter for Lucia's tricks up their sleeve.

Ash smiled, though to call it that was more to admire the snarl of a wildcat. The pressure at the back of his head vanished, all hints of Lucia gone. "The elder Sorceress does not take interest in you," she said.

"I think you have that backward," he said.

"Ash is Unseelie, Julian," Sorsha explained, nodding to the other woman in appreciation. "She can only tell lies, like Keegan and I are bound to the truth. So, the easiest way to talk to you is reverse what she's saying."

He scratched his head, feeling a headache coming on. So much to keep track of between their dire message and strange magics. "Does Lucia have something to fear for you being Unseelie rather than Seelie?" he asked Ash directly.

Her answer was crisp. "No."

So, yes, Lucia would have troubles because they had an Unseelie in the house. A relieved smile crossed his face. He made a mental note to befriend this woman quickly.

"But that's not what you wanted help with, was it?" Sorsha asked.

"No. This is." He held out his non-dominant hand to her. His fingertips were purple with cold, the rest of his skin dry. When she touched him, her hands felt like a heated blanket. He hoped she could figure out what was wrong from a brief inspection. Like a doctor might, but in a magical sense.

"Talk to me. When did you take chill?" she asked.

He explained his captivity to Lucia and all the pertinent information afterward, aware that these fae were likely conversing privately as they exchanged glances and crowded around him. While being held against his will, the cold crept in and hadn't left, except when he'd inexplicably shot sharp icicles from his palms.

"You do have a lot of magic in your system, like you are on the cusp of a vampire ascension. Are you close to gaining another ability?" Sorsha asked once he was done.

"I'm right between Master and Elder," he said, knowing he was somewhere in his third century of life. He'd stopped counting long ago, never expecting to make it to Elder status, which happened at age five hundred or so.

"Well, such things aren't unheard of. It would explain why you're so backed up with the cold, too," she said thoughtfully. "Something tells me Lucia has little to do with this. It's an odd coincidence, for certain. How about I give you some relief for now and we'll see how long it takes to return?"

"Please," he said quickly. He would do nearly anything to feel warm again.

Sorsha took his hand like they were shaking on a deal, humming a tune under her breath. Her occultarus flashed, and Julian felt a *pull* as if she were taking every iota of cold from him. Frost crept up her arm in a progression of crystals, but she shook it off afterward with a smile. "Better?"

Julian's skin was prickling and flushing all over, followed by the uncomfortable rush of heat that always came from entering a warm building after being out in the cold. He embraced that feeling, flexing his hands and feeling abused joints stop their brittle ache. "Thank God for you," he murmured.

"Hey, you're welcome. And if you need it again, well, you know where to find me," she offered. He nodded and took his leave to go rest, hoping he could find a peaceful night now that Lucia was temporary pushed from his headspace and the cold eased from his whole body.

He could hear the three fae's whispers follow him as he ascended the stairs in search of his loaned room in the mansion. He was too tired to acknowledge that they sounded worried.

Chapter 12
Olivia

She opened her eyes to a splitting migraine. Someone was screaming nearby, but the words passed in and out of her understanding as she pulled her pillow up over her ears with a groan. Yet she could still hear the woman who shouted like she wanted to shake the world.

"...corruption! Did you test...?"

Somehow, she knew it was about her. The woman sounded frightened.

A more familiar voice cut in. "Grandmother, it'll be all right..." Sorsha soothed her further, but Olivia's lids fell like the turning of a shutter.

She woke again some time later, like her mind wanted to dip its toes in the idea of being awake before taking the plunge to full awareness. Nobody had their voice raised this time. Her headache was easing to pressure toward the back of her head as she sat up, seeing she was still in the clothes she'd fallen asleep in. Someone had stashed her shoes to the side and drawn a curtain around her bed.

Testing her limbs, she realized she felt like she was just waking from a long nap. She wasn't weakened or tired, but she also didn't feel different. After tossing the thin hospital bed covers aside, she put on and laced her shoes before drawing the curtain aside.

She took a glance left and right, but the wing was empty save for one of the Gifted, the woman. It took Olivia a moment to remember her name, Melanie. She was at a computer, sipping from a mug to stave off the dark half-circles under her eyes. Glancing up at Olivia, she did a double take and nearly coughed up her next mouthful.

"You're awake!"

"Yeah. As long as no one starts yelling again," she said, knowing she sounded distracted as she looked for a mirror. "Did it work? Do I have silver blood?" She drew up her sleeve, realizing she hadn't even looked.

At first, she couldn't find her veins. And when Melanie approached, she wasn't quite smiling. "Your eyes seem normal. Why don't you have a seat so I can inspect you?"

"So, it didn't work." Olivia sat with a disappointed huff. Had she really just choked down a stranger's blood for nothing? Not to mention the impromptu nap. She thought nervously to what Charlotte would say to her next about being too trusting.

"Well, see for yourself." Melanie offered her a hand mirror.

Something was definitely different. Olivia brought the glass up close to her face to see what it was. "I'm going to need new makeup," she commented. Her complexion had darkened a full shade, like she'd tanned overnight. But with how pale Violet was, it was apparent her silver blood had done the opposite to her. Which meant for Olivia...

Well, she didn't know. "How about you poke me with something sharp?" she suggested. She would be immensely disappointed if her blood ran red, but it was the most straightforward way to see if anything had changed except for her magic tan. As preposterous as *magic tan* was to even consider.

"You know, that's not a bad idea," Melanie said, holding her hand out. A pack of sterilized equipment flew into her grasp, making Olivia gape. "Oh, come now. Your dhampir never did any mental tricks for you?" It sounded like she was teasing as she broke the seal on the tools.

"My...oh, you've met Charlotte?" she asked almost sheepishly.

"She and Julian spent some time here." She withdrew a scalpel and took hold of Olivia's wrist. They nodded to each other then watched the blade of the tool as she sank its tip into the middle of Olivia's forearm. She winced from a twinge of pain, watching the wound as a drop came to the surface.

Her lips parted as her blood made a trail down her arm. Its metallic glint didn't lie.

Something had happened during her slumber. Something was different.

But instead of silver, her blood was approaching a golden hue. She figured what red remained in the mix was because she wasn't quite done changing. She and Melanie exchanged a glance.

"I...ah...I'll call for Sorsha." The Gifted doctor seemed lost for words.

"Yeah, okay. She'll know what to do," she agreed quickly.

Melanie set the scalpel aside and wiped Olivia's skin clean with a square of gauze and cotton. The little hole was nowhere to be seen, neatly sewn up after leaking that single drop. It seemed a lot like vampire regeneration to her. She'd seen it in action a few times when Charlotte burned herself on the stove or had a papercut. Healed up in minutes or moments, depending on the severity, with hardly a mark to show for it.

Sorsha didn't arrive alone. She and Keegan flanked an unfamiliar silhouette that entered the medical wing with assistance from a cane. Looking like someone ready to tell some whippersnappers to get off her lawn, the newcomer was an elderly woman with a scowl making wrinkles sink deep in her face.

Olivia turned her gaze to Sorsha, who flashed a reassuring, megawatt smile. "Grandmother, this is Olivia. As you can see, she's fine."

She offered forth her hand. "Hello. I'm fine," she repeated.

"I'll be the judge of that," sighed the elderly woman, taking her hand in a gentle clasp. "I'm Gwendolyn. Usually the one to experiment and tinker. But it seems when Sorsha offers to take up my duties for a few days, she gleefully takes up *all* my duties."

The fae's expression held a distinct lack of remorse. "I knew you would be too cautious. We've been over this already."

"Indeed." Gwendolyn gave a tired sigh. A rolling chair shot toward her hand as she held it out, sitting down and laying her cane across her lap.

"So, full disclosure." Olivia was still excited and confused by what they'd just seen of her blood. "My blood is turning gold."

Gwendolyn shot back to her feet. "What?" she exclaimed.

Leaning back, her brow was drawn from such an emphatic reaction. "My blood is turning gold?" she said uncertainly.

"See, Grandmother? It's all right," Sorsha said as Keegan hurried forward to catch Gwendolyn before she could topple to the ground without her cane for balance. He placed it in her hand with care.

Olivia had to wonder if this woman was an elderly fae. Did fae ever get old? She had no idea. But the woman before her was trying her hardest to school her reaction, covering a trembling mouth. "I would not have allowed you to try turning had I known," she said quietly. "But...this is incredible. You are an answer to a long-uttered prayer, Olivia."

"So, I take it it's a good thing my blood is gold?" she asked.

"Oh, my dear girl." Gwendolyn uttered something between a laugh and a sob. "Yes. You're becoming something we so desperately need. An Alchemyst."

"Not...a Sorceress?" she said uncertainly.

"Something better than that." The older woman waved dismissively. "Your blood itself will become the most powerful catalyst in this world and the next. You will be able to brew potions like you wouldn't believe. Ones that can clear corruption and save our race."

"But...I won't have magic?" She didn't want to sound like a whiner, but this was certainly not what she'd signed up for. If her blood was the only thing powerful about her, what was stopping someone from stealing her away to be a kind of inkwell?

"Not the kind you fling around. You'll most likely develop one of the five virtues—empathy, true sight, druidism, mediumship, or future sight—as the Alchemyst before you did." She adjusted her glasses, finally seeming to notice the expression on Olivia's face. "What's the matter, dear?"

"I barely understood a word you said," Olivia admitted. "Virtues? What does that have to do with being an Alchemyst?"

"All powerful fae are blessed with an additional ability called a virtue. Vampire Sorceresses and Alchemysts gain one as well," Sorsha said, placing a gentle hand on her shoulder. Olivia pulled away, breathing harder as the reality of her situation sank in. "I promise, it's all right."

"Is this change permanent?" Olivia asked, looking down at herself. Her skin still had a healthy glow about it, but that wasn't the point.

She'd agreed so quickly when she thought she was getting magic and a shiny crystal ball. As Charlotte would call her, naïve. She hadn't asked what else might happen or what else she could become and what that meant for her future.

"It is permanent. Did you not know that?" Gwendolyn's glee upon seeing her was quickly morphing to a stern look that she turned on Sorsha.

The fae put her hands up. "Look, I told her what was going on, and she agreed. Some details might've gotten lost."

Gwendolyn held her forehead with a sigh. "We will talk later," she said in a tone that suggested the pretty, unfathomably old Archfae would be getting chewed out. Olivia managed a smile to think that even someone like that needed to listen to their elders.

Now that she was smiling, she just had to laugh. At them, but mostly at herself for how silly she was being. "Hey, no big deal. I should've assumed when I was drinking a vampire's blood to be a super vampire with magic that it was a permanent transformation," she said, scrubbing at her eyes. "And I probably shouldn't complain that I'm some rare version of super vampire with magic. So, what were those virtue thingies again? How will I know if I have one?"

"Trust me, all are pretty instantly noticeable," Sorsha said with a chuckle. "Future sight, like Lucia has, means you see snippets of the future. Violet and I have true sight, which means we can see through glamors and identify magic. It's more useful in Faerie." She glanced to Gwendolyn, who shrugged.

Both sounded useful, Olivia thought. "Then there's empathy —the ability to feel other people's emotions. Mediumship, where you can see and communicate with ghosts. And druidism, where you can talk to animals and encourage plants to grow at your command."

"Oh, like Doctor—wait, no. Like something from a video game," Olivia said, realizing she'd lost both women by attempting to make a reference. Neither seemed the sort to play video games, and she already knew that Sorsha didn't watch movies either.

Faerie must be really boring, she thought.

"Err, I look forward to seeing which one I get," she said. "So... what now?"

The other two women exchanged a glance. In the pause that followed, she figured there was some mental discussion taking place over her future. Sorsha offered her a hand up once they were finished. "Let me show you to your new room." She tugged Olivia along until she got the point, moving quickly from the medical wing before anything else happened to keep her there.

"It's not like Grandmother to lose her composure," a man said from behind them. Olivia jumped before realizing the smooth baritone belonged to Keegan, whom she'd already started over-looking as one of Sorsha's permanent shadows.

"You'd be on edge too if you were her," Sorsha remarked.

He cast a glance around as they took the stairs up to the second floor. "I'm always on edge in mortal lands," he said.

Olivia mustered her nerve to turn to him as Sorsha kept guiding her forward, arm-in-arm. "Is that why you're always with Sorsha?" She had to tilt her head back to look into his stoic face with how tall he'd been built. He wasn't particularly bulky, not like Julian, but moved with the sort of grace expected of a dancer, or perhaps someone very good with the blade on his hip.

He flashed a hint of a smile. "No. It's my job to protect her."

Olivia wore her confusion on her face. "You're a bodyguard. But she's an Archfae?"

"You should hope you never have to see what I am," Keegan deadpanned. In that moment, he reminded her of Julian. Stoic, strong, and honest about it—keeping himself in reserve rather than threatening with a show of power.

"Here we are!" Sorsha interrupted with a gentle tug on her arm as they stopped before a room with the door ajar. Within, Olivia could see an assortment of bags and boxes waiting for her, some looking like they came from expensive boutiques. Her friend had probably shared her sizes with the person who'd gone shopping for them, but she was struck dumb for a moment at just how generous that person was.

"I'll let Julian and Charlotte know that you're awake," the fae said as she parted from Olivia's side.

"Wait. Just Julian please." She knew her fiery friend would have a lot to say over Olivia's snap-decision to become a Sorceress. Especially because that plan hadn't worked out as predicted.

"Just Julian, then," Sorsha agreed, flashing a smile before leaving her to her own devices.

Olivia went into the room and locked the door, rubbing her palms as she started taking a peek at every garment bought for her with the same glee as a kid at their birthday party.

Chapter 13
Julian

JULIAN WAS IN THE MIDST OF A HURRIED INTERNET SEARCH when he heard that Olivia was awake and in her room. He didn't go to her right away, instead browsing various lists and scribbling down ideas on a notepad. A sense of pride refused to allow him to ask for help, not from Alex or any other man.

He surveyed what made the first cut of possible date options. *These are things I would find interesting,* he thought, about to crumple the paper with frustration, but stopped. Maybe he could offer her some options.

If they went on a date. Whenever that might be. Things already weren't going like he'd always thought when it came to his lifemate. And he'd constructed some grand plans indeed—taking her on a whirlwind trip of the world, showing her the places of old just like he remembered them in his own travels.

The idea of that crumpled in his mind when he weighed it against everything else going on. He had a new duty to contend with. Thoughts of Lucia remained heavy, even if her presence hadn't returned since Ash had scared her off. Though temporarily foiled, he knew Lucia plotted to torment him still. He just needed to wait to spot more threads of her machinations weaving together.

And finally, Olivia herself was going through a serious change. Not into a Sorceress, as everyone had expected from being turned from Violet's blood, but into an Alchemyst. Sorsha had warned him of this, but he supposed he didn't truly grasp what that meant. Alchemy was a dead art, long assimilated into modern science and medicine for what parts weren't superstition and hopeful thinking.

He didn't give much thought to the cold in him, which was still blissfully thawed, hopefully never to return. He was comfortable in a short-sleeved shirt as he finally left his loaned room and went to knock on the door of Olivia's.

"One second!" she called.

When she opened the door, it was all he could do to hold in a gasp. Her transformation was already taking hold, turning her skin a golden tan that would make supermodels envious. Such a shade was rare amongst those of the night, who invariably became pale as milk without so much as a hint of the sun to change it.

She wore an outfit he already had to acknowledge was much like her, a warm pink top with black shorts that showed the athletic lines of her legs. Her unruly curls had been tamed with a braid like a coronet, leaving the rest to fall down her back like a waterfall.

"You look beautiful," he practically blurted.

"So do...I mean..." she stammered back, a blush rising to her cheeks. "Thank you. It's nice to see you. Do you want to go out?"

He was glad he wasn't the only one with a case of nerves. Even though she didn't outwardly have signs of her vampirism other than the warming of her skin, he wondered if she was far enough along to have some sense of recognition of him as her life-mate. Maybe her forward-charging attitude was suddenly arrested by the same sort of nerves he had.

"I would love to go out. If you're not supposed to stay here for monitoring?" he asked.

"No one mentioned that. Let's go before someone changes their mind." She giggled sweetly as she stepped into the hall. They fell into step as he guided her out of the mansion. "So where do you want to go?"

A dreaded question he knew was coming. What sort of thing would she want to do with him? If he couldn't take her to some exotic locale to impress her, what close attraction would catch her eye instead?

"No, wait." She gasped, turning to him with a wide grin. "Could we go to Times Square? I've always wanted to go."

Mouth half-open to suggest something from his list, he instead closed it with a relieved breath. Times Square wasn't in Coven Rehnquist's territory, but it did belong to an allied coven. In this unique time, he very much could take her there.

"Do you go often? Have you gone there New Year's Eve?" she asked, her excitement growing with each question.

"I don't like the crowds. But I have been." He chuckled at her enthusiasm.

"Have you gone to Madame Tussauds?" If she knew an attraction by name already, she must really want to go, he thought.

"I plan to tonight. If they're open," he said, jumping on that idea before it could scramble away into her other thoughts. He checked on his phone but wasn't too surprised the attraction had late hours. The city was said to never sleep, which was ideal for vampires.

"Man, I need a phone too." She eyed his device. "Mine got lost."

"We can take care of that too. I have access to the coven funds." He held the door for her as they went outside and around to the massive garage that housed a vehicle for most everyone present in the mansion.

She seemed to have a moment of realization as he helped her into his car. "Is that what was used to buy my clothes? Who do I need to thank for everything?"

"I'll pass it along to Petra. She loves shopping and taking care of new coven members, so don't worry about being a bother," he said. He knew that very thing had lingered over Violet for a while, a modern mortal sense of guilt at being provided for rather than earning something of her own merit. As a whole, his coven was well-off. No one went hungry or homeless with Alex and his investment company at the helm.

"Well, I need to meet her and give her a hug, then." Olivia sounded humbled.

They lapsed into companionable silence as he entered city traffic. It didn't bother him, even when she started fiddling with his radio just like Armando did. Thinking of his nephew brought a sigh from his lips. He hadn't paid a visit to the hospital where he stayed yet, too caught up with Olivia and his own problems. And that was wrong, he thought, vowing that he would fix that as soon as possible.

"What do you do for fun?" Olivia, it seemed, couldn't take a quiet space for long. With thoughts of Armando fresh in his mind, Julian realized she and his nephew were alike in that way as well.

"I do not have much free time lately. But when I do, I travel. I have family in Florence I try to see." His mother was a coven master there, leading with a gentle hand that had been sorely lacking when his father was leader. "When that's not possible, I just try to get outside. Hiking, fishing, hunting, that sort of thing. How about you?" He was more keen to know what interested her.

"Oh! All kinds of things. I used to be active in my local theater a lot. I'm the full package—dancing, singing, and acting, and I used to do all three there," she said. Even knowing her for so brief a time, he wasn't surprised. His first glimpse of her was on a stage, mimicking a ballroom dance.

"Do you want to be an actress?" He wished he could see her perform in person.

By this point, he'd found parking and walked with her toward Times Square. It was early evening, the crowds still too thick for his taste. The only person he wanted to be near was Olivia, who stuck close to avoid them being separated. "Well, yeah." She had a sad chuckle at his question. "It's really competitive. I had my go at it when I was fresh out of college, but my folks cut me off when they saw it wasn't going anywhere. So, now I have a degree in theater performance that hasn't taken me as far in life as I'd hoped."

"It's not too late. You have the face for it," he said. He was also biased, thinking she was cute with her button nose carrying a hint of blush and a generous sprinkling of freckles.

"Yeah, but I need money to eat," she pointed out. "And...I'm special now."

She referenced her golden blood, which was turning her blushing cheeks a faint orange. She was special, and he knew she'd soon need intensive training for the new magic she'd be able to wield. He, too, would be very busy with his new job. So, in the meantime, he was glad they had a moment together.

"Folks like us have an advantage with age and looks," he said, mindful of the crowd around them.

She seemed thoughtful until their destination was in sight and breathed out an excited squeal. "So, what is so exciting about this place?" he asked, admiring the way her face lit up.

"You...really haven't been inside?" Olivia looked at him like she was perplexed by his existence without the attraction. "It's a wax museum. It has the likenesses of celebrities and other famous people."

"That seems creepy." He supposed he just didn't see the appeal.

"No, it's like you're there with the person. You can take selfies with past presidents..." she drifted off, propping her chin on her fist. "Have you ever taken a selfie before, Julian?"

"Definitely not," he said, laughing at the thought.

She rubbed her hands together gleefully. "I'm about to change your life."

He realized why the attraction was so popular as Olivia took him through, posing next to several wax figures of modern celebrities for him to take pictures of. His eyes were on her having fun, pretending she was with the real people, whom she knew on sight. "Okay, c'mere. Let's take a picture together," she said next to one figure.

"Who is this person?" he asked.

"Don't listen to pop music either, huh?" She sounded amused as she waved for him to come closer. He inched into her personal space until she pressed to him instead. "You gotta slouch a bit or something. You're a lot taller than me."

She took hold of his phone and held it at the right angle to get a shot of both their faces with the wax figure. "There! Your first selfie," she said, immediately bringing it up.

His eyes drifted to her likeness on the screen, affecting a big grin. Next to her, his face reflected back. Usually, he could pin several flaws the moment he saw a picture of himself. But in this one, he saw something elusive instead. A smile, with his gaze straying toward her brightness. Visibly enamored with her energy.

"That was...fun," he said. "Will you tell me who this person is now?"

He followed her through several levels, snapping pictures and being a more-than-willing audience as she revealed the depths of her knowledge on pop culture. There were actors, musicians, television stars, and even movie characters. He recognized a few, glad he wasn't completely out of his league here. But Olivia gladly informed him of what he was missing anyway.

They took several pictures together, with and without the wax statues. What he found most amusing was the flexibility of her face. She acted for the camera while he...well, he tried. It was hard not to smile with her.

When it was announced the museum was about to close for the night, they weren't even done seeing what was on offer. "Ah, downsides of night owl hours," Olivia sighed, trudging back the way they came. He checked his watch—they'd been there for hours, but it hadn't nearly felt that long.

"We can always come back," he offered.

"I would love to!" Though once they left the building, she turned back to him with her smile faltering. "You had fun too, right?"

He felt his heart start to drop with her expression. "What? Yes, of course," he hurried to say. "I fear I may have showed my age, though."

"It's okay, I showed mine too." She drew her shoulders together in a half-shrug, brightening back up. "Well, what are we going to do with the rest of the night? If it's midnight, most things should be closing down huh?"

"The city always has something open." He fell into step with her as she strayed toward a different building. There was a brush against the back of his hand and he nearly jerked away before realizing it was her. She laced her fingers with his, palms brushing.

Warmth filled his chest from the simple gesture. When was the last time he'd enjoyed another's touch, even in the platonic sense?

Alex told him not long ago that he was going cold in his old age. He'd feared such a thing was true, but if so, Olivia was the gift of gentle summer nights, warm and peaceful. Looking into her eyes, he knew he would thaw. For her, only for her.

They were nearly to a new destination, the M&M Store, when his cell phone buzzed with an insistent ringtone. It was programmed only to ring when one of his closest friends called so he would know it was worth answering. "Sorry, I should take this," he said, glancing at the screen and seeing that it was Melanie.

"You want any...?" She pointed at the store, and he shook his head.

"I think it's closing," he said.

"Oh, well, I'll be fast!" She went in as he answered the call.

He heard general chatter and a clatter of equipment in the background. "Julian, come quick," Melanie said in an excited rush. "It's Armando. He's awake."

Chapter 14
Julian

Julian sped them across the city, back to their coven's territory. He'd offered to drop Olivia off, but she'd insisted on coming with him like this was part of their date too. She munched contently on her candy, having snagged and paid for it right before the store closed.

"You sure you don't want any?" she asked, rattling the chocolate shells within.

"I'm fine, thank you." He didn't need to consume human food, but he liked to in limited amounts. The vampires who didn't ended up turning into lean slips, relying purely on their preternatural strength. He ate the occasional protein-heavy meal to help keep up his bulk and weight but steered clear of sugary sweets on most days.

When Olivia leaned in and batted her eyes, he felt his will being tested. "It's a limited edition flavor," she sing-songed.

He bit his lip. "Okay, one." What could it hurt? He was about to see his nephew again at last.

"You can't have just one." She placed a few in his palm. He chewed and savored the treat, a rare taste of sweetness with the peculiarities of his diet.

She cupped her jaw as she waited for his reaction. "Good, right? I'm usually a plain kind of gal, but I like trying new things."

"It is…enjoyable." *Just like her company,* he thought. He let her feed him more candy so he could remember the sweetness of the evening.

They arrived at the hospital as Olivia asked, "So, what's your nephew like?"

She took his hand again on the walk in. "He's a lot like you," he said, looking into her eyes. Her brown irises were flecked with gold, shining back at him in the reflection of the nearest street-light. "Very personable. I think you two will get on like a house on fire."

"Does he have an accent like you?" she asked.

"Not so pronounced." Armando, unlike Julian, enjoyed talking for the sake of it. He'd taken to English later than Julian and still ended up speaking it clearer.

"Well, I like what you have." She gave his hand a squeeze, and they shared a smile before they were in public again. Few people were here at this hour unless it was serious.

Once they were checked in, he took her up to the third floor. Melanie was a surgeon here, operating on mortals and vampires alike. The hospital did not have any special, secret wings for immortals, so Armando was in a regular hospital bed, receiving more responsive and better equipped care here than he would have in the mansion's medical wing.

He parted ways with Olivia, leaving her with her candy and a promise to be back soon. She waved him off and sat, thumbing through a magazine with a somewhat familiar face on the cover, leaving him to wonder if he'd "met" that person in wax earlier.

He checked the room numbers as he hurried down the hall, looking for the one that held his nephew. Excitement and nerves warred in his chest, though the latter had no right being there. But he just couldn't help worrying that after his week-long coma, Armando would wake up different somehow. Or, even worse, would hold his affliction against Julian, who'd been powerless to stop it.

The door to the right room was open a crack, and Julian pushed it in, swallowing a lump in his throat. Seated on sheets of white was his nephew fiddling with the cuffs of a casual shirt. Their gazes met from across the room. Despite a week of sleep,

Armando wore dark, half-moon bruises under his eyes like none of it had refreshed him.

Julian froze, his apology slipping from his tongue. It felt so inadequate. He'd been so caught up in his own world that he hadn't even visited. Armando got to his feet. The next moment, he was across the room in a blur of speed, giving Julian a back-slapping hug. "Uncle! Hey, man, look at me! I'm still alive," he said with a laugh. "I looked into a Blood Prince's eyes and lived to tell the tale. What's going on, huh? What did I miss?"

"How are you?" he asked in a quiet voice, pulling back to inspect him. Elandros had hit him with a cloud of something to cause the coma, and it looked like he was fully recovered.

"Tired. Bored. Nobody has time to chat," he said, breathing a long-suffering sigh. "I've been waiting for you. Boss wants me to relocate to the mansion. Said that's where you're staying now?"

"Until further notice, for my protection."

Armando shot him an incredulous look. "For *your* protection?"

"It's a long story," Julian sighed.

"Hey, man, I got time."

Mindful that they had someone waiting for them, Julian told Armando almost everything he'd missed. His nephew sat in a state of shock to hear that Julian had been stolen away and enthralled by the same man who'd incapacitated him, not to mention that he'd witnessed the destruction of the Eye of Worlds on Nyixa and found his lifemate through a lead generated by the woman who hated him most.

"So wait...you found your lifemate?" Armando interrupted.

"I did. She's in the waiting room right now." Julian wondered if he wore his infatuation on his sleeve from the big grin his fellow wore as he looked him over.

"Yeah? What's she like, huh?" He clasped his hands under his chin and batted his eyelashes playfully.

Julian's lips curled in amusement. "Just like you."

Jumping to his feet, Armando pumped his fist. "I knew it! You need someone like that!" When Julian only lifted a brow, his nephew continued, "Someone to get you out of your shell. I don't know this girl, but she already sounds perfect."

He couldn't help a chuckle. "Because she's like you? That's all I've said."

"Yeah, and how long have we been partners? Exactly. It's a match that works. The straight man and the funny man. Tall and brooding verses color and charm!" Armando breathed out a sigh as if he'd spoken a poetic truth. "Have you taken her on a date?"

"Technically, we're still on it. I took her to Madame Tussauds, and that was when I got the call to pick you up."

Armando laughed. "Whose idea was that? Hers? No, no, man, you gotta pick the place next. If she digs learning things, then take her to the spy museum."

"There's a spy museum?" he asked.

"See, this is why you got me. You can live not knowing a thing about pop culture, that's fine, but you're not going to impress a chick being uninterested in statues of people you don't know. Look it up. Take her to the spy museum. She's going to be mega impressed with you." And Julian was inclined to do just that, considering Armando had a way with ladies that he couldn't help but envy.

"So...she's here now? How about you fill me in on the rest later, after you get us to 'safety'?" He put the word in air quotes with a smirk.

"You're lucky I like you." Julian laughed. His heart felt fill in that moment as they left to get Olivia.

When he pointed her out, still reading her magazine, Armando turned a grin his way. He walked over with his hands in his pockets.

Julian didn't hear a word either of them said, his hearing suddenly washed out as cold washed up his back.

She would like him better.

He glanced around, thinking someone had whispered in his ear. Had he really just compared himself to his nephew? Olivia was his lifemate, his ray of starshine in the endless night. But now that he'd had the thought, he watched the two get acquainted with cool dread curling in his gut.

Julian woke the next evening, cold. He cursed the shivers that wracked him as if saying, "Remember me?"

Yes, he remembered. Bitterly. Lucia's touch on him lingered, meaning he would need another magical intervention. But first, he needed to get back on track with his job. Sirius was none too pleased that he'd taken a day off and had made it clear yesterday morning that he was gathering up the head enforcers of every allied coven to have a meeting.

Which meant leaving Olivia to her own devices. By how golden her eyes were when they parted, he assumed she would have magic to learn. He still wished he could spend the night with her instead.

Armando insisted on going with him as they piled into the car to meet in a more neutral, centralized location. Along for the ride were Adrius and Sirius, both looking quite uncomfortable as they squeezed into the backseat.

Julian turned the music down and filled in all the gaps in his nephew's knowledge of what was going on in a mental conversation. Once he was done, Armando sat in uncharacteristic silence to process it all. *"So, she's targeting you because of your dad. That's messed up."*

"And she's not done. I can feel it." He literally could in the cold that crept from his core out to his limbs, making his joints ache and fingers stiffen.

Their centralized meet-up location turned out to be a bar. Julian frowned in distaste but knew there was no better place to hide a group of burly men who needed to look like they belonged. As he parked, his headlights briefly illuminated someone too small to be hanging around a bar. He bid the others go inside as he checked on that person.

If his eyes didn't deceive him, it was Cossette, the reigning Ancient vampiress of New York. He went directly to the bench outside of the seedy old establishment for a closer look. The little girl had an elbow on the bench's worn armrest, her snowy hair braided in a long tail. Red eyes much too old for a girl's face peered up at him.

Cossette Deveaux was permanently crippled in the form of a child, but she'd inherited and grown the largest coven in New York City. She was the name behind the Deveaux Accords, the one who kept some semblance of peace when twelve different covens of vampires lived uneasily in the same area. To see her here was so unusual he had to keep himself from blurting a question at her.

"Ancient Deveaux," he said instead, bowing his head in respect.

"You're finally here. I've been waiting, Mister Fairfax. Or should I call you Mister Marcuson now?" Her smile didn't quite meet her eyes, so he knew she was in a serious phase.

"Please, Fairfax will do just fine," he said hastily. "I changed it for a reason."

"Do you remember what I told you about your lifemate, Mister Fairfax?" Cossette was unique even past her appearance. Those albino-red eyes could see the future, though she delivered it to her friends and allies in barely decipherable hints and riddles. He blamed it on the damage done to her mind when forced into permanent girlhood. When she was serious, as he saw before him, he had a brief window to talk to the Ancient rather than the girl and seek some answers.

"Of course," he replied. "In the midst of my darkest hour, she will save me." After centuries of searching, it was the only hint she'd decided to give him, letting him stew in his uncertainties rather than throwing him a lifeline.

"Do you feel saved?" She tilted her head curiously.

He considered that and the chill that flowed over his skin with her question. "No. It must not be my darkest hour yet."

Her expression grew solemn. "It's everyone's darkest hour. You may not see it, you may not feel it, but shadows surround us. They block my sight."

"You cannot see the future anymore?" He reeled from the implications. Though she had a hard time sharing what was in store for everyone, her sight was still an asset when their primary enemy also saw into the future with an eye to change it to suit her own goals.

She shook her head slowly. "The last thing I saw was Olivia holding a fistful of gold."

"Gold. Like...her blood?" Olivia bleeding from her palm, he thought. Using the special Alchemyst powers he'd heard whispers of in the mansion.

"Maybe she will save us all. Protect her with your life." She stood and clasped his hand in both of hers.

This was the longest he'd seen a serious Cossette, and he nearly didn't know what to say. "Of course," he decided on. A shiver ran up his spine as he wondered what could be ahead. What did Lucia do to smother Cossette's future sight? What dire warning was he missing because of it?

"You feel really cold." Her expression lightened as she let off a girlish giggle. The tension in him ratcheted up as he realized he'd gotten what he could from the Ancient. "Maybe you should go warm up inside, Mister Fairfax. I'll be fine."

"Do you have an escort?" His eyes roved the darkness for any sign of someone listening in.

"I called for him," she said, tapping her forehead. "Don't you worry about me. You have enough on your plate."

She certainly had that right. He left her reluctantly, sure that an Ancient of nearly nine hundred years could take care of herself, and went inside, his thoughts a jumbled mess as he blundered into one of the serving staff. Barely noticing the dirty look he'd earned, he walked to an enclosed booth where he saw the back of Armando's close-shaved head.

When he sat, he felt the scornful attention of at least one person. The booth sat several vampires he recognized, strong men and women who wore different coven crests. If he wasn't consumed with cold distraction, he would've felt the heat of hostility that close proximity provided. It was the first time he saw this crew of enforcers together in one place, there to somehow become a cohesive fighting force on the decree of their coven masters.

"You're our new leader?" scoffed Cossette's head enforcer, a man twice his age and half his size.

"Do you have a problem with that, Luis?" Julian *saw* his eyes flash with a glow of power this time. Cold crept up his hands, ready for a fight, to be used now that he knew some of its potential.

The Frenchman forced his lips into a displeased line and glanced away. "I hear it's only temporary anyway," he drawled. "The highest ranked will lead us when they understand the city." He gestured toward the two vampire royals.

One of the women spoke up. She was trim, with the lean muscle he would associate with a model. She wore Coven Taylor's wolf head insignia on either shoulder, showing allegiance to the newest, smallest coven that existed in a pocket of territory. "Bloodhound, where are your badges?"

He glanced to his shoulders, realizing he hadn't had time to add the lion of Coven Rehnquist back as his own insignia. Everyone else, save for the vampire royalty, wore some indication of what coven they were from. As he looked around at all of them, taking in their hostility and contempt for each other and for him, he thought fast for an angle to explain himself.

"I think the better question is, why are you still wearing yours?" He drew a throwing dagger, the smallest blade secreted on his person, and offered it to her handle-first. "Look around you. We're gathered today to become the leaders of an army united under one purpose. If you don't get along with the person next to you, that's tough. We're allies now, and we'll crumble if we can't work together. Let's make a symbolic agreement of our new cooperation."

The vampiress eyed his dagger. There was a sound of ripping thread before a pair of lion badges hit the table. Armando smiled over at him, picking out bits of string still attached to his shoulders.

A pair of roses followed from Coven Rosas, followed by a pair of skulls from Coven Washington sliding across the table. The vampiress from Coven Taylor took his blade and cut the wolf insignia free from herself, adding them to the pile. One after the other, they all took that first step together.

Chapter 15
Olivia

Olivia nursed a headache with a cup of tea they'd gotten from a drive-through on their way across town. Keegan drove, Gwendolyn up front, with her sandwiched between Sorsha and Ash in the back. She was worried to have a fae behind the wheel until they'd reassured her that they crossed over to Earth often enough to understand modern technology. "Why are we going to the hospital again? I thought we had a perfectly good medical center in the mansion," she asked.

The elderly Gwendolyn had knocked on her door early in the evening, looking upon her with such hope in her gaze that she'd agreed to everything asked of her. Go to the hospital, let them test her blood, mix some potions. Apparently, all she was good for was mixing potions with her new supernatural blood. Her eyes were shading into a lighter and brighter gold as time passed and her body settled in its transformation from human to vampire. She might not feel any different, but she was something extraordinary to these people.

"We're expanding our operation," Gwendolyn answered. "Instead of keeping all of our people in one place, we're extending you and several others to one of Coven Rehnquist's other safe zones."

"It's so if someone wanted to attack us, we're not all in one spot," Sorsha whispered behind her hand.

Olivia blinked owlishly. "Are we expecting...an attack?"

From the grim expressions all around her, the answer was an unspoken but resounding *yes*. She fiddled with her thumbs. "So, the coven owns the hospital? There aren't people who are going to think it's weird that a group like ours comes and goes? I mean, Keegan has a freaking sword, and you wear daggers like a fashion statement." She gestured to Ash with her full bandolier.

"Money and a bit of influence go a long way," Gwendolyn answered with a sigh. When they arrived and went into the building, Olivia had to do a double take at the entryway. Other than an obvious vampiress behind the front desk by her beautiful glamor, the first floor was completely deserted of people. Even when she'd visited last night, there had been a scattering of folks waiting for emergency services.

"What about the people that need help?" she protested.

"Only the first floor is ours, and only in the late evening. During normal hours, the whole hospital belongs to mortals. Come along now." Gwendolyn allowed Keegan to support her weight, walking further inside.

Olivia rubbed a chill from her arm and followed. Hospitals weren't her favorite place on the best of days. She didn't like the smell or the uncomfortable chairs. It reminded her of the long days before she'd lost her grandfather, waiting and waiting with nothing to do by the side of her perfumed and coiffed mother while he had his treatments. She was expected to be perfectly behaved in public. Now, all she remembered was the hours that felt like days, the clock ticking arduously while she watched the minute hand or fish swim around their tank.

As she passed by a window-sized fish tank and the sanitized smell of her surroundings sank into her nostrils, she felt like she could've blinked and been transported back into that moment. A slim, firm hand landed on her shoulder. She jerked her head up, expecting her mother's stern face, just to see Ash's instead. The fae gestured to where the others were disappearing into a section marked off for laboratory and x-ray.

"Is it true you can't tell the truth?" Olivia blurted, hooking into anything that would distract and remind her that she was an adult now. An adult who had blood turning gold, who kept the companionship of three fae and many other seemingly mythical characters straight from the wildest fantasy movie.

Ash's expression grew sly. "It is not a question of whether the truth can fall from my lips, rather that you perceive it as such."

Olivia perked up as she changed course to the laboratory. "Oh, is this a fairy riddle?" She repeated the words to herself. "You mean that you can tell the truth as long as I don't believe it's true?"

"Something like that." Ash held the door for her. Concern seemed to shadow the woman's hooded eyes as she watched Olivia pass by.

She found Keegan standing at the end of the hall, gesturing toward a section marked "For Employees Only." *Guess I'm an employee now,* she thought, heading into the first room, where Sorsha and Gwendolyn stood together beside a table they'd cleared of most modern equipment.

Sorsha hefted a burlap sack that appeared half full and started fishing within it with her tongue tweezed between her lips. She drew out a book that fell to the counter with a heavy thud. It was a tome akin to three encyclopedia volumes in one, bound in thick leather. Then she followed that up by drawing out various smaller bags, vials, boxes, and a few potted and growing plants. Together, it was more volume than she expected from a sack of that size, but Olivia quickly attributed it to magic.

"I didn't expect a vampire Alchemyst. I only brought enough for myself and any mistakes I might make," she was saying to Gwendolyn as she drew out a wooden rack next and lined up glass vials within. Petri dishes and corks followed.

Gwendolyn eyed the bounty of items in front of her. "It will have to do."

"At least I brought plenty of ground mayroot?" She lifted a vial about as thick as her wrist and gave the powdered contents a shake.

Gwendolyn lifted her head to Olivia like she was just remembering she was there. "I do not plan to advertise you or your skillset. You are capable of so much." She gestured to the massive tome. "But I will pay you handsomely to sit here, night after night, and make as many of one particular potion as you can."

"Wait...I'm getting *paid?*" She hooked into that knowledge eagerly.

"If you do as I ask, I will empty my bank account for you." Gwendolyn nodded, holding out her hand. A chair skidded over to her, and she sat with a heavy sigh.

Olivia dragged another over the old-fashioned way, sitting across from her with a formal, straight posture. The older vampiress—or fae, whatever she was under her glamor—seemed on the verge of explaining something big. Like hopefully why her Alchemyst identity was worth so much to the older vampires when she couldn't even cast spells like a Sorceress.

"Has anyone told you that in the time of old, there was only ever one Sorceress and one Alchemyst?" Oh yes, she really was about to spill the beans. Olivia leaned in eagerly, shaking her head. "They were both turned from the blood of a Fell Sorcerer, freely given with all of his magic within it to Lucia, in a pact where he was offered safety in exchange. She had him killed instead and suffered a curse from it that lasts to this day. We cleaned and sanitized the remaining blood so my daughter Nyah, the true Queen of Vampires, could also drink it and wield magic. She became the Alchemyst, and we barely had time to explore her magic together before she met her untimely end."

Olivia remembered the name Nyah referenced a few times before she'd taken Violet's blood. Her heart dropped when she saw the pain in Gwendolyn's gaze to speak of her lost daughter. "For many long years, I wondered why my daughter's blood ran gold. Why her powers ultimately manifested in the ability to change and help others. I wondered why...why did I think her gift was weak? When I also admired Lucia for her great feats of magic. Fast forward to now, and I saw that same reaction in you. Why are you an Alchemyst when you signed up for Sorceress power, right?" Her piercing gaze flashed up to Olivia, who recalled thinking something similar.

Nerves tangled in her throat. "I, uh, yeah. I thought I'd be throwing fireballs by now or something."

"Vampire society fell apart when my daughter died, when her Alchemyst powers were lost. She was far more important than any Sorceress ever will be," Gwendolyn stated matter-of-factly. "Her blood was the only cure for the one affliction that hides in the heart of every vampire. Now that we have you...we may be able to rebuild ourselves and chase away the stain of our blood curse."

"Blood curse," Olivia echoed.

"You know that vampires come from Fell, fae cursed to eternal hunger?" she asked, earning a slow nod. "Vampires of all walks have a piece of Fell within them. A twisted, hungry kernel of instinct that calls for them to feed their dark hunger. As they grow older, they grow stronger. But so does that instinct, eating away what was good and human within them until the hunger starts to take over. They twist and mutate within first, wanting to feed their darkest tastes. And when it consumes everything, it transforms a man to a monster with shark-like teeth and fingers like rending talons. Their very blood runs black. We call the end result Fell Madness."

"And I can cure that?" she asked.

"You, and you alone." Gwendolyn leaned in, taking Olivia's hand in both of hers. They trembled with her conviction. "We *need* you."

Olivia felt her heart swell to hear those words spoken so earnestly. She reveled in the feeling of being needed and, more importantly, that she could make such a big difference to a race as secretive and seemingly self-sufficient as the vampires.

"Then I'm ready to get started," she said.

Chapter 16
Olivia

Olivia breathed in the night air, enjoying a stroll in the dark with Julian. "So, I'm very special, and you should remember that," she said with a wink his way, finishing a recapping of events.

"I didn't need Gwendolyn to know that," he said, flashing her a smile.

They'd barely seen each other in the past few days, relegating their time together to walks in the neighborhood in the wee hours of the morning before the sun was due to rise. He was more and more exhausted every night, dark shadows deepening under his eyes. His job seemed much harder than hers—coordinating and training people for the mysterious danger to come. Julian threw his everything into the task, so much so that she worried he'd burn out within a week.

His aura wrapped them both in a cool blanket, chasing away the summer humidity. Despite the pleasant fatigue that lingered over her from a hard night's work, she was glad of this time with him. As her eyes turned to molten gold to reveal her magical vampire nature, she recognized she had a strange sort of pull toward him. Taking a walk with him was more interesting than staying in and gossiping with Charlotte, who seemed to have almost forgiven her for jumping headfirst into the idea of becoming a vampire.

Julian was a quiet man, but she wanted to crack that shell and get to know him. Maybe that was the lifemate bond at work, saying they would make perfect forever partners. She tried to put that out of her mind when they were together, though, not wanting to point toward that as any proof that she would settle with someone in a ritual as irrevocable as a full vampire mating bond until she knew for sure.

"How many potions have you made?" he asked, drawing her out of her thoughts.

"Hmm? Oh, uh, one," she admitted. "Not for lack of trying. But apparently magical Alchemyst mojo takes some time to recharge, and I'm still new to this." Not like she hadn't noticed Gwendolyn's disappointment when she hadn't produced more than a few drops of concentrated golden blood. Maybe she just wasn't as good an Alchemyst as the mythical juggernaut that was the woman's memory of her daughter.

It didn't help that the fae were splitting their time and effort between her and Violet, training at a different, secret location to harness more of her magic. Without Sorsha's calm presence, Olivia could practically feel the hope and anxiety warring within Gwendolyn. She studied the massive tome the fae had left behind to better understand her magic in general, finding some interesting tidbits that she'd already shared with Julian.

"Things would be much easier if Sorsha could make this potion too," he remarked. She nodded emphatically in agreement.

In fae society, it turned out that Archfae were Sorcerers that had grown so powerful in their magic that it suffused their blood. It meant that Sorsha was a Violet and an Olivia *combined*, but her Alchemyst skills didn't extend to vampire-related potions, making that uniquely Olivia's bag. Instead, she had spells to create occultari, which Olivia wouldn't be able to do since she had no way to harness and place fae magic within one of the glass orbs.

"If you listen to Gwendolyn talk, it's because vampires weren't meant to be. We're getting lame, watered-down versions of fae magic." She sighed wistfully for the power she would never have.

He considered thoughtfully as his eyes roved the night. "That does make a sad sort of sense. The more I hear about where vampirism came from, the more I agree with her."

"Well, vampires are here, and nothing's going to change—" The next thing she knew, she was crumpled on her side in someone's lawn, the wind knocked out of her. She sat up with her brow furrowed, about to tell Julian just what she thought of his sudden push.

A blur flew by where she'd been standing. There was a snap like the closing of an animal's maw. It sounded like the kind of chomp that would shatter bones. A figure skidded on the sidewalk with its momentum, turning quickly for another leap.

"Olivia. Stay down." Julian whipped a dagger from his thigh, bearing his fangs in a furious snarl.

Her would-be attacker crouched, its features obscured in the dark. She got a hint of too many fangs and black smeared across moon-pale skin before it jumped at Julian. The two of them rolled in a tangle of limbs, nearly faster than her eye could track. She curled up with a whimper, hoping there weren't more out there waiting to attack while her protector was distracted.

She heard the sound of tearing, a grunt of pain, and the smack of flesh on flesh. It was done within moments, with the same supernatural speed it'd started with. Julian limped back to her, holding his arm with his teeth gritted. Red streaked down his skin past his fingers. "He's dead," he said in a sharp burst. "Help. Call someone."

His eyes rolled back, and he collapsed a couple yards from her. "Oh, God. Oh, God," Olivia said, drawing in on herself as her breath came in short pants. She fumbled her new cell from her pocket and brought up a list of contacts. Several were important names from the coven, leaders she could call. Her thumb found Melanie Rainey's name.

Three long rings followed. Olivia felt lightheaded. She couldn't get enough air as she watched Julian's form. His chest rose and fell, so he was alive, but blood was starting to puddle under his arm and leg.

"Hello?" Melanie's curt voice came over the speaker.

"Melanie!" She grasped the phone with two hands. "Come

quick! It's Julian. Some...thing just came out of nowhere and attacked him, and now he's unconscious—"

"Slow down. Where are you?" the healer interrupted.

"I don't know! He's losing—"

"Stop. Take a deep breath with me."

They wasted precious seconds as Melanie took an exaggerated deep breath over the phone. "Okay, girl. Are you close to a house?"

"Yes."

"Go read the house number to me."

She rushed across the sidewalk to the closest mailbox, reading its number to Melanie. She tried to ignore the dark figure in the street, lying motionless. A sour feeling lingered at the back of her throat, her dinner threatening to make a reappearance.

"You're not very far..." A troubled note entered Melanie's voice. "I'm sending help now. Stay with me."

Melanie didn't say anything else. She figured she wanted the line open just in case help couldn't find them. Heading back to Julian, she crouched down, wishing now that she'd accepted Jaromir's initial offer and become a regular old vampire. She would be Gifted now, able to heal the worst of another vampire's wounds.

As she steeled herself to take a closer look at him, she gasped. "What? What is it?" Melanie demanded.

"His blood. It's...freezing?" The puddle beneath him was iced over like a pond, turning into pink ridges where it lay. Her hand shook with more than nerves as she reached for his torn shirt to see where this was coming from. It felt like he was surrounded by a cloud of dry ice. "God, he's so cold."

She lifted the torn edge of his shirt, fighting the urge to vomit as she expected the worst. With his blood freezing, the wounds she spotted were sealed under a sheet of ice. She spotted two sets of punctures, set in a perfect half-moon fan as if he'd been bitten by something with a perfect set of fangs.

"I...I don't know what's going on," she stammered.

"Stay with me, girl," Melanie said. She sounded far too calm for the situation. "Look out for a black van."

Olivia forced herself to look to the street. The promised black van came speeding down the road, skidding to a sudden stop a few feet from her. Several people poured from it as the line went dead against Olivia's ear. Melanie herself rushed past her, kneeling beside Julian. She placed her hands on his shoulders.

A man cursed from further down the street. "Take a look at this...thing." It was Armando's voice, a relief to know someone else familiar was on the job.

"Bloody hell. It looks like it used to be a person. I'll get another team out to gather it up." She recognized the other man's voice as Samuel Rainey, Melanie's husband and the coven deputy. He was usually around in the mansion somewhere but too busy for more than a hello and a smile.

The two of them returned to the van, both looking disgusted. Samuel, a pleasantly chubby man with a halo of curly brown hair, pulled out his phone to make a call.

Armando startled her, placing his hand on her shoulder. "Hey, he's going to be all right *ragazza*. He's taken a lot worse."

"Why is his blood turning to ice, though?" she asked, watching his brow draw together.

"That's...unusual. I don't know," he admitted.

Melanie lifted her head. She huffed as she hefted herself to her feet. "We need to get him to the hospital. His internal temp is dangerously low. Help me chip him from the ground?"

Rushing to help her, Armando ended up punching the ice around Julian's arm and leg to free him. Both of them carried Julian with Olivia's scant help, fitting him in the back seating of the van. "Why don't you ride shotgun?" Armando offered as he secured a seatbelt around Julian's limp weight.

"I would rather ride with him," she said. His big body occupied both seats in the back, meaning she had to get in the middle with Melanie while Armando sat up front. Sam sped off with the squeal of tires. The world flashed by as he took the van to its limits, pressing Olivia flat into her seat as he took a sharp turn, and then to the limits of her seatbelt with another.

She turned her body around, hooking an arm around the headrest as she peered back at Julian. "Do you know why he's so cold?" she whispered to Melanie, her worried gaze scanning him head to toe. His arm hung limp over the seat, jostling with every bump in the road. Inexplicably, as she looked at him, she felt a chill over herself despite the lingering humidity in the car.

"No idea, love. I suspect it's magic," the healer replied. "He's always had a cold aura, though. And it's almost like it had an over-reaction to seal his wounds and save him. He had a couple wounds over major arteries."

She nodded slowly, wondering how it was possible that his aura had the power to ice him over like this. It *had* to be magic of some degree, though. "As a matter of fact, I'm going to call Sorsha," Melanie continued, pulling out her phone.

As she placed that call, Olivia felt her belly rumble. She rubbed it, her brow furrowed in confusion. She'd had dinner not too long ago, but there was a growing pain inside like she hadn't eaten in days. It prickled her insides like sharp needles. But she didn't say a word, since the unpleasantness of being cold and hungry was nothing compared to the emergency behind her.

Melanie's voice faded to background noise as she turned to Julian again to see his lips and fingertips turning blue. She leaned over and reached, grasping for his frozen hand to hold between her own. The hunger in her sharped to a stab as her skin stuck to his like trying to hold a dry ice cube.

A shiver passed over him, turning to a twitch of tendons in her grasp. His fingers curled. When she felt the point of some-thing sharp against her palm, she checked what it was and nearly dropped his hand.

It twitched in her hold again, twisting further out of shape as nails turned to talons and lengthened before her eyes. A whis-pered curse escaped her lips. Something was *very* wrong, but what was going on? She noticed a bloom of color under his shirt and realized she could reach that far to inspect.

"What are you doing?" Sam asked, noticing first when Olivia unclipped her seatbelt and climbed into the back, her body jostling as he hit a pothole. She ducked in the foot well in the back, just in case he took a sudden turn.

Melanie was still on the phone, turning to watch her with a

confused brow furrow. "I just...have a feeling." Olivia couldn't explain now, she just knew there was something under his shirt on the side where he hadn't been attacked. It wasn't iced over, but darkness bloomed at the corner of his collar. She jerked it aside, falling back on her behind with a shocked gasp.

In the pattern of a crescent moon on his undamaged side, black veins worked under the surface of his skin, nearly hidden with how cold he was. Melanie cursed as she saw it too. "Black veins," she said into the phone, waiting a moment. "Sorsha wants you to check his teeth."

"His teeth," she echoed, feeling it click into place for her. What did everyone mention first when it came to the Fell? The teeth, sharp, serrated, and lined like perfect interlocking triangles. The wounds on Julian resembled that kind of dentition.

But she didn't think they'd been attacked by a Fell. They hadn't existed on Earth for a thousand plus years.

Yet Gwendolyn had told her directly about another threat. She recalled the words as her shaking hand reached for Julian's lips.

Please don't be sharp. Please, she begged, gingerly tweezing his upper lip and lifting.

Julian breathed a groan, shifting away from her in his sleep. But she'd seen enough.

When it consumes everything, it transforms a man to a monster with shark-like teeth and fingers like rending talons. Their very blood runs black.

Gwendolyn had described Julian. All his teeth were developing a point. His fingers sharpening...his blood black.

"Melanie," she said, her voice a frightened squeak. "Tell Sorsha it's Fell Madness."

Chapter 17
Julian

When Lucia had bitten him the first time, he'd dropped unconscious with a vision as vivid as reality. It showed him Olivia in a yellow gown, ballroom dancing with another man as her lips moved to the lyrics of the song playing over them. They were on stage, and Olivia was younger, a college student, he suspected.

This time, he was the one dancing with her, effortlessly gliding through steps he didn't know outside of this split reality. One moment, he was protecting her from a man with teeth like Lucia's, and the next, he was falling and opening his eyes to her younger face as they danced. He wanted to enjoy the moment, but his eyes roved the bright spotlights on them, obscuring any hint of an audience.

"What's wrong, Julian?" Olivia whispered under the music.

His gaze returned to her. In thick stage makeup, her eyes stood out brown and doe-like from her face. But it couldn't be the real Olivia. She was years older and somewhere in New York, unprotected while he dreamt of her.

He'd played this song and dance one too many times. Different dreams, same nightmare. "What do you want, Lucia?"

Young Olivia's sweet face curled into a venomous smile. "I'm impressed. Every time we do this, you catch on faster." Despite wanting to recoil, his body was stuck in the motions of the vision,

"

twirling her around while her skirts swished gracefully. He knew he'd be forced to hear her out, as he always was when she walked through his dreams. "You're about to give me everything I want, young Marcuson."

"Don't call me that," he snapped.

"Oh? Does it hurt to be reminded of the man you slew in cold blood?" she asked smoothly, her hands tightening their grip on him to the point of pain.

"My father nearly killed me more times than I can count." He felt a chill come over himself in lieu of a flush of anger. "He was a danger to his own people. He would've seen the world burn so he could rule the dregs—"

"Silence." With her hiss, his lips sealed shut. He glared at her as his body moved on autopilot, trapped on an endless loop as the music repeated itself and they started the dance anew. Lucia liked the sound of her own voice, to the exclusion of anyone getting a word in edgewise.

"Much better." As they moved, she shed Olivia's face, becoming the raven-haired beauty she would be if she weren't hopelessly corrupted into a black-veined monster. She pined for the looks she'd lost, if her vanity was any indication. "As I was saying, you're about to hand me victory. Do you feel it yet? The hunger?"

As if her words summoned it, his belly growled, pain building there like he hadn't fed for weeks. Considering the bites he'd taken earlier, he was also in desperate need of mortal blood to replenish what he'd lost. But he couldn't answer her, so he simply stared and waited. "You will soon know the same wretchedness all Fell knew. The hunger every vampire to fall to their corruption felt. You'll show your true colors at last."

Her vicious smile was back, much more appropriate on her features. "My curse has morphed, you see. I produce a venom now, and it's flowed through your veins this whole time, waiting to be activated."

The bites from the other vampire, he realized. If he could consider a man with Lucia's affliction a vampire still.

His breathing constricted in his chest. Would he be the same soon? Ruled by the hunger mounting within him, like he'd never fill its bottomless pit?

"Oh yes, I see you understand where this is going." Her eyes gleamed, her feelings of triumph apparent. "When you awaken, you will be Fell Mad, ready to consume and spread your venom to others. Don't think you can resist it—I'm your dark mistress now, your matron of the damned. The friends you've cultivated will fall to my influence. And your sweet little lifemate..." She licked her lips.

Horror seized him. What was she implying, that he would *eat* his own lifemate? "Maybe you should've begged for my forgiveness while you had a chance," she purred.

He forced his eyes wide, glancing downward multiple times in the hope she'd understand he wanted her to remove the spell so he could speak. She waved a lazy hand, and he felt his tongue loosening from the roof of his mouth. "It's not too late. Beg, Julian. Tell me just how much you regret slaying my lifemate."

"Will you allow us to stop dancing?" he asked, working on not slurring his words as his mouth tingled like coming off a shot of novocaine.

The music stopped. They were still on the stage, but there was silence now. Lucia drew herself up as she stepped away from him, like a queen waiting regally for her due. "Go on. Grovel. Maybe I'll let you free of my influence."

He knelt, biting back his pride and inching forward until he was at her feet. He could've kissed the sandaled toes before him if he were so inclined. "My father told me of you once," he said, knowing that, no matter what he did, Lucia wasn't the type to ever relinquish control of him. Instead, he had to hope to buy as much time as possible.

"Just once?" Every word oozed with relish.

"I was his fifth son. He didn't have time to chit-chat with the likes of me, especially on the matters of love." Ever since he'd first heard of Lucia coming to New York, her good looks and silver eyes were a topic of whispered conversation between the vast majority who didn't know she was a monster beneath the perfumed veil she wore. He'd wracked his brain over and over, trying to remember centuries in the past when his father had mentioned loving a silver-eyed woman. In the midst of his suffering at her hand, he'd finally remembered, the moment buried under the trauma of what his father had done as he spoke.

He looked up, seeing Lucia waiting patiently for him to cry and beg for mercy. For all her future sight, for everything she thought she knew about him, she hadn't realized such weak behavior was ripped out of him long ago by the man she yearned for.

"Once, I took it upon myself to love a woman, and we had a chat, man to man. She was there too...my Rosa." His memory of her was hazy at best, but he didn't want to recall her face while staring into Lucia's. "He told me of a silver-eyed woman who'd taught him all he needed to know about love. She was the most beautiful creature he'd ever had in his bed, he said. Her eyes were as radiant and full as the moon."

Her face creased with pleasure. She closed those very same eyes as she leaned in, stroking her neck like remembering the touch of a lover. "Her voice was like silk sheets. The kind he just wanted to get buried in," Julian continued, fighting the tide of resentment that threatened to choke him. Lucia looked like she'd completely forgotten why they were there and that she was waiting to hear him grovel. "And a body like an hourglass. Skin smooth, bathed in milk and honey."

He took a deep breath, hand creeping up his thigh. "He said that her love opened his eyes to the possibilities in the world. That, in her arms, he saw what could be his."

"Yes. Yes, Marcus, my love," Lucia whispered, her hand drifting down her collarbone.

"He said that the taste of her ruined other women. Ruined what he had," he continued, feeling his hands bunch into fists. "He wanted to prevent me from making the same mistakes, because the woman with silver eyes was everything love embodied. Everything he wanted, he could only have without her. She made him *weak*."

With her lost in her own fantasies, she didn't react until after he'd unsheathed his dagger and buried it in her heart. Her eyes flew open, stunned with the same betrayal he'd felt when Marcus had put his sword through Rosa's innocent chest. "He said the most important lesson I could ever learn was that love makes you weak," he said from between gritted teeth. Every tendon in his neck stood out as he breathed like a bellows. "*This* is the man you mourn. The monster you left behind. And I understand him so much more now. I'd be a monster too if you were my lifemate." He twisted the dagger, feeling the dream fall apart around them.

He woke with a jolt, sitting in an unfamiliar hospital bed. His arms stopped short, throwing the rest of his body forward with the crackle of breaking ice.

"You will regret that. This isn't over," Lucia whispered in his head.

He had a more pressing problem, though. At the foot of his bed stood Adrius, holding an unsheathed sword. His expression shaded solemnly as Julian fought his restraints in futility, hissing like an animal.

Chapter 18
Adrius

EVER SINCE HE'D WOKEN FROM HIS THOUSAND-YEAR REST, darkness had been his constant companion. It wrapped him like a covetous lover, answering his every beck and call. But everything, even the mortal, modern world full of unnatural light and noise, was dulled from his shield of shadow.

Maybe that was why he, too, was numb. He couldn't bring himself to act against Lucia's scheming until moments before she'd called the Fell back to their world. She'd destroyed the Dark Eye, something he saw his fellows mobilize to fix. They had countless impassioned meetings. Friends new and old tackled the problem.

He didn't care. He sat there and made the right faces, but it felt like a farce. *There's nothing you can do to help,* the shadows whispered. *Why even bother? You'll just get in the way.*

Adrius let his brother take over in learning who their new men were and organizing them into a proper army. He'd only get in the way after all.

When Gwendolyn told him of the new Alchemyst, his numb heart had nearly torn itself into pieces. *This world forgets Nyah. It has replaced her.*

His beloved mate was no more than a fading memory to him now. He couldn't remember the sound of her voice or how she'd smelled. The world wasn't just forgetting her...so was he. He would sit for hours with a pencil and paper, writing down every detail he could remember.

Staring down at a crumpled page, he knew it wasn't enough. He had five things scrawled there. *Pathetic. Was she really the light of your life?*

So, when Gwendolyn returned to him with a golden potion in hand, he hadn't drunk it in front of her. It was Olivia's first and only purification potion, hopefully one of many once her powers settled. He rolled it over his desk, back and forth against the wooden grain as he watched flecks of gold swirl within.

He didn't deserve the first potion. He didn't deserve one at all.

He'd failed Nyah all that time ago by not being at her side when she was locked away in the Fell Lands on a diplomatic mission gone horribly wrong. *You cannot gain forgiveness from a corpse. Her death will be your burden forever.*

The shadows were right. He kept the golden potion secured on himself for someone else who needed it more. All the Blood Princes had the same problem as he—too much power taken directly from the veins of a Fell. They were the most likely to turn and go Fell Mad at the drop of a hat. Two of their numbers had suffered and returned from the edge of madness before Gwendolyn condemned them to death by eternal rest to avoid it becoming permanent for them all.

Can you blame her?

"No. I suppose not," he said aloud.

He did that sometimes, talking like someone else could hear him. As if he wasn't just speaking to his subconscious come alive to torment him for his mistakes.

He'd had the purification potion for days before Gwendolyn returned to him, looking more worn than usual. She hadn't been feeding, something the former nephilim often forgot since her body didn't require it in the same way as other vampires'. Unlike everyone else, Gwendolyn did not have a kernel of Fell hunger inside her. She only needed blood to maintain her age. If she forgot it much more, she would be too frail an old woman to function.

"Come with me," Gwendolyn said. Her lips trembled, as did the hand on her cane. As he followed, he considered asking when the last time she fed was.

Why bother? She will just lie.

He sighed in agreement. The woman did what she wanted, regardless of his input. Some things didn't change.

"What is the hurry?" he asked as she ushered him into the backseat of a car. An unfamiliar vampire—another of his new allies, he had to assume—was behind the wheel, taking off the moment they were settled.

Gwendolyn sat next to him in the back, her gaze shadowing. "It's the Madness."

He sucked in a surprised breath. "Someone fell victim? Who was it?"

She shook her head slowly in disbelief. "Julian Fairfax. There is an unidentified corpse of another who displays the same symptoms."

Julian, the spitting image of a man he remembered as a friend. But he was not nearly as powerful as the Blood Princes, thus under no danger of turning into one of the Fell Mad. Or so he assumed, but now he understood the grim twist to Gwendolyn's lips. "How is that possible?"

"That's what we're going to find out," she said. He nodded, though he wondered why she even bothered to bring him rather than someone more versed in medical studies like Jaromir. Unless she knew there was still a potion burning a hole in his pocket.

She can't find out. She will just force you to drink it.

And he was unworthy of it, he already knew.

They arrived at a hospital and rushed inside, him nearly carrying her there. Her bones pressed against paper-thin skin, and again, he nearly said something, almost offered his vein so she could regain her strength. Doubt stopped him. She didn't need his help, else she'd have asked for it.

Gwendolyn took him to a back room where a corpse was laid out under a thick tarp, a grim sight neither of them flinched from. She started putting on a pair of thick gloves, muttering, "Just like old times."

"Where is the Alch...Olivia?" he asked, finding it too hard to refer to her by his wife's old title.

"With Sorsha in the back rooms of the laboratory. They're trying to make a new purification potion." She paused to pick out a scalpel, turning to frown up at him. "Apparently, my energy was negatively affecting Olivia's focus, so I am here instead to figure out why Madness sickened this man."

"And why did you bring me here?" He didn't really mean to ask it out loud, but it slipped out.

She shot him a long-suffering look. "I don't know, Adrius. Why don't you think on that? Why would I invite the King of Vampires to witness a mysterious resurgence of the most deadly thing to afflict us?" she snapped.

Drawing himself up, he lifted his chin proudly. "There is no need to take that tone. I will just see if my assistance is needed elsewhere."

Gwendolyn was already turning back to the corpse. "Julian is restrained a few rooms down from this one," she said with a vague wave of dismissal.

True to her word, he was, hooked up to several modern machines he presumed were keeping him alive. Unnatural cold wafted from the bed despite the technology in the room making it as hot as possible. It felt like he'd stepped straight into a hot spring's humidity.

On the bed and restrained with nephilim chains lay Julian, passed out. The chains themselves were as old as he was, made with Gwendolyn's power before she became a vampire. Wearing the golden links suppressed a vampire's preternatural strength and abilities, allowing them to be restrained just like any mortal.

The man before him needed to be controlled in such a way. Even with his eyes closed, his skin bore the telltale black veins. Adrius drew his sword on instinct.

We do not suffer a monster to live.

Julian woke a moment later, his eyes flooded with Fell darkness. They resembled endless dark pits, ringed by prominent lines. As he opened his mouth, two rows of fangs were revealed.

Monster, he thought. Just as much as Lucia, who was cursed to find the Madness completely inescapable.

Julian, however, was not damned to the same fate. Even as he hissed and worked his restraints like an animal, chomping at the air like he wanted a taste of Adrius, he was not as far gone as he seemed.

"Did you know I also fell victim to the Madness?" Adrius asked, knowing he wouldn't get an answer. The newly succumbed were usually no more than instincts and hunger, incapable of sane conversation.

He sheathed his sword. Old habits died hard. In the modern era, as he understood it, a sword was as antique as he was. Unnecessary to the contemporary mortal.

"Now that's a tale. But I had a way out that no one else has," he said, holding up his hand, where the Shield Key glinted. "You are lucky, actually."

Julian gnashed his teeth. "Yes, lucky," Adrius continued. "You do not need to die to remove the corruption. All you need is a potion."

Pulling the vial from his pocket, he stared at the other man's salvation lying in his palm. *If he takes it, Gwendolyn will know I didn't drink it,* he thought. But what if the new Alchemyst couldn't summon the power to properly mix another? He'd heard she was weak in her magic, unlike his beloved Nyah.

Julian needed the cure *now.*

Was his secret worth more than this man's life?

Protect yourself at all costs.

He shook his head. This time, his subconscious was wrong. He had to come clean and give the potion to someone else. That was why he saved it in the first place.

Uncorking it, he felt his fangs unsheathe as its intoxicating aroma filled the air. It smelled just like the potion Nyah used to brew for him, another punch to the gut. He swallowed on a suddenly dry throat and lunged forward, grabbing the back of Julian's head so the other man wouldn't be able to bite him. He roughly shoved the glass past his fangs, watching the golden fluid drain into his hungry maw.

Julian choked on a sound of pain. "Sorry, friend. It burns," Adrius murmured, drawing back once the vial was empty. The other man's body seized, twisting in pain as he clawed at the air in futility. He *screamed*, shaking the walls in his agony.

"No! What have you done?" Julian yelled, turning a sneer of perfect rage Adrius's way. "How did you have the cure?"

He stood there, dumbfounded by the sudden coherency of Julian's rage. The truth didn't register until Julian arched his fingers and something shot from his palm. Luckily, Adrius moved in time to avoid a wicked-sharp icicle now quivering where his neck had been. No hint of the room's heated conditioning remained as Julian gestured, throwing a gust of freezing air like a cutting gale.

With pain wracking Julian, he was clumsy. He couldn't hit the King of Vampires with any sort of projectile. Rather, Lucia couldn't. Somehow, he knew she was directing his movements until his body slumped in its restraints, unconscious as the cure stripped away his corruption internally.

Adrius stood in a corner, taking a slow look around the room. The walls, ceilings, and floor were all coated in sharp-edged ice, spikes stopping inches from him. And the door, well, it was frozen shut.

<h1 style="text-align:center">Chapter 19
Julian</h1>

Julian opened his eyes after a sleep as deep as death, finding it a surprise that he was even still breathing. Reality crashed in to find he was still in a plain white hospital room.

Actually, he was in a different one than the last time he'd woken. There was a curtain around his bed for privacy, and the quality of sheets he lay under was different. He was in the mansion's medical wing, no sign of golden chains or any other restraints.

He lifted and flexed a hand. No talons. It was the same hand he'd always had, free of darkness in the veins or any other sign of transformation. Like he'd only been Fell Mad in a dream, a terrible second nightmare where Lucia had used her magic through him like some kind of frost puppet.

There was no ice now. He was warm.

He uttered a quiet curse. What was real—and what wasn't?

"Julian? Are you awake?" It was Sorsha's voice on the other side of the curtain.

More magic, he thought, laying his head back and scowling at the ceiling. The last thing he wanted was to see the Archfae and her silent entourage.

"Are you feeling up to a chat?" she asked a minute later.

His lips lifted sardonically. Would he really have a say in this? "No," he responded.

115

There was a pause as her shadow shifted on the cloth barrier between them. "Are you sure?" She sounded taken aback. "I have good news. I know why you're having trouble with the cold."

As he'd expected, no matter his answer, "no" wasn't the correct one. "All right. What do you have to say?" He sat up with a grumble, seeing that someone had changed him into a clean set of clothing. The shirt was something baggy, comfortable, and white, not a choice he'd make for himself.

Sorsha parted the curtain only long enough to slip in, dragging a chair behind her. Her occultarus orbited behind her back in slow circles, its light dimmed so he could look at her without blinding himself. The fae wore a scarlet dress of velvet and dark lace, a matching jeweled butterfly pin in her perfectly coifed hair.

She inspected him, cocking her head. "How are you feeling?"

He had to chuckle at that. "Remarkably normal, all things considered."

Silence lapsed between them, something he was in no hurry to change. Her expression was far away, like she was counting her worries and discovering how numerous they were.

"You avoided the swing of fate's axe a second time," she said finally, her gaze refocusing on him. "It is my people's belief that all things, good and bad, come in fours. If I stuck to faith alone, I would see you as a good omen."

He heard the catch in her voice. "But?"

Her voice lowered as she shook her head. "You are so lucky, Julian. I'm going to leave it at that because I think you need to hear good news. To that end, this ordeal has made me finally start asking the right questions. I understand you so much better now. Follow my logic for a few minutes here." He nodded cautiously.

"Your nephew recently experienced a week-long coma after being attacked by one of Lucia's men," she said.

Lips tightening at the reminder, he nodded again. "So I could be captured for torture without any interference."

"Ah, that is the most logical conclusion, isn't it?" Her lip quirked as she called her occultarus to her hand. "Hopefully, you remember my history lesson on the Fell Keys."

The magical tool projected an image outward as she gestured, showing the likeness of something he didn't quite understand. He'd seen the Eye of Worlds on Nyixa before it was destroyed, how it resembled a desk globe with a house-sized black marble in place of the world. The holder had been a crescent moon etched with several symbols, and its likeness is what Sorsha showed him now, with the portraits of several people next to each symbol.

"That's my father," he said, pointing to a symbol not unlike a snowflake. Next to it, like a picture, was Marcus's perfect likeness. Except the big blond man was...smiling?

Marcus never smiled.

His brow drew together as he turned to Sorsha for some sort of explanation. "This is a visual representation of the leads we have on each Fell Key. You notice Gwendolyn and Adrius next to their Keys."

"And *her*," he practically snarled, stabbing a finger toward Lucia next to a triangular symbol.

"Yes...she has one too." She sighed. "But that's not the point right now. Your father was the last known holder of the Winter Key, which controls the weather and the element of water. The Keys representing the Seasons are the strongest, so considering how long it's been missing...I worried we would have to turn the world over to find any hint of it."

"He must've done something with it before he died." Julian's face drew grimly. He wondered if his father had been forced to trade it for money to pay his mercenaries and debts.

She eyed him anew, wetting her lips as if there was something on her tongue she didn't quite know how to say. "Did you know Marcus like I knew him?" she finally asked. Before he could open his mouth to snark, she held up a hand. Unlike Lucia, she didn't silence him with magic, but he let her speak her mind. "When he first learned I had stars in my skin, we spent nights outside together, tracing the constellations. My mom would come over and make ones up just to make him laugh. And his laugh...he laughed with his whole self. He didn't care what others thought of him."

"No," he murmured. "I didn't know that man."

"There's something I want to show you. One of my most cherished memories of the man who raised me." She offered it tentatively, a fragile gift from one of the last people he'd suspect to carry tender remembrances of his father.

"I'm a captive audience," he said, waiting for more magic, and she didn't disappoint. She projected her memory like a movie from her occultarus.

He had the feeling of antiquity. Flower petals drifted around the point of view, making him picture Sorsha as a flower girl as she flitted here and there. She was in a church, moonlight filtering in from a set of stained glass windows. Waiting in a fine suit for his intended was none other than Marcus.

Behind him was Jaromir draped in a dark robe, ready to officiate. A man hissed Sorsha's name, drawing her to the side in the first pew as the music began. She looked up into Keegan's face, the two of them sharing a smile. He was in the gangly, awkward stage of a teenage boy, with limbs too long for his torso, bouncing a leg with nervous energy.

Cloth whispered as a small crowd stood and turned as the bride walked in. Julian's fingernails dug into his palm as he caught sight of a feminine figure draped and veiled in silver and white. Sorsha wouldn't make him watch Lucia and his father wed, would she?

The memory of Sorsha scattered petals in the woman's wake as she joined Marcus. He looked over her dress and laughed heartily, saying just loud enough for Julian to hear, "Is this the first and last time I'll see you in a dress, Prince?"

His battle-scarred hands lifted her veil with a tender smile. Julian held his breath.

"Ah, my beautiful lifemate, my bride-to-be," Marcus said, looking straight into the eyes of the only female Blood Prince, Neala. She wore no glamor to hide her flaws, and under the loving gaze of the man she was about to wed, why would she?

Julian blinked rapidly, glad he was lying down, else he would've fallen over in shock. The memory paused there as he looked to Sorsha, who watched with him wearing a wistful smile. "It grows more bittersweet every time I watch it."

"I need you to explain," he said, voice strangling in his throat.

"Isn't it obvious? They were wed before their peers. My adopted mother and father."

"But Lucia is his lifemate." As he voiced those terrible words, Sorsha's expression fell from its nostalgia to sober reality.

"So she says. But I know otherwise. I was *there*." Their gazes locked, hers beseeching. "Forget the venom Lucia tried to drip in your ear. I know it's hard to believe, but your father was a good man before she ruined him."

He thought of the vampire royalty he'd gotten to know. All of them spoke of Marcus as a fond friend. Somehow, he'd missed every inkling of that, knowing only the man who slipped closer and closer to the void of Fell Madness, everything good in him eaten up. The laughs, the late-night constellation studying, every shred of love.

Bowing his head, he wished he could've met the Marcus she'd shown him. Only a brief memory proved that he had been different once. "What did she do?" he whispered.

"Somehow, she's always believed Marcus belonged to her." He felt her pitying gaze on him but didn't turn to acknowledge it. What was done was done. All she was doing was stoking the anger in his heart by proving that Lucia had somehow had a hand in the downfall of a good man. "She severed the mating bond between him and Neala and forced herself upon him. There's evidence she used the Mind Key and an attempt at a powerful love potion to make him forget what he had and accept her. It didn't last.

"But most pertinent to you, she gave him the Winter Key as a wedding band and a token of her affection. It was still on his hands when her magic wore off and he realized what a massive violation he'd just endured. He stole the Fell Keys in her possession and, well, made my current job really hard, frankly." She crossed her arms, lips quirked with her pique. "He sold them like common jewelry and made sure they would never be in the same place together again. But he didn't sell the Mind Key. He threw that one in the ocean. It was retrieved, before you ask. And the Winter Key..."

"He wouldn't keep it," Julian said immediately. Why would

he? It was a token from Lucia. If Marcus had been anything like him at all, he would've been revolted by the very sight of it.

She nodded in agreement. "He destroyed it. I have the proof right in front of me."

Glancing around, it took him several moments to realize she was looking pointedly at him. "Me?" he asked.

"Did you know, when a Key is destroyed, its power transfers to the person who smashed it? Nothing is lost, but the vessel changes. It happened with Gwendolyn, the sole wielder of portal magic." As she spoke, Julian shivered. It was a chill of certainty that, somewhere inside of him, that cold core of magic leapt to confirm her words. "Without a stone to return to, when your father passed away, his magic went to his heirs. You, and everyone else who shared his blood."

"But how did I not feel it? Why is it happening now?" he asked.

Sorsha lifted a shoulder. "You were born with it. As his fifth son, he'd already split the magic between the rest of your siblings. But as they started passing away too..."

"It became stronger," he finished for her with a slow nod. He thought of his cold aura, so much at odds with everyone else's, which always manifested hot. His family was an anomaly, but not for the reason he'd expected. "His only living descendants are Armando and I."

"Circling back to Armando's coma. He's only alive out of sheer stubbornness. The magic within him was convinced he was dying—and it jumped to you. You're generating so much magic and cold that it could kill you without intervention and practice," she said soberly. "Your magic is so strong that not even nephilim chains can hold it back. It's the only explanation that makes sense. Julian, *you* are the Winter Key. And it would be my pleasure to teach you how to master the storm inside you."

Thoughts and ideas swirled in his head, reconstructing Lucia's plan as he considered. She hadn't expected him to be free at this point, giving him the lucky break he needed to have this moment. "When do we get started?" he sighed.

"Why not tomorrow? It's urgent, but I see you need some

time." She stood, clearly ready to dismiss herself. "I'll get Melanie and tell her you're awake."

With her hand on the curtain, she turned back to him. "Two things—you should go to your lifemate. She hasn't seen you since you were attacked and beginning to turn."

His heart dropped. While he was glad she didn't see him as a monster, he still needed to see her, reassure her that he was all right. Better than that, actually, even though his emotions were a hopeless tangle from this conversation that he had little hope of ever unwinding.

"And...don't tell Neala what I showed you. She remembers Marcus but not that they were lifemates. No one should ever remind her of that one detail." She studied a pattern in the ground, her shoulders slumped. "I...I failed a long time ago in fixing the damage Lucia did to her. Neala went Fell Mad and nearly rampaged when she re-learned what she'd lost. And after experiencing the same, I figure you would understand why I don't want her to have that fate again."

"I won't tell her. But I will have revenge on her behalf. Some-day," he promised. Sorsha smiled sadly as she left.

Chapter 20
Olivia

Olivia was sandwiched between Charlotte and Violet before a flat screen television, all three of them taking big handfuls from a jumbo-sized bowl of popcorn they'd scrounged up. She was grateful that, in a giant vampire mansion, there was popcorn, movies, and a comfortable lounge set aside from the main entrance to enjoy them.

Despite that, her thoughts kept skipping backward. Julian was supposed to be doing okay now, but he'd been asleep a long time. She wondered if he'd been gripped by the same queasy nerves she'd had when she was resting off her transformation. It felt worse because, while her sleep had been self-inflicted, he was resting off the aftermath of saving her life and having a brush with something truly evil.

Fell Madness. The not-so-mysterious affliction now that it was practically in their backyard. Gwendolyn's boogeyman, the one thing she wanted an Alchemyst for. Maybe the only reason an Alchemyst was needed at all in a world full of modern medicine and science.

Despite the reassuring presence of her two friends, Olivia couldn't help but linger on the other thing that'd happened that night. She hadn't told anyone about it despite it playing on repeat in her head.

Not even one? You can't make one right now?

With Julian suffering in a hospital bed a few doors down from her, she hadn't been able to summon the power to infuse one drop of blood with the magic it needed to become a purification potion. Gwendolyn's pleading had turned to a sigh and a bowing of her head. But not before Olivia had seen the heavy disappointment creasing her face. She'd practically felt it.

She, Olivia, the first Alchemyst in a thousand years, couldn't even save her own lifemate. With *one* drop of blood. It'd taken a different miracle when Adrius had produced his unopened vial, saved just in case.

With Fell Madness a real threat instead of a rumor, Olivia needed to do better. A lot better. Gwendolyn was stacking her up mentally against beautiful, golden Nyah, and she was coming up short to a memory.

She bet *Nyah* didn't have trouble brewing a life-saving potion for her lifemate.

"Aww, c'mon, kiss the girl already," Charlotte said, tossing a kernel of popcorn at the screen. She was particularly unhappy to be in the mansion in the first place rather than helping the groups patrolling the neighborhood and Coven Rehnquist's territory at large for any more signs of additional Fell Mad. Olivia could practically feel the pent-up energy in her, ready to move if the full-blooded vampires would give her a chance.

"Hey, you'll have to clean that up," Violet protested. "Alex's maid quit. Do you know how hard it is to find a vampire to do that? They don't necessarily have it *maid*."

Exchanging a glance, the three of them had a chuckle. Olivia liked the silver-eyed woman and her puns, even if she fiddled with her fingers nervously as they waited. She seemed like the type that couldn't stand a tension-filled room. That made two of them, so she embraced the distraction Charlotte provided as she shrugged and tossed another kernel.

"I'll clean it up. This guy deserves it anyway."

Olivia chuckled. "That's romantic tension, Char."

"Girl, I know. You've given me an honorary theater degree by now." She nudged her playfully. "You're good at picking apart the acting."

Violet glanced over in surprise. "You have a theater degree? Alex just took me to Broadway the other day."

Charlotte sat back, scrolling on her phone while the other two immediately dropped into the finer points of different, famous shows. They only refocused on the movie occasionally, following Charlotte's lead to boo and throw popcorn when the male lead flummoxed himself again. They giggled together afterward.

That was the moment Julian walked in, his gaze darting between them and the screen that had sustained such an assault of flying grain. Olivia gasped and pushed the bowl into Charlotte's lap.

"Am I interrupting something?" he asked. He seemed like his usual self, dressed in dark-washed jeans and a casual shirt that would show the outline of hard muscle if he flexed.

Dodging around a coffee table, she flung herself into his chest to hug him tightly. After a few surprised moments, he wrapped his arms around her. "You're all right," she said into his shoulder. She drew back to look him over more closely, fixing the wrinkles in his shirt. "Right?" she asked more hesitantly.

His face was as neutral and unreadable as ever. But somehow, she felt sadness wreathing him like a cloak. "Yes, I'm fine," he replied, pitching his voice to a private tone between the two of them. He brushed a curl from her face, forcing a half-smile that didn't fool her for a moment.

"Usually, 'I'm fine' is code for something being secretly wrong," she pointed out.

He shrugged. "It's been a trying few days. Thank you, by the way." He took her hands and gave them a squeeze. "Your potion saved me. In more ways than one, I think."

Drawing breath to tell him just how much of a failure she actually was, she stopped when she saw his expression. Those cold blue eyes seemed to glimmer with their gratitude. "Well, I..." she started to say, drifting off as a kernel of popcorn flew past her, tapping Julian on the forehead.

She turned around, ready to demand an explanation. Charlotte had sat up, her hand cocked back to throw another. "C'mon, kiss the girl," she said with a grin.

Julian's brow crinkled for a moment before he turned back to Olivia. He shrugged to himself before sweeping her forward. Their lips met for the first time with the familiarity of old lovers. She could've kept going without hesitation if they didn't have an audience, and from his side glance her way, she figured he would agree.

I need to get this man alone, she thought.

"Olivia and I need to discuss a few things," Julian said to the two women, turning away and offering his hand to her.

Charlotte made air quotes behind his back. "Bye, guys!" Violet called.

Olivia waved farewell, feeling all tingly as he took her upstairs, toward his room. Her heart pattered harder in her chest, hoping he was thinking what she was. After they got busy with their jobs—his going much better than hers, she presumed —they'd barely had a moment together. But if no one was looking for Julian and she was cooped up for her own protection...

"I've been placed on house arrest," he said, a troubled twist to his lips.

His unhappiness was the last thing she wanted to see in that moment. "I have too...sort of." When he turned to quirk a brow, she sighed. "Well, Gwendolyn probably thinks I'm useless. She's off doing important things and 'giving me time to mature into my blood,' whatever that means."

"Why would she think you're useless? Your blood saved my life." He smiled at her in full, his aura pleasantly cool as it caressed her like a refreshing wind on a hot day.

"Well, um..." She forced the truth out like she hadn't earlier. "That was the only purification potion I've successfully made. It was almost like beginner's luck. Alchemyst magic is apparently more than cutting yourself and putting the blood in a mix of herbs and water."

"Of course. If anyone could do it, she wouldn't have been overjoyed to see and train you. It's hard to excite a vampire as old as her," he said, giving her side a squeeze.

"Yeah, well..." She didn't really want to argue against that.

Hopefully, her blood would "mature" and she'd start shooting out purification potions like no one's business.

They stopped before the door to his room. He turned to her, in no apparent hurry to go inside as he tucked his hands in his pockets. "It chills me to know what she would've done to me and, through me, you."

"We don't have to talk about it," she murmured, feeling that this might be a tender subject coming off the trauma of his ordeal.

He nodded readily in agreement. "Well, thank you for walking with me. That seemed like a good movie, so have a good evening—"

He wasn't seriously suggesting they part ways? "Wait. Aren't you going to invite me in?" she blurted.

From the change in his expression, he looked ready to cover his face with a broad palm. "Of course. I didn't know if you wanted to go back to your popcorn throwing."

She swept by him as he unlocked the door, hiding an eye roll. Maybe he wasn't feeling the same anticipation as her. It'd occurred that maybe he was out of practice with courting in his older age. She'd just need to take the lead for both of their sakes.

"What would you like to do?" she asked, smiling coyly over her shoulder. She wondered how much of a hint he'd need.

He didn't seem to notice her glance, heading past her to the kitchenette his room came with. "I'm about ready to get drunk and watch TV. Can I get you something?"

"Don't drink too much now," she said, smiling a little wider. "We can watch TV, I guess."

"Did you have another idea?" he asked, already pouring them both a glass of wine.

"Oh, no, that's fine." She accepted the glass, a deep red. Knowing him, it'd be a dry vintage he had saved. They toasted and she sipped it with a, "Cheers!"

He replied with a phrase in his native Italian.

"I knew you'd pull that out eventually. What does it mean?" she asked curiously. As she'd expected, the wine was quite dry, but she appreciated the dose of courage she was about to have.

He winked. "To us." And just that made her heart do a little excited flip. Maybe he was more keen on this private moment than she thought.

They relocated to his couch, where he lounged back and started flipping through channels. She sat close, their thighs nearly brushing, while his gaze was on the television. That sense of sadness was still about him, seeking some form of relief or distraction. She wanted that relief to be *her*.

Getting his attention would need something bold and obvious. "I need to use the restroom," she said, earning a distracted nod.

Part of her said this was a bad idea as she headed deeper into his room, past a bed made with military crispness.

The other part of her said he was just like that bed...in need of someone to come along and ruffle it invitingly. Draw back the comforter, get a peek at what was underneath. She downed her entire glass in front of the bathroom mirror and wished she'd gotten more in her system before going for this. But she shook herself off and then flushed the toilet to mask the sound of her clothes hitting the ground.

Sauntering out in her underwear, she knew the moment she had Julian's undivided attention. Wine glass halfway to his lips, he froze with a look of open-mouthed surprise.

"I had another idea of something we could do," she said, taking a nervous swallow despite herself.

His gaze drifted downward as he sat straight. A slow smile spread across his face; she had his full attention now.

Chapter 21
Julian

Julian woke before Olivia, watching the shadows of sunset lengthen on his bedroom wall. The heavy shutters outside would be lifting soon, and he hoped the sudden rattle wouldn't startle her. Her head rested opposite of his, her curls piled over her face like a screen. Sometime before they'd passed out together, she'd claimed one of his shirts, which tented around her curves like pajamas.

For an evening, he'd forgotten his troubles in her arms. They niggled at the edges of his consciousness now, threatening to remind him why he was supposed to spend a couple days in the mansion while others worked. His friend Luke, Alex's brother-in-law from his first mate, had taken over his duties with Sirius, and last he'd heard, the two of them got along quite well. Since Luke was a shapeshifter of Sirius's bloodline, it wasn't too much of a surprise.

It left Julian at loose ends to recover. As he played with a lock of Olivia's hair, he thought this was the most pleasant recuperation period he'd taken in a long time. If he didn't have the uncertainty of the Winter Key magic inside of him, he'd extend this time-out as long as possible.

Olivia stirred, arching her back as she muffled a yawn. Multiple pops came from her joints. She released a pleased hum as she opened eyes of liquid gold and smiled at him.

"Goooooood evening," she said with her usual pep.

"*Ciao, bella.*" He'd seen her face light up at his toast last night as it did now from the simple phrase he spoke in his mother tongue.

"Oh, baby. Speak Italian to me."

He obliged and got a few sentences in about her beauty before she laughed and pushed playfully at his chest. "Sorry. I didn't mean it. I don't understand what you're saying!"

He clasped her hand, whispering, "I said...you've given light to the eternal night of my life. I don't know what I'd do without you, and I'm completely unsurprised you wake up with energy." Her eyes seemed to sparkle as she listened and fluttered a hand to her chest.

"Does it make me a morning person if it's technically evening?" she asked.

"I'd say that counts," he said.

She released a short giggle, resting her head on his shoulder. "So, what do you want to do?"

"Is this another trick question, bella?" His hand smoothed down his shirt on her, tracing curves he vowed to learn every nuance of.

"Maybe we should get up," Olivia said some time later, laying out in a satisfied sprawl beside him.

He shrugged, not wanting her to stop her idle stroking of his chest and sides. "It's not like anyone is expecting us."

It was, apparently, the wrong thing to say. Her brows drew together as her eyes dimmed from their supernatural brightness. "Yeah, I guess you're right. Gwendolyn gave me time off too." From how she spoke, it didn't seem like she thought it was the kind of break she'd earned.

"What's causing you trouble?" he asked, recalling she wasn't so excited about her Alchemyst abilities as when she'd first started despite creating the potion that'd saved his life.

"She keeps comparing me and my progress to what she

remembers of Nyah," she grumbled. "I can't do the very basic stuff yet. When I cut myself, my blood isn't pure gold unless I, like, magic it to be that way. I've only been able to do it once. Gwendolyn and Sorsha go on and on about all the things they could do with my blood—if I could only get a grip on this part."

He pressed a kiss to her temple, drawing her close. "I don't think they know how to teach you." She opened her mouth to protest before giving it some thought, her lips quirking. "Gwendolyn has thousand-year-old memories to guide her, and Sorsha is of a completely different race."

"There's a book of formulas to reference," she said. "Fae Sorcerers have magical blood too. But you're still right. I can make purification potions, and she can't. Maybe there are more differences."

"Undoubtedly."

She huffed a sigh, sending her curls scattering as she shook her head. "While you were unconscious, I heard them talking about you. How you're being targeted. But they wouldn't tell me why."

Rather than stiffen at her remark, he reminded himself that he was alive and safe, in the one place Lucia wouldn't dare show her face for fear of the other Ancients who now called it a temporary home. "The Sorceress we won't name is doing that, yes." He didn't think to hesitate, though the reasons for his targeting could change how she saw him. "She was in love with my father."

"What, a thousand years ago?" she asked with an uneasy laugh, which faded as he nodded.

"A thousand years ago." He found his tongue slipping around the words to begin to share the terrible truth he now held after Sorsha's bedside revelations. "She coveted him, but he was not destined to be hers. His lifemate was another, and they were happily married. Have you met Neala?"

"I mean, she's been around with Sorsha, but not really. Are you saying...?" Her eyes widened as the implications of his question sunk in.

"I just learned it myself," he said, feeling like a great weight was leaving him to have someone to share this with. "She stole my father from her, using magic. This damaged Neala's memory, so she can't remember him as her husband without going Fell Mad. He was apparently a great man before this, but the Sorceress ruined him; and he spurned her by stealing the Fell Keys from her." He looked down at his hand, warm and free of any sign of the cold magic that was his inheritance.

"So, what does that have to do with you?" she asked, her fingers flexing at the injustice as presented.

"She wants revenge," he said quietly. "Because many years later, my father met his end on my blade."

Olivia gasped in shock. "What? Why?" she asked simply. He felt he had one chance to explain himself and dredged up his memories of that day and the chain of events that'd caused it.

"I have a story to tell," he said, waiting for her to nod. "I was born in a different time. Keep that in mind, all right?" Maybe a disclaimer would soften this for her. "I was my father's fifth son. He was a warlord human history never wrote about, but at one point, he held a good portion of Europe as an empire-sized territory. His coven was an army and the strongest, most ruthless of them all."

"Wait. How come humans didn't know about that?" she asked. "Wouldn't the fighting be noticed?"

"Vampire politics are more subtle than that. Many would put down their arms and join my father when they knew he was coming. Vampires bow to power, and power comes with age and influence. Any battles happened late at night, the bodies laid out to burn away with the dawn of the sun." He grimaced, remembering doing such gruesome work himself, finding secluded areas and stripping the corpses of anything that would remain. No one was the wiser.

"Brutal," she murmured.

"With such a vast territory and reach, my father could take anything he wanted. And he did." He sighed. "He and his coven landed on *Italia's* shore in the late seventeenth century. There on the shore was my mother, then a mortal. She was maybe your age." Olivia shifted uncomfortably, immediately seeing where he was going with this.

"He claimed her for himself before turning her. They later found out that she was with child. I was the first son born with his features. I grew up Julian Marcuson and only later changed my last name to Fairfax," he continued.

"My father did not like children. He had a whole harem full of women." Olivia winced at this, and he gave a solemn nod of agreement. "So, I rarely saw him, growing up. I did have more mothers than I could count, though. Since the vampire gene is dormant until adulthood, I spent a lot of time playing in the sunlight with mortal children." Just barely, he could remember that time, when light had been pleasantly warm instead of burning at a glance.

"My father ignored me until I was about thirteen, then he told me I would be trained to fight. I wanted to please him badly, so I threw my whole effort into the work and got my friends involved as well. Strangely, he encouraged them, and he ended up drilling a couple dozen mortals in the finer points of combat.

"I was about twenty years old when my body started to turn. The fangs grew in." He rubbed his jaw in remembered pain. "I became stronger and more sensitive to everything. Shortly after I turned, he turned all my friends, the ones who had trained with me. He had made us into young soldiers, there to fight and die in his war. I enjoyed it back then. Fight all night, feast until sunrise.

"I did this for many years. My mother would pray for me every time I visited her, coming back with tales of war. I buried some of my friends, but thus was their sacrifice for our ultimate goal, spreading my father's coven as far as possible. Then, everything changed. I met a woman."

Olivia let off a snicker. "A special one," he amended. "I was used to warrior women who I could spar with, who liked how rough I was. One night, I decided I wanted a frail mortal's blood. She was painting in the moonlight, lovely in her own way. When I jumped her, she stabbed me with her brush. I looked down at that bit of color on my clothes, and she said, 'Try that again. I will paint you to death if I have to.'"

He realized her smile was fading, shading to concern. Picking up how he spoke wistfully of a woman that wasn't her, he realized. He was lost in his own memory of Rosa, seeing that moment so clearly, even though most of his memories were faded like an old mural. "Rosalia did not fear like everyone else did. She was alone, without means to protect herself, and I grew fascinated with her. What was it about the coastline at night that brought her out to paint it? We met in the same spot every night until her work was done there. I did not know it at the time, but I was courting her like a man should court a woman."

Olivia was holding her breath. And so was he, releasing it on a slow sigh. "Rosa knew her time was brief. Briefer than most. Her heart was damaged." He tapped out a regular heartbeat on his wrist and then changed its tempo, sometimes fast, skipping beats.

"With her, I learned to be gentle. I would spend all my free time in her room, disrupting her sleep. She was appalled by the violence I held inside myself, so slowly, I let it go. Anything to please her. My coven noticed, and eventually, I was followed.

"I begged her to let me turn her, but she would always refuse. She told me my life was not for her. Just like her life was not for me." He paused, finding the rest stuck in his throat. His tongue wouldn't move to tell the rest of the tale. Worry flooded in, like he'd already failed to convince Olivia that he'd ultimately done the right thing.

She placed a hand over his chest, flashing a concerned look. "Take your time."

He took a deep breath and forced the rest from himself a few minutes later. "When my father learned of Rosa, he demanded she be brought before him. I dreaded what he meant to do and said anything I thought would sway him. He knew me too well—when I told him she was my lifemate, he recognized it was a lie. The most mercy he was willing to offer was five minutes alone with her. Rosa made me promise two things—that I find my life-mate and that I never settle for less. It was all we had time for."

Olivia shook her head in denial as he continued, "He had two men hold my arms and shoved Rosa to the ground. 'Do you love this woman?' he asked me. I said yes." He took a shuddering breath, closing his eyes to block out the moment.

"He took the time to tell me of a woman he once loved. The Sorceress who'd shown him that love made him weak." He couldn't bear to repeat any of the compliments his father had paid Lucia for fear he might vomit. "He drew his sword and slew her right before my eyes. I felt the loss down to my soul. And since then...I made sure to keep my promises to her." Julian reached over and brushed the trails of wetness from her cheeks. He forced a smile now that the worst of it was over. "It's all right. It was a long time ago," he murmured.

"He killed her because you cared about her," she said, shaking her head. "If I were you, I'd get him back for it too."

"That was why I abandoned his cause," he said. He felt his heart lighten once more as she flashed him a sad smile, knowing he *had* shared the right thing after all and that she was still with him and his tale. "I left everything I knew and went to England, a territory outside his reach. I didn't know English, but I got by. My nights were spent mesmerizing mortals, forcing them to give me lessons in their language.

"One such night, I met Alex Rehnquist, who had watched me for a while. He approached with a deal of mutual interest. We both spoke French, so he could teach me English, but I had to show him how to fight in exchange. I accepted and became the fourth member of his budding coven. Alex was a reluctant leader. He was little more than a wily rogue with a knack for dodging his enemies. Look at him now." He chuckled, smiling more fondly on those memories. He had so many stories for her about his old friends.

"Thing about Alex, though. While he had never led before, he was rather good at it. His enemies became my enemies, and when he eventually fled England for the colonies, I went with him. Sometimes I would write letters to my mother. Most probably didn't reach her, but she did write back. Things were not going well in my father's coven. As an Ancient, my father had his most powerful ability, which was being able to connect mentally over long distances. Every couple of years, he would reach out and demand I come home. I ignored him.

"I'm going to skip about fifty years here. Coven Rehnquist

was pushed from America by circumstances and was traveling across Europe, steadily growing larger. One day, my father tried to talk to me again, but it was different this time. He'd said please." Olivia chuckled, rolling her eyes, as if it wasn't the direst of circumstances to prompt a hint of begging from *the* Marcus Hartson. "I'm serious. I knew he was desperate. So, I brought my new friends back home, where the coven was almost completely wiped out. He'd driven our family to ruin. Armando was the only blood kin I had other than my mother. All the friends I'd trained with were dead. He was so happy to see us, thinking we'd bolster his ranks. His army was so decimated that his harem had taken up arms. He'd put a sword in the hands of my gentle mother and told her to fight."

He shook his head, still furious at the image of it. "I was treated like the prodigal son. After so long, I was a walking myth—the man who'd turned away from his father's war. But I had not come there to fight for him. I'd come to challenge him to a duel, in the old way of things. A fight to the death." He touched his chest, where he still bore numerous scars under his glamor, all from that battle. "And I *won*. Briefly, I was coven master to a crumbling empire. But my heart wasn't in it. My friends were bound for another try in America, and I went with them. My mother took up the mantle, making peace with my father's enemies and settling a small territory for the survivors." A feat he admired, wishing he knew that kind of diplomacy.

"I took a couple of people from my mother's new coven with us, most notably Armando. He was the son of my eldest brother, barely twenty-five when he came along. He'd grown up hearing about me and was most unimpressed by the real Julian," he finished, chuckling quietly.

She giggled. "The start of a beautiful friendship."

"Indeed. So, this...woman. She's been sleeping for a thousand years, seeing the future and watching my father, covetous of what she cannot have. She's targeting me because I took away the possibility of a future with him. I think it makes it worse that I look just like him." He sighed, flexing his fingertips. "Because of her, Sorsha thinks my bloodline has the powers of the Winter Key. I assume she wants a piece of that too."

He thought of the long nights of tormenting half-remembered nightmares where she kept confronting him for his crime. "She doesn't have any reason in her, does she?" Olivia played her fingers over his muscles, her light touch distracting. "Like, she probably doesn't care why you did it, just that he's dead."

"Exactly." He released a weary sigh. He hadn't shared the story of Rosa with another since commiserating with Alex over the death of his first lifemate. Just the act of telling had left him worn out but so relieved in the same breath that Olivia was still there. She seemed to know it by instinct, holding him close as the evening shaded darker and stars winked down upon them.

He didn't know how long they lay together like that before Sorsha checked in with him mentally, sharing that she wanted to start his magical training the next day. He accepted that. All he wanted was Olivia for the rest of this night.

Chapter 22
Olivia

Olivia and Julian barely left his room the rest of that night. They showered alone in their own rooms the next evening, else Olivia figured they'd miss Julian's first training session for his magic by being otherwise preoccupied.

With the story about his father out in the open, it was like a great weight had left his shoulders. He spoke more openly with her in his arms. Now she knew he was the living embodiment of the Winter Key. She hated how Lucia had manhandled him and Armando to make it happen and how the Sorceress kept looming over him like a wrathful shadow.

From what else he'd told her of Lucia's plans with Violet, she hoped they weren't playing into her hands unwittingly. When facing someone who could see the future—who just happened to seem certifiably insane—there was no way of telling.

Olivia was sure of one thing, though. Lucia wasn't done with Julian.

She wholeheartedly agreed that he should be training his magic for the day he would see her again. They were pulling Sorsha in yet another direction, but it sounded like she could train him and Violet together.

Which left Olivia at loose ends. She was supposed to train with Gwendolyn in the hospital, but the older woman wanted to watch Julian practice his magic instead. Olivia was glad for it, because she'd also get to see the secret place Sorsha had set up for magical training.

She went downstairs wearing jeans and a light top, knowing from Julian that the location was out in the middle of the woods somewhere. Waiting in the entrance foyer was Gwendolyn, flanked by Adrius and Sirius. Sirius approached and bowed over Olivia's hand like a gentleman of old. "We are blessed to have you," he said.

She felt a blush creeping up her neck. When had anyone been *blessed* by her presence? "Thank you. I'm trying my best, but I have big shoes to fill."

"So do we all. Those who came before us cast a long shadow," Sirius said. His gaze narrowed on his brother. "Isn't that right?" His tone held a biting edge.

Whoa, she thought, edging away on instinct. Adrius didn't look up, like he hadn't realized the question was for him.

"Hey, good evening!" Violet's voice called across the foyer, coming from the master bedroom suite in casual clothes and her hair done up in a swinging ponytail. Her shimmering eyes took in the scene, darting between them. A frown tugged at her lips. "What did the sun say to the sky as it set?" She put on cheer for the question.

"What did it say?" Sirius sighed, working his jaw.

"I need my beauty rest! I'm *evening* up appearances." Olivia managed a chuckle for her.

To her surprise, so did Adrius. He swung his bulk around so he had his back to Olivia but acknowledged Violet with a nod. His smooth voice held some relief at her appearance. "Hello, Sorceress. Will your mate be joining us this evening?"

"You know it. But I'm not the main attraction tonight." She lifted her hands in an exaggerated shrug.

Julian's boots hit the stairs as his voice preceded him. "Does that make me the show, then?"

Violet grinned. "I, for one, would love to see you throw some ice."

He waited until he was in the foyer with them to reply rather than broadcast talk of his magic out to the whole mansion. "As I understand it, Winter magic itself is more than ice." The air chilled in his presence. Olivia knew now that it wasn't his aura causing it but the Winter Key within him, flushing him with cold as it grew more concentrated.

"It is. It's water and weather, actually." Violet responded automatically. "Winter magic makes rainstorms and blizzards alongside ice and lightning. It's the domain for a lot of spells."

Julian laced his arm around Olivia's hips as Violet spoke. "Sorsha suggested it was one of the most powerful Keys," he murmured.

"She would know," she said, seeming more interested in watching the two of them with a knowing look.

They waited a few minutes for the fae, who arrived as a unit, like always, with Sorsha in the lead and Ash and Keegan flanking her like armed guards. Olivia wondered if they slept in the same room, too.

Alex came in not long after, sharing a glance with Sirius. There might've been some mental communication between them as Sorsha worked a spell by circling her arm. What happened next defied explanation, except Olivia knew it was magic. A doorway shaped hole appeared midair. Its surface rippled like black ink as the others started to go through it.

Sirius turned away from the group, leaving Olivia and Julian to be last. Julian gave her side a squeeze. "I know it looks intimidating, but it works. It's a portal—you go through it and end up somewhere else in the world."

"Anywhere?" she asked, turning an incredulous look up at him.

He kissed that expression from her with a laugh. "Just try it. You'll see."

She only tried it because she trusted that he and everyone else in their group wouldn't use this dark doorway if it didn't actually work. After a gut-wrenching moment of complete silence, her feet landed in a patch of ankle-length grass. Her first thought was *I don't like this.*

"This isn't Kansas anymore," she said under her breath, looking around. They were in a clearing somewhere far from people. She was in the middle of a football field's worth of space, grass and weeds as far as she could see, surrounded by a silent crowd of trees on all sides. Things were too quiet here, lacking the song of nature.

Then Adrius came up to them, and with him, a strange sensation passed over her ears, like she was suddenly in a room full of whispering people. "I need to show you something," he said shortly, his gaze on Julian.

"Sure," Julian said, glancing toward her with a shrug.

He turned his back, speaking over his shoulder. "Her too."

She pulled a face, walking hand-in-hand with Julian as they followed. "Can you hear that?" she asked.

"Hmm?"

"It sounds like whispering," she said, pitching her voice to be a dramatic whisper to match. He raised a brow but shook his head.

Maybe she was just imagining it. The feeling was fading anyway, her ears ringing faintly as if trying to pick up on something that wasn't there. "We have a couple of rules," Adrius said, stopping abruptly and holding up a fist like he was a commander and they, his soldiers.

Julian stopped quickly as well, pointing out why. Resting in the grass was a piece of glass as big as she was, surrounded by jagged edges. There were more of all sizes around it, scattered like the wreckage of a window factory around a bent piece of metal that could've been a skyscraper's support if it weren't mangled beyond repair. In the shadows of a tree, several stone slabs were stacked.

"Is this the Eye of Worlds?" Julian asked.

"What remains of it," Adrius said, swinging a grim look on them both. "The rules are thus. We do not mention a particular Sorceress by name in this place *ever*. And you do not touch, nor take, any piece of the Eye of Worlds away from here."

Olivia nodded slowly, eyeing the remnants and imagining the real thing must've been absolutely massive. "Why did you take it from Nyixa?" Julian pressed.

Shadows seemed to dance in Adrius's eyes. "There is no

Nyixa anymore. The explosion finished the job of a thousand-year plunge into the ocean. The palace collapsed, and the island itself will sink soon, I've heard. For good this time."

"There were mortals studying that island."

"Sorsha worked some magic on the ones we rescued from the explosion. They will share tales of an accidental catastrophe they caused. But the rest of the world will wonder." He toed a piece of glass to turn it over. A wisp of smoke rose with the barest of sounds, like a voice spoken from far away.

Olivia scrubbed her ears, but the sound was already gone. "Let them wonder." Adrius sounded like his mind was elsewhere. It took him a few minutes to turn back to them. Even then, he was still only looking at Julian. "Good luck with your training."

Training, it turned out, was quite the boring affair for someone watching. Olivia ended up needing to stand a "safe" distance away as Sorsha and Gwendolyn drilled Julian in the basics of harnessing his magic. She was glad Violet needed to stand far away too, so they passed the time together. "Why does it look like he's practicing for a sign language class?" she asked the Sorceress.

Violet muffled a giggle. "That's what casting spells looks like before you get an occultarus. I wonder if he'll need one..." She glanced up to the simple golden orb circling her head like a halo. "Sorsha was going to decorate mine when she had time. But judging by how things are going, she's not going to find a spare moment."

"Maybe if the three fae separated and split the work..." Olivia offered a shrug. "Especially since they want to bring new Sorcerers on board, right?"

"That's not how they work."

"So, it always takes three fae to screw in a lightbulb?"

Violet raised a brow. "You haven't asked them why they're always together, have you?"

She felt heat creep up her neck. Usually, she was the one to ask a hundred questions of everyone she met, but with the fae, it'd felt more disrespectful. Especially since they were never apart. "Luckily for you, I've asked," Violet said. "Fae society is a lot different from ours. Sorsha's a rare and powerful fae as an Archfae and was assigned Keegan to be her protector. It's his job to be by her side any time she's in public. He called himself a Blade—a master of physical magic and martial skill."

Considering the sword he carried on his hip like he, too, was stuck a thousand years in the past, his title didn't surprise Olivia. "Is she important enough to have *two* bodyguards?"

"Ash is unique. I asked how an Unseelie got through the veil when we were told only Seelie could come to Earth on midsummer day. That's all they'd tell me on that subject. 'Ash is unique' and that spells she doesn't approve of die in her presence. She's our anti-Sorceress. I don't think she or Keegan will find anyone with magic like theirs to train here."

They both startled back as Julian lifted his arms, palms facing out. A sharp, icy breeze buffeted them even from a distance. "Yeah, well, that makes sense," Olivia said. "It's just weird, you know?"

"To our standards," she pointed out. "Alex has been trying to convince Ash to go hunting the unfriendly Sorceress, but she won't entertain the idea of leaving the other two."

"That sounds like a great idea...where is Alex, by the way?" It occurred to her that it was odd to see her without any hint of him around.

Violet glanced around before lowering her voice. "Sirius asked him to keep an eye on Adrius. He hasn't been acting right."

She thought of the Vampire King's gruff manner and turned back. "You're saying he's normally not a donkey's rear end?"

Violet hesitated a moment too long. "He hasn't been."

"All right." Olivia wasn't about to argue. Not when Julian was sweeping his hand and making a line of jagged ice spikes appear a few feet from him. She sighed wistfully.

"He's something else, huh?"

"You have no idea." She knew her friend meant in the physical sense. But a wave of longing hit her with how much she wished she, too, could throw ice and summon storms. To be able to do something more useful than make potions.

That is, if she could even get that right.

Chapter 23
Olivia

JULIAN TRAINED HIS WINTER KEY-GIVEN MAGIC FOR DAYS, but Olivia wasn't there past the first session. She and Gwendolyn returned to the hospital and their borrowed back room with all the tools to make potions.

Sorsha and the other fae didn't come with them, so instead, they had two Ancients standing guard close by. This evening, it was Adrius and Neala, who was glamored in public to look like a long-legged beauty with a crown of red locks over a flawless face. Julian had entrusted her with a secret and warned what had happened the last time Neala was reminded of what she'd lost. It was uncomfortable to look into her flaming maroon eyes and say nothing of the deep well of sympathy she felt for her.

Considering how difficult producing purification potions was turning out to be, Olivia didn't want to risk any guaranteed Fell Madness. She sat with her hand poised over a petri dish, a scalpel millimeters from her thumb. "Remember, focus on your blood. You are the only one who can control the magic within," Gwendolyn said, watching her intently. "Can you feel the influence flowing through your veins?"

Honestly, no, she thought. From day one, that explanation hadn't made sense to her. But when she nodded and cut her skin, the truth bubbled to the surface. Without magic, her blood was the same color it'd always been. Not even a fleck of gold. She nursed the little wound, waiting for the tingle that signified her vampire healing sealing it back shut.

Without that bit of magic, she would've believed she was still a human. She had special eyes...so what? She set the scalpel down with a clatter.

Useless...

Her brow furrowed. "I'm not useless," she snapped.

"I never said you were." Gwendolyn eyed the single drop of blood in the dish, shaking her head slowly.

"You just did. I heard you with my own ears." But the old woman had an honest expression of confusion on her face.

"I didn't say that, because I don't think that. Why don't you take a break?" she suggested.

She scratched the back of her head. "Yeah, that's probably a good idea." She got up and went to the door. Sitting outside was Adrius, who seemed wreathed in shadows even under the neon glow of the fluorescents above. Their eyes met for a moment before he flinched away.

The sense of whispering returned for an uneasy moment. She turned from him to Neala, who had a gun disassembled on a table next to her. "I'm taking a break. Want to step outside?"

The other woman lifted a shoulder and stood, leaving her experiment where it rested. She didn't say anything, just gestured that she should lead on. Olivia abandoned the hospital and its uncomfortably clean smell to the outdoors, enjoying the song of the crickets instead.

Neala rested her back against the hospital's side, and Olivia paced close by. "*Something troubles you?*" The woman's mental voice startled her. Being mute, it was the only way she could communicate.

"No. I mean, maybe. Do you hear that?" she asked.

Neala tilted her head, brow creasing. "*The crickets? The wind? That man's footsteps?*" A doctor in scrubs was coming in from the parking lot, barely sparing them a glance.

"No, the—" she clammed up before she could blurt that she was hearing things. The last thing she needed was for this near-stranger to judge her too. Especially because as she looked at Neala, she could feel that sensation returning, like several someone's were whispering at once just out of earshot. "Never mind. It's nothing."

Shrugging in return, Neala gazed up at the sky. On a whim, Olivia leaned against the wall next to her. She strained her hearing.

Then, it happened.

Remember long nights looking at this sky? Just you and him, under the stars.

It was Neala's voice, but she wasn't speaking. At least...Olivia didn't think so. She was hearing a whisper rather than a distinct voice speaking in her head.

"Sorsha and I would study the stars together when she was just a girl." Neala's actual voice came a few moments later as she lifted a finger and traced a constellation. *"Different times. Same stars."*

Was she going crazy? Olivia rubbed her forehead as she looked up too. "It must be nice to know that some things don't change."

"It is a great comfort, girl."

They stood there in companionable silence for a few minutes, though Olivia was hyper-aware that the whispers were continuing. Buzzing like a maelstrom of thoughts that she caught bits and pieces of.

...through his heart...

You never said goodbye.

She took him from you.

Olivia's skin crawled the more she heard. "I'm ready to go inside."

"Very well." Despite the whispers around her, Neala herself seemed perfectly placid.

When they went inside, Olivia made a point of brushing past Adrius's knees, making physical contact with him for the barest of moments. The whispers around him solidified for her to hear one thing, and it made her pale and rush into the room with Gwendolyn pouring over the tome of fae potions.

She startled as the door slammed. "What's wrong? You look like you've seen a ghost."

All Olivia could focus on was a tendril of shadow winding its way around Gwendolyn's arms, brushing past her ear.

"Look at this child, standing in for your flawless daughter," it whispered.

Olivia shook her head rapidly. The last thing Gwendolyn needed to know was what she'd just heard—that the whispers had just confidently told Adrius he should end his life. Something was wrong. So wrong she couldn't tell anyone here. All three had something literally whispering in their ears, and somehow, she could hear it too.

Her throat felt like ash. "Let's try again. I have to feel the magic in my blood and force it out of me. I'm ready."

"No, not force. Have you been listening?" Gwendolyn pinched the bridge of her nose. "Control it. Coax it. But if you try to force it, you won't get anywhere. Obviously." She made a dismissive gesture toward their Alchemy station, where several murky vials waited for a drop of Olivia's golden blood.

Olivia started with her breathing exercises to calm her racing heart. She closed her eyes, feeling it begin to calm just to jolt into double-time as someone else's voice entered her mind uninvited. *"Olivia?"*

Her fingernails bit into her palms as she broke out into a nervous sweat. She recognized the desperate businessman voice of Elandros, the very last person she'd expect to reach out to her.

"W-what do you want?" Even in her head, she knew she hadn't concealed her sudden fright.

"It's okay. I'm not contacting you because of her. This is my agenda," he said.

"Uh-huh?" She cracked her eyes open to see that Gwendolyn had turned back to her reading.

"I need your help."

"Me?" Somehow, she doubted she could do much to help someone as Ancient as him.

"Yes, you. The Alchemyst. The first one in a thousand years."

"How do you know—?"

"How do you think?" Well, he had a point. And she'd already gotten into the habit of not mentioning Lucia by name, so she just waited with anxiety creeping over her skin like an army of insects. *"I need two things. A potion that breaks blood oaths and for you to tell me where Adrius is."*

"Hold on. Why? I know what you've done. Julian's told me." She injected her mental voice with as much scorn as possible, an easy task as she forced herself to imagine Julian's pain at seeing Armando knocked out by a mysterious disease borne from Elandros's mouth.

A sigh passed over their mental connection. *"I wish to... change. I will offer you a boon if you assist me. Anything you ask of me, you will have."*

"Tell me what she's planning!" she blurted. *"Every step, every word! Then I'll help you."*

"I already plan to do that. And I would now, but—I need that potion." She heard a bitter chuckle from him. *"She holds a secret over me. One your allies would gladly destroy me for."*

"Why would you worry about that? It's not like they'd believe her," she pointed out. *"In fact, you could've gone completely under the table with your secret if you hadn't said anything about it to me."*

"What...?" His confusion was palpable. *"I...That doesn't matter! She held it over me when it was important, a thousand years ago. She kept saying she'd forget about it if I'd do one more thing for her. One more thing turned into another. 'Elandros, wouldn't it be a shame if someone found out what you did?'"* He mimicked Lucia's silken voice with practiced ease. *"I swore a blood oath to her to make it stop. It's saved my life up until now."*

"But now you want out?" she supplied.

"I don't want to be her errand boy anymore. But I must also look after my own interests. So, before any alliance is struck, I must speak with Adrius."

She glanced over her shoulder at the closed door. *"I'll set up a meeting between you two at a coffee shop or something, okay?"*

"How soon?" he demanded.

"I'll let you know."

She pulled away from the mental contact, feeling her awareness of him fade. She took a deep breath, picking up a new, clean scalpel and drawing a glance from Gwendolyn to see how this round went.

You are Nyah, Vampire Queen, Alchemyst, and leader of an ancient people, she told herself. The sharp edge of the tool trembled with the jitters in her arm.

Taking another deep breath, she lowered it before she accidentally skewered herself. No, this wasn't going to work.

You are Olivia, the next Alchemyst. You have big shoes to fill, and you're only a size nine. You hear voices and know something's not quite right here. The blood in your veins may be the cure...

On that thought, she drew the scalpel over her thumb. A bead of liquid gold glowed on the surface of her skin.

Chapter 24
Adrius

Adrius was glad of his errand, as menial it was, to get everyone coffee from one of the modern stores that specialized in such things. He'd only had "fast food" a couple times, finding the experience of combining fresh vegetables with a greasy, meaty patty pleasing. This was supposed to be another such fast place. Gwendolyn had handed him a few bills along with a golden purification potion and sent him on his way after making sure he left his sword behind.

He repeated the name of the location he sought, supposedly only a short walk once he left the hospital grounds. The green bills in his fist were dollars, the currency of this country. Someone had written down a list of exotic-sounding coffee blends for him to repeat to the coffee servants.

This is all you're good for.

No one wants you around.

Heaving a sigh, he tilted the vial in his other hand, watching the thick, glittering liquid within shift. He was supposed to drink this and present the empty vial back to Gwendolyn by the end of this trip.

You still don't deserve it.

You failed Nyah.

His grip on the glass tightened. Maybe he should save this one as well, to ensure one was on hand if the new Alchemyst continued to have spotty success with her powers. But how? Gwendolyn would hound him now that she knew he wasn't drinking it down. She wouldn't understand that he just... couldn't.

What does she look like?

Why can't you remember?

He couldn't look the new Alchemyst in the eye. It sent spikes of pain straight to his core to see her golden blessing as a reminder that Nyah was fading from him. He couldn't recall what she looked like, how her voice sounded, what she preferred...only those eyes, as luminous as Olivia's but twice as mysterious. Why couldn't he remember?

Arriving at the coffee shop, he took a glance around. Mortals awake at this hour gawked as he passed, heading up to the servant behind the counter busying herself on a phone with how quiet the store was. "Excuse me, fair lady," he said, waiting for her to look up. She turned a bored expression his way, giving him a once over with a lift of a heavily plucked brow. "I wish to procure a number of your pastries and coffee items."

"Okay," she said, drawing out the word as silence stretched between them. "What can I get for you, sir?"

He read off his list to her and offered his whole fistful of bills. She gingerly unrolled them and slid one back before offering more bills and coins in exchange. "Nice cosplay, by the way. Very convincing," she said as she passed all of this back with a slip of paper.

"What is a cosplay?" he asked, earning a laugh from her as she went farther behind the counter to mix his coffee.

He was gathering up the order and placing the money within a container meant to carry multiple drinks at once when a long-fingered hand reached out to snag one of the drinks.

"Mortals sure hate the taste of coffee," remarked the last person he'd expect to cross paths with as he stole a sip. Elandros, dressed in a fine suit with a cravat.

Adrius slammed down the laden tray and swung to face him, feeling his face crease into a snarl. "What are you doing here?"

The other man held up his hand. "I just want to talk." He

took another sip of coffee before placing the cup back in its holder.

His voice dropped to a quiet rumble. "You've got a lot of nerve showing your face."

"I've seen the error of my ways." To his credit, he looked contrite.

He lies!

Another one of Lucia's schemes!

"I'll do anything you want," Elandros continued, dropping his voice too. He glanced down at his clasped hands. "Just get me away from her."

Adrius glanced up to see that the three other people in the coffee shop were all turned their way. One had his phone up and pointed at them. "Let's take this outside," he muttered, swiping up the coffee and pastries in one hand. He started walking away from the hospital. The last thing they needed was to bring Elandros of all people to that place of sanctuary and healing. "You have five minutes to convince me before I slay you where you stand."

"Lu...the Sorceress forced me to swear an oath of loyalty to her long ago," Elandros said, hands in his pockets as they walked abreast, forcing mortals to go around them to pass on their own errands.

"You mean all those times you've gleefully supported her have been lies?" Adrius wasn't impressed with the idea of rewriting facts.

"No. When it was just politics, I was behind her fully. Can you blame me?" He smirked. "You may be a king, but you're a terrible politician."

"Shockingly, this is not endearing yourself to me," Adrius deadpanned.

The other man shook his head. His slicked-back hair remained stiff with the motion. "I can't tell you much. But she's working with powers beyond the political now, and I've seen things I don't want to be a part of anymore."

"You fear the Fell Madness?"

Elandros's face darkened. "That, and so much more."

They passed by a club, its thumping beat immediately giving Adrius a worse headache than he'd started with. Thoughts swirled in his head. Possibilities now that he had one of Lucia's lackeys inches away. He could finally rid himself of this simpering pest.

Do it. If he betrays her, he'll betray you too.

"Breaking a blood oath means you die," he said, holding back those urges for the moment.

He held up a finger. "Ah, not if your Alchemyst brews me a potion for it."

Distrust painted every pore of Adrius's skin. So he, and by extension Lucia, already knew they had an Alchemyst. That wasn't such a surprise. But the leap of faith Elandros was asking him to make was still simply too much. His tale could've easily been concocted by Lucia to tug on Adrius's heartstrings just right.

A thought occurred to him. "I need a sign of your loyalty. Something that'll prove without a doubt that you wish to change sides. Luckily, I have something in mind."

Elandros circled his hand to beckon him to continue.

The arrogance. This fool doesn't deserve your mercy.

Adrius fought to speak through a sudden wave of fury. "Bring me Qin. We need to have words."

Despite himself, Elandros released a deep belly laugh. "Qin's gone! Took his bribe money and left the rest of us to fight."

He'd suspected Qin would do such a thing, and was glad to have confirmation. One of their own was already trying to find Qin, after all. Without skipping a beat, he went to the next, bigger target. One he doubted Elandros could take down on his own. "Fine. Taryn, then. We have an Alchemyst, just like you said. Maybe we can free his mind at last."

Elandros's laugh cut short as he paled. "You want me to bring Taryn to you?"

"Alive, unharmed, and preferably unconscious." Adrius punctuated it with a nod. "We'll have the potions waiting. One for him...and one for you." He watched the brief flare of hope cross the other man's face before it was schooled back into a polite mask.

"Where shall I bring him, then?"

"You manage it, you get in contact with me. We'll figure it out." He glanced around at their surroundings. They'd reached a quiet part of the city, shopfronts shuttered to hibernate through the night. Not a mortal in sight for the moment.

"Now, a parting gift," he said, punching Elandros square in the gut. He went sprawling to the sidewalk, gasping for air. "That is for working with *her* for so long. You deserve so much worse."

"I...suppose," he wheezed, picking himself off and dusting off his fine clothes.

Adrius extended out his hand, the vial of golden potion resting in his palm. *Two birds, one stone,* he thought. "And drink this so you know what you will have working with me instead."

Elandros's eyes widened. He wasted no time in snatching it and popping the cork, taking a deep breath of the fumes that rose from it. "You're sure?"

"Drink it before I change my mind. And give me back the vial."

Chapter 25
Julian

Julian sat back in his recliner. After several long nights of training, he was feeling sore but warm and secure in the knowledge that he finally had a hold over the cold magic that was part of him. What made him less confident was what Olivia had shared, seated in his lap as they tested the balance of his chair.

"Do you think you're hearing their thoughts?" he asked.

She rubbed her lips together. "They didn't *seem* like thoughts. It was like something else was whispering in their ear and I could hear it too."

"Can you hear my thoughts right now?" He concentrated his thoughts on how much he wanted her to kiss him. It'd been a long night. He'd summoned his first storm, feeling the power flux up his arms as wind, water, and electricity met in a perfect symphony overhead.

Olivia pressed her lips to his, so much better than the feeling of power. "So, you did read my thoughts," he said, pressing his forehead to hers.

"It wasn't hard to figure out what you wanted when you got all smoldery. Is smoldery a word?" she mused. "Oh well, it is now."

He laughed and let her lips distract him for a few more minutes before getting back on topic. "I see why you're worried. Especially if this outside force is encouraging Adrius to end his life. But the good news is your magic is showing at last." He tapped just under her eye.

"Hearing whispers isn't one of the five virtues, though," she said, though she brightened. "Did I tell you I made five purification potions today?"

"That's incredible news," he said. With how it seemed that Lucia's bite spread Fell Madness, they'd need as many potions as possible.

"And!" She gave the declaration a dramatic pause. "Adrius drank one. Hopefully, it helps him out."

"Hopefully, it does." His hands crept up her side as he spoke. "Tomorrow, you and I should have a chat with the fae. You talk about your whispers, and I'll share that I can track the Sorceress." Except there was something wrong with his vampire trait when he tried to focus on her. Instead of having his gut point in one specific direction when he focused his awareness on her, it was pulled in many, like tracking multiple people at once.

"When did you get a taste of her blood?"

"Not too long ago. Her blood was foul." His face crinkled in remembered disgust at having to choke down the rotting taste of it. "But it hasn't been helpful because I think her magic is interfering. I can't get a bead on her."

"Maybe the fae can fix that," she said, shrugging. "What do you want to do until we see them next?"

That was starting to become his favorite question. "I have a few ideas..." He grasped her hip with a meaningful squeeze.

WHEN THEY LEARNED THAT THE FAE ALL STAYED IN THE same room, Olivia nearly choked on her breakfast of cereal and milk. "They're literally *never* apart. Wow."

Julian sat across from her with a mug of coffee, watching Armando struggle with the coffee machine while Charlotte pushed him aside, fiddling with it to get their stream of slightly burnt caffeine flowing again. He smiled despite himself to see them. With his preoccupation with Olivia and his training, he'd barely seen his nephew, who patrolled with a different partner for the time being.

Julian had paired him with Charlotte, thinking they'd either get along well or kill each other with their clash of personalities. He was glad to see it was the former. Charlotte had been so eager to get out of the mansion and do something. Having her work with his more experienced partner seemed like the most logical choice.

"Yeah, dude. They got a room next to mine," Charlotte said, continuing what she was saying as she tinkered with the machine. "Dead silent inside, though. Helps me get my beauty rest."

"So important, *amica*. I sleep with neutral sounds. Best discovery of my life." Armando's good cheer faded as the smell of burning coffee wafted from the machine. "That's it! I'm buying the boss a new coffee maker!"

"Finally," Julian remarked, sipping from the last good cup it'd produced.

Olivia rolled her eyes as she finished her bowl, going into the kitchen to rinse it off. "Ready to go when you are," she said to him. She swallowed, rubbing her arm nervously.

He put an arm around her as they went upstairs. "They're not going to think you're crazy," he murmured.

"Yeah. They deal with crazy magic stuff all the time. Right?"

"Right," he agreed. He knew the trio had been given one of the corner suites, big enough to house them all comfortably.

Ash answered the door on the first knock. She was dressed in her usual leather but without the weapons. "You're early," she said shortly.

"We need to talk to you. Privately," Olivia blurted, taking a half step forward. The fae raised a brow but stepped aside and beckoned.

The room had a small balcony attached to the comfortably large living room. Sorsha and Keegan were standing together outside, the sliding glass doors askew. He turned before she even noticed they were there, nudging her to come inside. Her occultarus flapped behind them on its clockwork wings.

They waited until Sorsha spoke. "To what do we owe the

pleasure?" She wore a gray gown, the layers on it progressively darkening until it looked like billowing smoke around her.

"I think you need to sit down for this," Olivia said.

Without questioning it, Sorsha tossed decorative pillows off the couch and sat, letting the other two fae flank her. Julian took a regular chair, and after a moment's hesitation, Olivia sat next to him rather than in his lap like he figured she wanted to.

"I've heard your Alchemyst blood has come in at last. Congratulations," Sorsha said.

"Thank you. With it, something strange I think you'll want to hear about." She drew a deep breath, seeming to steel herself for the tale ahead. "I'm hearing...voices."

She shared with them what she had with Julian, about hearing whispers when close to the three Ancients yesterday. As well as the shadowy tendril she'd seen close to Gwendolyn. The fae exchanged glances as she spoke, some sort of urgent mental communication passing between them. "I'm not crazy, am I?" Olivia finished.

"Not at all." Sorsha gave her a brief nod. "We will look into it."

Olivia turned to Ash. "You cancel out magic, right? Can you go make whatever this is stop?"

Wetting her lips, Ash lifted her shoulder. "Spellbreakers have many capabilities," she said in a neutral tone.

"But—"

Sorsha held up her hand. "I'm sorry, Olivia. When it comes to this kind of thing, we can't give you any answers until we observe the magic in question. It could be magic from the Night school or an Unseelie curse or...something else. Let me talk to Adrius, who sounds like he has it the worst. Okay?"

She sat back with a huff. "That's reasonable. Just don't wait too long. It seems serious."

"I'll make it a priority," the Archfae promised. "If that's all?" Above her head, Keegan and Ash were having some sort of mental argument, their brows creased and gazes locked.

Julian shook his head. They were probably in a hurry to rush them out to discuss whatever was going unsaid in this room. "I have some magic to talk about as well. You're aware of my blood tracking ability?"

"How could I not when you're the infamous Bloodhound?" Sorsha's smile was strained.

"I haven't mentioned this before..." Suddenly, he was punched with a fistful of nerves. What if his erring tracking was more tampering from Lucia? A way for her to worm her way into his already existing magic and ruin it permanently? "I've gotten a taste of Lucia's blood. But I'm unable to track her. If I try, it feels like I'm trying to track dozens of people at once."

The back of his neck prickled. All three fae were staring at him. Sorsha in particular looked aghast. "You drank her blood?" she whispered.

"He did take a purification potion already," Keegan pointed out.

"You...you're right. I'm just thinking of Marcus." By her accounting of the man he'd used to be, Julian came to a realization then and there.

"He drank her blood. That's why he changed," he said.

"I think it accelerated his Fell Madness, yes," Sorsha said, shaking her head. "We'll just need to test your blood more often. Don't go changing your personality on us."

Their reaction sat with him as well as a lead weight in his stomach. "I'll try not to."

"As for your blood tracking...have you tried following that awareness to one of the people your magic seems to be trying to find?" she asked.

"I have not. Do you think I should?"

"Yes. But take a Blood Prince with you. Maybe Sirius." Sorsha glanced to Olivia. "How about you test him for whispers first. If not Sirius, Korin's around somewhere. He would work as well." Prince Korin, the Bane, was a man of deeds rather than words. He existed by Sirius's side as a close friend, but Julian hadn't seen him since the Ancients had settled in the mansion.

Breathing out a sigh, Sorsha added, "Now, if you'll excuse us, we have much to discuss."

Chapter 26
Julian

THEY FOUND SIRIUS IN THE BACKYARD OF THE ESTATE WITH Neala. Alex's mansion was set in a secluded area, which was fortunate with the noise of swords clashing coming from the two Ancients. At some point, someone had gifted them the weapons, which they used while practicing dueling skills with near-impossible agility. "Do you hear whispers?" Julian asked Olivia as they watched from the covered patio.

"Not from here. We'll have to get closer." Her golden eyes shone with admiration. "This is so cool. I never thought I'd see a *real* swordfight!"

He chuckled into her hair as he placed a kiss on her crown. "Real swordfights were at about half this speed. This is a marvel of how different being an Ancient makes you."

"Too darn cool. Do you think they could dodge bullets, too? Like those slow-motion action shots?"

He snorted with amusement. "Probably not. They may be superhuman, but there's still limitations to the *human* part of it. Which means I wish they were practicing at a range right now."

"Oh well," she said, sounding a little disappointed. She stepped into the manicured grass, cupping her hands to call, "Hey! We want to talk to you!"

The Blood Princes parted after one last scrape of parrying swords, their shoulders heaving. Neala drew a towel from her belt

159

to mop at her face as she turned toward them. Here with an old friend, her glamor was down. Her homely face with its unsightly mouth scar was on full display for a few moments before she remembered herself and put it back up, replacing uneven features with a beautiful mask.

He wished he could pick her brain. The woman who'd won his father's heart...before tragedy had befallen them both. If her mind hadn't been tampered with, what stories could she tell of the man he wished he knew? But it wasn't meant to be, not if reminding her of her lost mate would turn her into a bloodthirsty Fell Mad from the spike of extreme emotion.

"What can we do for you, Lady Alchemyst?" Sirius's voice brought Julian back from his thoughts. He was dueling without a shirt on, causing a blush to creep over Olivia's neck. Blood marked him in lines where he'd been struck and mended with vampire regeneration. Still, Julian stiffened to see the other man's lean, perfect physique on full display before her.

Olivia drifted closer while Julian caught his attention by speaking up. He watched her progress, wondering just how close she'd need to get. "Sorsha suggested you could help me with my tracking." He explained how his blood tracking ability got confused when trying to find Lucia as his lifemate inched closer before finally flashing Julian a thumbs up.

"I wanted to track one of the people I'm sensing, but I worry that...a certain someone may see the opportunity of me leaving on my own to trap me again." How it burned his pride to admit he couldn't go do such a simple task alone.

Sirius's eyes narrowed to animal slits. It was an expression he was familiar with. Alex did the same thing when his inner beast was close to the surface, urging him to act with instinct rather than reason. "You wish for me to hunt with you, with the possibility of finding the Sorceress at the end? This is one request I would gladly fulfill."

Both he and Neala went inside to shower. "No whispers from him," Olivia said, biting her lip. "But for Neala...they were talking about a husband. Mentioning details about him."

His heart dropped. "If she remembers what the Sorceress did

to her, she'd go on a rampage..." There was no question these whispers were malicious.

"Where do you think they're coming from?" she asked, drifting into his arms with a shiver of fear.

He held her and sighed, looking to the heavens. "It has to be her, waging a new war she knows we can't fight. Sitting back and waiting for our allies to go off like ticking time bombs." He just hoped the fae could thwart her.

"When you focus on her, just how many people do you sense?" Sirius asked. Julian drove them both deeper downtown, his focus miles away, toward the closest tether of awareness that said *Lucia*.

"My ability is a little less precise than that. It could be thirty... forty," he admitted. "All in different places. It's the exact right thing to ensure I have to guess which one is the real one and probably come up empty-handed."

"Hmm," was all he said, staring out the window. Julian had turned off the radio at his request, so they sat in silence as the city scrolled by.

It was Julian who spoke up some time later as he felt they were nearing their quarry. "Have you noticed anything strange with your brother recently?" If anyone needed to know that there might be something plaguing with Adrius, it was the man sitting next to him, who released a snort of derision.

But Sirius didn't think Julian was watching him, because the sharp sound was accompanied by a troubled frown. "Nothing that a purification potion hasn't fixed in the past."

"Has he seemed...depressed?" Julian hoped he wasn't overstepping any boundaries as he looked for the opening he needed.

"What does that mean?"

He figured a thousand years ago, few were thinking of the mental health of a soldier. "As in feeling sad or helpless, avoiding others and accomplishing little. Those are some signs."

Sirius tapped his fingers on the dash. "He's been depressed

since his wife died, then. A thousand years of regrets, even though we've slept through most of that time. Something seems different now, like there's nothing going on in his mind."

"Or perhaps too much?" Julian suggested. "Olivia is developing an ability. She's hearing negative whispers around some of your fellow Ancients, like some outside force messing with their heads."

He pulled into a parking lot as Sirius frowned over at him. "What has she heard from Adrius?"

Shutting off the engine, he turned to meet the Blood Prince's feral gaze. "That he needs to commit suicide." Pain and weariness etched across Sirius's face as the implications sank in.

"What about from me?" he demanded. "What do these whispers tell me to do?"

"You don't have them, apparently," he said.

"I have enough voices in my head with the inner beast," Sirius muttered. "What about...Gwendolyn?"

"How worthless and unworthy Olivia is as an Alchemyst." He felt his fists ball up that the whispers would target his lifemate.

Sirius blew air from his nostrils in a distinctly animal-like chuff. "Anyone else?"

"Just Neala..." Julian wanted to leave the vehicle before Sirius could explode with his rage. His fingers were morphing to wicked-sharp claws and back, as if imagining raking them over an imaginary enemy. But he spat out the rest anyway. "It's giving her details about her marriage to my father. Marcus."

To his surprise, Sirius relaxed with a deep breath, releasing the tension in his body and the partial shifts taking over in his anger. "We are being sabotaged. Thank you for telling me." He cleared his throat awkwardly. "Are you aware of Marcus and Neala?"

"They were married, raised Sorsha and Keegan as adopted children, and the Sorceress tampered with Marcus, turning him into the monster I knew. The man before her is a mystery to me." He sighed as he got out of the car, stretching his limbs and tracking sense alike. His quarry wasn't far, a few blocks at most.

Sirius checked his weapons, which were a set of blades along with his sword. He'd refused a gun, turning his nose up at the more modern device. "If you're curious, he was a good friend of mine," he offered in a low voice. "I went to sleep not long after his betrayal. My memories of him are like yesterday."

"Maybe we should grab a drink sometime. If things ever slow down." He knew he wanted to pick the other man's brain, but then he'd need to nurse his feelings deep in a glass of spirits.

"Indeed. Lead on...Bloodhound." Sirius quirked his lip in amusement at the title.

They took to the sidewalk. They were deep in a nest of office buildings, most with darkened windows except for the offices of the most dedicated of workers. He worried he would track someone straight into a locked door, but as they got closer, his gut tugged downward, the angle changing to imply they were about to walk *over* the person he was tracking.

He turned to Sirius and pointed downward. "We need to find a subway station." Luckily, he thought he knew of one not far from there. He followed his gut to the subway tunnels rather than the sewer, considering how trouble always followed Haven and its mastery of the abandoned nooks and crannies of the city's underground.

This particular line had cars running after midnight, so he and Sirius slipped in amongst a sparse night owl crowd. His ability told him they were close and on the same level as the person he was tracking. However, now they had an audience. He met the eye of one curious mortal, charming her with a hint of vampire influence.

Sirius caught on, and together, they made the few mortals aware to meet their gaze just sleepy enough that they might miss two tall, muscular men jump onto the subway tracks. Once his boots hit stone, Julian ran. Sirius kept pace with the loping stride of a hunting wolf, his lips pulled back with anticipation. They both knew that whatever they found would likely end in a fight.

He stopped before a door marked "For Authorized Personnel Only" with a keypad on the knob. Sirius kicked it with all an Ancient's brutal strength, denting the metal before Julian could warn him of the alarms they might set off that would alert either mortal authorities or Haven to their trespassing. Uttering a growl, he kicked again, snapping the lock and sending the door into stone with a hollow *boom*.

Pitch blackness lay within. Julian's eyes adjusted as he saw someone jumping toward him face-first from the dark. He ducked, whirling as it landed on the tracks and hissed through a maw of fangs. "Fell Mad!" he called, drawing his daggers.

"Take care of it! I've got my own," Sirius grunted.

He trusted that the Ancient could handle himself, holding up a blade to impale the creature that leapt at him. It was slower than the one that'd sent him to the hospital, unable to best him or deliver a devastating bite before Julian ended its life. He left his blade, leery of the black blood coating it. Drawing another, he turned to see Sirius's training doing him well. He killed Fell Mad with militaristic efficiency, bodies piling up as they threw themselves at him.

Then...quiet.

Sirius stepped over the grim pile, his nostrils flared. He stabbed his sword straight up, catching another of the afflicted individuals before it could ambush him from the ceiling. "Older, stronger beasts have tried that one before," he muttered, sidestepping the corpse. He turned back to Julian. "This room is clear, but there's a tunnel beyond. What do you sense?"

He checked his ability for Lucia, who felt far away now. Where one tendril of awareness was gone, three more took its place. "We've killed whatever I was sensing."

"She was a part of these people...wasn't she?" Sirius growled.

Julian knelt, turning over the one he'd stabbed from the ceiling, looking for any clue as to who these people were. A parasol insignia was embossed on this former man's jacket, the symbol of Coven Rockefeller. "She's turning her allies into monsters."

Chapter 27
Olivia

Alex's boardroom was beginning to grow crowded. Between the Ancients, the fae, and numerous vampires, there was barely enough room for everyone to have a seat at the table. The personalities felt like they were suffocating her.

She'd figured out her virtue all on her own. It was like the whispers had flicked the switch inside of her and everyone's emotions came rushing into her head at once. She felt the tension from the room, enough to give her a splitting headache. Beside her, Julian warred with fatigue and a desire to be anywhere but there, his hand entwined with hers under the table.

He and Sirius told the whole story of what they'd found. A cell of Fell Mad seemingly sitting around waiting to ambush them the moment they'd opened that door.

"Lucia predicted you'd find them and placed them there to kill you," Gwendolyn said immediately.

"Why wouldn't she send triple the amount if she'd also seen that Sirius would be there to effortlessly nullify the ambush?" Julian replied.

The tension ratcheted up a notch, but no one spoke their mind. The Ancients in particular seemed to wait for someone else amongst their ranks to provide some explanation. It took Sirius to do so, punching the table with a snarl. "This always happens!

Every time! We sit around building up our defenses just for Lucia to worm her way around them. She's about to hit us in the one way we can't counter." He leaned over until he had eye contact with Adrius. "I remember when you went Fell Mad."

Adrius had his usual accompaniment of darkness, his face blank of worry or thought. He blinked slowly, feeling like he woke from a deep sleep. As Olivia looked him over, she felt a great... nothingness, and that was enough to chill her. Everyone around her was full of emotion, most of it combining into a negative spiral in her head. But with them, she could tell they were aware of the significance of their conversation.

"He went out of control," Sirius continued to the group as his brother stared at him. "Feasting on blood without restraint. If a group of Fell Mad happened upon modern mortals...your technology would not let us scrub the memory away from everyone. Lucia has a knife to our throat and has been waiting for us to notice. No wonder she wanted you dead." He said this directly to Julian.

"Because I can track them. But she didn't want me *dead*. She wanted me Fell Mad too. I think she had some control of them," Julian said.

"Some? Try complete control," Gwendolyn spoke up, tapping her cane on the ground thoughtfully. "Most in this room has not seen a true Fell Mad. They are...animals. Lucia has no use for anything she cannot manipulate to her favor. We have proof from her attack on Julian that these new Fell Mad are produced from bites."

"From venom in her bite," Julian corrected.

She nodded. "With her as the source, yes. Most Fell Mad in our time succumbed to a spike of great negative emotion or drank too deeply from the veins of a true Fell and gained their unholy hunger as well as their preternatural gifts. I fear that she's introducing a different, more contagious strain that's linked to her." Gwendolyn's gaze was far away as she steepled her fingers.

"That seems like a bit of a jump," Olivia ventured, sitting up when the room's attention turned to her. "How do you *know* they're being controlled by someone?"

"Easy," Gwendolyn said, her thin lips pressed into a line. "You are invested into the theater arts, yes? Put yourself in the shoes of someone like Lucia."

Though she rather wouldn't, she did. *I'm a megalomaniac Sorceress with a bad case of shark mouth and future sight...*

"You have two covens who've sworn to you, full of individuals you have no time to bribe or coerce to your side, with a mission that secretly goes against the morals of many of them. Do you trust the two leaders you have under your thumb to whip them into a proper army for you?" she said. A few in the room murmured, apparently seeing where this was going ahead of Olivia.

"Well, yeah. Isn't that how armies work? You trust the chain of command?" Olivia asked.

Gwendolyn held up a finger. "But introduce another option. You could wipe away all of the pesky morals of those who don't agree with you so they don't run to your enemies and spill what they know. They become monsters just like you, but as long as you keep them on a short leash and out of trouble, they're your enemy's problem, not yours."

Olivia's face fell. "Oh. So, logically, as a megalomaniac Sorceress with a bad case of shark mouth and future sight, I'd go for the turn my people into monsters option. We're on the same page now." There was a brief uplift in the room, amusement and a couple chuckles coming from her blunt description.

Now would be a great time to mention Elandros and the possibility he was about to come to their side once he could, possibly because of so-called "pesky morals." But she held her tongue as she watched a curl of shadow circle Gwendolyn's ear like the caress of a lover. With those whispers in her ear, and others' at this table, how well was she expecting that to be taken?

Alex spoke up as she thought on it. "Now that we've cleared up that that's the most likely explanation, we haven't answered one very important question. What the bloody hell are we going to do about it?" His gaze swept the table. "What's Lucia's next move now that we know what hand she holds?"

His phone buzzed on the table. Taking a glance at it, he tilted his head. "My head of security says we're about to have a visitor." He said it so mildly, it couldn't be much cause for concern. Yet when a man built a few inches taller and wider than Adrius muscled his way into the room, breathing hard like a work horse, she nearly startled right out of her chair.

The newcomer saw Adrius at the head of the table and marched up to him, slapping something down on the table. She leaned in, watching him pick up a ring set with a stone as dark as obsidian. "You found him," Adrius said.

Sirius glanced over and grinned wide enough to show fangs. "Olivia, meet my good friend Prince Korin, the Bane. The *original* Bloodhound." He jerked his chin to Julian. "Your father's blood sire."

"Who did he find?" Julian asked, shifting forward in his seat like he was presented with competition.

"Qin," Korin answered. His voice was low and slow, like a rumble of thunder. He bowed in Olivia's direction. "Lady Alchemyst. A pleasure."

"Likewise," she said. He turned back to Adrius, who'd set the ring aside. She whispered behind her hand to Julian. "Who's Qin?"

"Another Blood Prince. He was an informant for Lucia, took payment from her, and ran, far as we know," he said, seeming impressed by the big man. "If Korin's my father's blood sire, he must be the most accomplished blood tracker in the world."

"Well, what happened?" Sirius demanded, nearly vibrating with impatience. "Why isn't he here with you? What did he say?"

Korin remained standing, cracking his neck as he looked over his audience. "He spoke of a blood oath he was forced to swear to keep Lucia's business close to his chest. But he told me where he was heading and everything he could share after a little...encouragement." Out of nowhere, he was flipping a white coin. Sirius gave a vicious smile at seeing it.

"He said Lucia is not working alone but instead has found an ally with a heart as wicked as hers. She's temporarily pursuing an agenda with this ally's goals in mind, as she has yet to prove her worth to him." He scratched the back of his head with a shrug.

The idea that a Sorceress as powerful as her hadn't been able to impress someone was baffling to Olivia. "Her new allies are already miserable. She promises much and delivers little. Qin decided to get out before he could be sucked into the same kind of orbit. Since he showed his true colors to us, he was of little use to her anyway."

Sirius sighed. "We could still use him as a fighter."

"We don't need a snake, no matter the circumstances," Korin replied. "I made him surrender his biggest treasure and a blood oath to us in exchange for his peace." He turned to Adrius, his brow crinkling as he saw the Vampire King staring off into nothingness, the ring now resting on the table. Sweeping it away, he showed it to Sirius, who passed it to Gwendolyn, on down the table until Sorsha was admiring it.

"Fantastic job," she breathed. "The Night Key, keeper of shadows and herald of darkness. It needs a wielder."

Olivia saw a chance there in the gleaming facets of the obsidian ring. If it could control shadows, maybe it could chase away the whispers that plagued a few of the Ancients. She focused her mind, going through all the steps to speak to someone mentally. She'd only felt comfortable doing it to Julian, invading his thoughts with idle questions and fun distractions when they were in a more relaxed setting.

But now, she felt strongly enough that she spoke to Sorsha before she could hand it to anyone else. *"I have an idea for the ring."*

The Archfae's gaze snapped toward her, halfway to handing it back to Korin. *"Tell me."*

"I want to borrow it. Just for a couple days. Maybe use it when I next hear those whispers." She held her breath as Sorsha's eyes flickered with thought.

The ring rolled back into her palm as she curled her fingers around it. "If you don't mind, I'd like to experiment with it," she said to Korin.

"Go right ahead. I understand you're our magic expert now," he said. Olivia wondered if he ever raised his voice, as mild as he seemed.

"Come to the field with Julian tomorrow. I'll train you on the basics of using a Key, and you can see if it'll work," Sorsha told her privately.

"Thank you. Thank you so much." Olivia really hoped she could pull it off. If she could lift the curtain of malicious shadows around Adrius, she'd consider it a big success. At the same time, she wondered why Sorsha would let her experiment with a Key when she herself had power over every kind of magic. Maybe she already knew it wouldn't work, but it was still worth a try.

"Let us return to the question at hand, shall we?" Alex asked as Sirius promised to fill Korin in mentally. "If you haven't forgotten, Lucia has us over a barrel with her army of monsters. She knows that we know what she has cooking. What do we do?"

"Unlike us, Lucia does not care about concealing vampire kind from mortals. At any moment, she could let her Fell Mad off their leashes to feast on the city," Gwendolyn said grimly.

"Obviously, killing them should be our first priority," Neala agreed. *"But we will have to do it on Lucia's terms, in these tunnels her allies hide in. We lose our numbers advantage. Also, many of our fighters are not actually warriors. I'd expect them to turn and run at the first sight of a Fell Mad."*

"Wait." Olivia spoke up tentatively, seeing where this was going. "I could cure them."

Gwendolyn shook her head, not even skipping a beat. "When you only make five potions a night, your efforts would be a spit in the desert. We have to keep your potions for our wounded."

"So, what are you going to do? Kill all those vampires? It's not their fault Lucia bit them," she said, seeing the truth on everyone else's face. Even Sorsha was shaking her head.

"We have to act quickly and decisively," Gwendolyn replied. "Put out the infection before it can spread any farther."

"Have you had the misfortune to partake in Lucia's blood?" Julian asked Korin, who shook his head. "So...only I can help find those infected."

"We will need you to sit down with a map and pinpoint as many locations as you can," Sirius nodded. "We will mobilize our army and move as soon as possible."

"I'll do that now," Julian promised, giving Olivia's hand a squeeze under the table. "Sorry. If there was any other way..." he murmured for her ears alone. She felt his sincerity. The fight bled out of her until she felt hollow, because it seemed like she could've saved these people were she a better, stronger Alchemyst.

The group planned, but most of it was noise to her except for numbers. She needed to somehow make not five, but hundreds of potions a night to have a chance of saving anyone before the combined coven army would remove the infected permanently.

The meeting ended, Alex lingering with an air of weariness at the necessity of calling in the other coven masters and explaining what they'd discovered. Gwendolyn caught Olivia's arm as the group disbanded, and Julian went with Sirius to map out where he sensed the infected to be.

"I'm sorry for how that went," Gwendolyn said. "You remind me so much of my daughter. She was a pacifist, too. Always trying to make peace with our enemies."

"This girl is just a weak copy," a whisper hissed.

"Unfortunately, the time for such things has passed."

Olivia took her frail hand in both of hers. "I mean this from the bottom of my heart. I am not Nyah, and I never will be. If you keep finding ways to compare me to her memory, I will always come up short. Please. Stop."

Gwendolyn's lips trembled. Whispers seemed to swirl around her. *"Disrespectful. Being compared to Nyah is an honor."*

She hastily added, "I don't mean you any disrespect. I just want to be measured up to my own self."

The Ancient bobbed her head, swallowing hard. "Of course. Forgive me. I just look into your eyes and they're just like hers. The most unique in this world and the next."

In that moment, her empathy told her the right thing to say, tugging her awareness toward the loneliness and heartbreak hiding within this woman's unbreakable façade. "You must miss her greatly."

"Every day," Gwendolyn murmured, parting from her. "I would do anything to bring her murderer to justice."

Olivia was left standing alone in the hall. Bringing a hand to her chest, she nursed the echo of heartache that lingered in Gwendolyn's wake. Maybe this was progress. She felt like she understood her hyper-critical mentor better.

She took that knowledge back to Julian's room, which he'd left unlocked for her. She practically lived with him at this point. Though they usually saw each other only at the end of a long night's work, it was those few hours together and the days in each other's arms that made this room special to her.

She wondered how long Julian would be planning tonight. It was possible to ask him with mental communication, but she forewent that for a little fun. She dimmed the lights and programmed some soothing instrumental music into the clock radio. Ruffling his perfectly made bed, she peeled the comforter back before tapping a finger to her jaw.

Going back to her own room, she picked a discrete garment bag she'd put aside with a blush earlier. Now, she took in the lacy underthings with a smile. "Perfect."

She brought them back to his room in the bag, only changing once she'd drawn a bath and located a dusty bottle of lotion under his sink. It'd have to do.

You are a European masseuse at a high-class massage parlor, she told herself, teasing out her curls in the mirror and trying on a few sultry looks and eyebrow waggles.

She heard the door open in the other room, her heart leaping. She'd just started getting into character! But Julian was already there; she heard him sigh and call her name.

Olivia came sauntering out, saying in her best European accent, "Hello, weary traveler. Welcome to my parlor. I am, uh..." she searched for the first name she could think of. "...I am Olga! Here to serve your every need."

He looked her over, seeming bemused. Under that, she sensed his confusion and fatigue washing away on a wave of amusement and affection. Her heart beat harder to feel just how much fondness he had for her. "Are we roleplaying now?"

"You are wearing too many clothes, sir. How am I supposed to massage those guns if you cover them up?" she asked, fighting her laughter until she felt red in the face. She let out a titter, and he laughed with her. Then she was in his arms, their lips meeting, and her little game didn't matter so much as the pleasure they shared and the warmth in her heart as she later drifted to sleep, feeling safe in his arms.

Chapter 28
Olivia

The Night Key was cold, even hours after placing it on her finger. Olivia's thumb brushed the smooth underside idly as she waited for her turn with Sorsha. When the Archfae had given her the ring to wear, she'd expected a massive surge of power and awareness once she slipped it on, but instead, it was inert, like a solid, heavy piece of jewelry. No wonder she'd need training on how to use it.

Today was Violet's day to train her magic, which meant she had little reason to be here. Gwendolyn was certainly displeased at her choice, but Olivia wasn't about to tell her about the whispers until there was some sort of solution. She hoped the Night Key could answer their problem.

Julian was off coordinating his men for war. She imagined he wouldn't get any more time to train his own magic while his tracking skills were in such high demand.

That left her mostly alone, sitting on a towel in the grass and watching the lightshow of Violet and Sorsha dueling with fire. They were training shields, as far as she could tell. The Archfae was capable of summoning a curved wall of light in front of her, which stopped spells with a harmless sizzle. Violet was attempting to replicate the same.

Alex was there, meeting with Neala in a quiet conference. Her presence seemed almost obligatory, there as a bored bodyguard with so many of their important people amassed in one place. But Olivia was secretly glad it was her rather than a different Ancient—she had a feeling Neala was the ideal candidate to try the Night Key's powers on first.

She sighed, turning her attention back to the tome of fae potions. There were thousands of pages straining the leather binding, full of cramped, hand-written instructions she was surprised to see in English. She'd finally gotten to borrow it and now flipped through page after page in search of something that could break a vampire's blood oath. This was another thing she wished she could tell Gwendolyn, especially since Adrius hadn't mentioned a word of meeting with Elandros...or not. She had a feeling the elderly vampiress could find what she was looking for without breaking a sweat.

"So, you have an ancient book of knowledge too." Squinting closely at a page of writing, she hadn't noticed Alex approaching until he was already sitting on the towel with her in one graceful motion. On the surface, he looked fine, but she felt his fatigue pulling at her the moment they made eye contact.

"Yeah. Long night?" she asked.

"Yesterday was. I am hopeful today will be better," he said, lifting the cover of her book to take a glance. "Potions. That must be dry as dirt."

"Try as dry as the mirage of a desert oasis that turns out to be another stupid cactus and you just want something to drink."

"Oh my. Now I need to find a bottle of water," he said with a chuckle. "Why don't you put that down and talk to me? A little birdy mentioned I should be asking you about whispers."

"Julian?" she asked, earning a nod. She placed the book aside and told him everything—the whispers and who their victims were, what they were saying.

When she showed him the Night Key's obsidian stone glittering on her finger, he was shaking his head, his eyes narrowed down to catlike slits. "You don't like this," she said.

"Of course I don't like it. I think I know why the fae dismissed you so quickly...and something about what you're trying to face." He rested his weight back on his hands in the grass. Her empathy picked up troubled emotions and a hint of anger starting to bubble to the surface. "Did Violet ever tell you that the Eye of Worlds talked to her?"

"It *talked?*" she echoed.

"The other Sorceress had it opening a portal to the Fell Lands, but Violet took control of it at the last moment. She told it to stop, and the bloody thing said, 'Are you sure?'" He gritted his teeth. "It showed her a vision of Nyah, alive, in the Fell Lands and suggested she could still be saved. When Violet insisted, instead of just...slowing down, it destroyed itself and thanked Violet for setting it free."

Olivia's eyes bugged wide with this information. "You've never seen the thing intact, but it was full of darkness," he continued. "Violet described its voice as a chorus of *whispers*. It fits too perfectly, wouldn't you agree?"

"A shadowy something that whispers to people? Yeah." She felt the blood draining from her face.

"I sure hope your fancy ring has the power to scare it away, but I would put my cards toward a no," he said grimly. "There's something the fae aren't telling us. Maybe what you're sensing is something they have no answer for."

Her heart dropped somewhere in the vicinity of her knees at the idea. The fae seemed so invincible as a unit, but their leader also couldn't lie except by omission. "I think you might be right," she said, grasping her head in both hands. "What are we going to do?"

"I'd like to suggest a purely speculative course of action." She glanced toward him, hopeful he had some cure-all answer for their woes. "What if Nyah really is still alive?"

"Well, I'd probably pester her to death with Alchemyst questions," she said.

"What if you could do exactly that?" He chuckled, his gaze on his mate as she put up a shield long enough to stop a fireball. He gave a polite golf clap since there was no way she could hear him from that far away. Yet Violet's blonde head turned, and she flashed a thumbs up.

"It would be amazing if she was around. Can you imagine?"

Olivia said, her mind's eye supplying the scene and her best approximation of what the legendary first Alchemyst looked like. "Adrius would have her back, so he'd be happy again. She could help me make potions. Maybe we could even turn the tide on the Fell Mad with two Alchemysts."

"You're closer to the magic fairies than I am, so I think you should suggest my idea," he said, turning to her with a serious expression erasing the pride at his mate's success. "The Dark Eye kept everything bad from our world, according to them and Gwendolyn—Unseelie, Fell, demons. What if, with its destruction, they could use some fancy magic to try to make contact with Nyah in the Fell Lands? I've seen their spell books. I know they're capable of some incredible magic."

"If that were possible, why hasn't it been done before?" Much as she wanted it to happen, she had her doubts that the true Queen of Vampires had survived in such a hostile location for a thousand years.

"According to Sorsha, the Fell Lands are a one-way street in Faerie as a necessary quarantine. Since the portals from Earth closed, the people there have been completely abandoned both physically and magically. From how she describes it, Sorsha and the other fae believe there's nothing left down there except Fell and sand."

"But you don't think that's the case?" she asked.

"I'm a simple vampire. I didn't believe any of this until I saw it with my own eyes," he answered, palms up in submission. "All I'm saying is that it's worth a try."

"It would be nice. What's the harm in trying?" she agreed. "Can I ask you a question? Something completely unrelated?"

He offered a tired smile. "You can always ask. No guarantees I'll have all the answers."

"Why does Haven hate the coven so much that it allied with the likes of...you know who?" she asked.

"Well, love, that's a personal grudge. Haven's leader, Bryant Collins, has hunted my bloodline for centuries. He succeeded for a time in getting it reduced down to one person...me. But I've been too wily for him, thriving in places I shouldn't like a weed.

He's made his own pseudo-religious cult by feeding mortals lies so they'll join him to hunt vampires when they're really only trying to kill me or other coven members." She wondered how it was even possible to have stacked up such a house of cards when the vampires Collins turned would eventually learn the truth. Maybe that's where the *cult* part came in.

"But why your bloodline specifically?" she pressed. That was the part she didn't understand. The level of obsession it took to take this grudge to present day astounded her.

"He wants to be the only daywalker, the only vampire who can walk in the sunlight and not get burned," he said, shaking his head. "That's what I don't understand about him. Why does he have daywalker traits when the rest of his abilities seem like they're from the Legion bloodline rather than the Dawn one like myself? He's old enough to have been turned by Elandros himself or someone directly descended from him as blood sire."

"I don't know. But if he does it for a grudge, then it sounds like an extreme grudge."

"One that will topple his organization. That is...if we are the eventual victors in this war. That's another reason we *have* to win." He drifted off, watching Sorsha and Violet approach them. He got to his feet and offered her a hand up, going to meet them halfway.

Alex went straight to Violet, sharing a brief kiss and a murmur of praise. "Are you ready to train?" Sorsha asked Olivia, motioning to her hand. "I hope this will be quick. I'm eager to see if you have any results."

Olivia waved goodbye to the other two as the Archfae drew her a safe distance away to practice. Using a Fell Key, it turned out, was a more user-friendly experience than drawing the Alchemyst magic from her blood. She first needed to learn how to identify shadows she could control. The Night Key was all about manipulating those shadows, which was an open-ended prospect, but she quickly picked up on how to scatter and make darkness dissipate like mist.

"Do you think I should try this back at the mansion? There's a lot more light there," she suggested once she'd gotten a good grasp on that aspect of the Key's power.

"That's a good idea. We should retire for the night soon anyway." Sorsha nodded, glancing up at the sky. It seemed early to do so...but there was concern and an eagerness to get back to something else brewing under the surface, according to Olivia's empathy.

"Hey...I had an idea." Olivia didn't mind taking credit for it, at least. "Have you ever tried talking to any of the folks stuck in the Fell Lands?"

Sorsha turned away, beckoning to Keegan and Ash, who were sharing some sort of fruit as big as a melon but bright green and as juicy as a peach. Ash was still taking bites as they wandered over. "The Fell Lands aren't something to mess with, Olivia," Sorsha replied quietly.

"But have you tried?" She didn't hear a straight answer in there, just a fae that could only tell the truth hedging. Her empathy stabbed her in the chest with pain and loss as she looked into Sorsha's perfectly schooled poker face. "Look...I was thinking it could be time to try again. See if Nyah is there."

"It is incredibly unlikely Nyah is still there. Or anyone else we've lost to that hell."

As the other two fae flanked her, Olivia felt her hold on Sorsha's emotions fading. The three of them were unreadable and foreign to the magic seeking to understand their true feelings. "Do...you want to talk about it?" Olivia had to rely on her own self, recognizing the pain of loss in the Archfae's stiff motions, if nothing else.

"Don't worry about me. While you wish for a second Alche-myst, I remember my mentor who willingly returned there to assist any survivors. She's been through so much." Sorsha glanced up to Keegan, whose expression turned grim.

"Izell. I still can't believe she left Faerie the way she did." He sighed, scratching the back of his head. "If anyone would wipe out the Fell hordes and laugh about it, it'd be her."

"Well, if she did, then maybe you could contact her?" Olivia knew she was grasping at straws now. They seemed convinced that they were remembering the dearly departed.

"With the Dark Eye out...I think it would be possible," he said, glancing to Sorsha. "Right? The veil is already weakening."

"It's false hope. You know it," Sorsha murmured.

Over the Archfae's shoulder, Ash flashed Olivia a wink. "I think she's still alive," Keegan said. "You were right about Mother. We have her back. Now let me prove myself right about Izell."

"All right. Fine." Sorsha put her hands up. "I'll get the mirror set up, and we'll try tonight."

"Good. Great."

"Great," she echoed, making a portal and gesturing. "I'm sending her in after you, Olivia. We'll give you a few minutes to try removing her whispers."

Olivia stepped through with a nod, steeling herself. Both ideas—scrying to the Fell Lands and using the Night Key to combat the whispers—could end in success or flaming failure. She held her breath as she watched the portal rippling.

When Neala stepped through, Olivia heard the telltale whispering like a second voice in her head. "Hey, Neala. Can I ask you a question?" she said, beckoning the other woman over.

"What is it, girl?" She sounded impatient after half a night of idle nothingness.

Olivia waited until she physically saw the darkness moving to whisper in her ear again. "Can you feel this?" she asked, lifting her hand. The Night Key glimmered on her finger as she used its magic to disperse the shadow into nothingness.

The moment before it was gone, she felt a presence turn and notice her. Her empathy was seized by a hatred so fierce and fiery that she knew it belonged to something that desired to see her dead in the most painful, slow way possible. She flinched away, but it only lasted a split second. Neala rolled her shoulders, cracking her back with a sigh of relief.

"I'm not sure what you did, but I do feel better. Some Alchemyst magic?" she guessed with a half-smile.

"You could say that." Olivia's heart fluttered in her ribcage. It felt like she'd just had a brush with something far more evil than she realized.

Chapter 29
Adrius

WORTHLESS.

Selfish.

Nobody wants you around.

Why would they?

You ruin everything.

There was a knock on the door. He turned slowly toward it, wondering what someone would want with the likes of him. The shadows lengthened, throwing the world into grayscale as he opened it and peered down at the person who'd bothered to check on him.

His gaze met the only pop of color in his world, a set of golden eyes in a face that wasn't hers.

You failed her.

You lost her.

"Hello, Adrius," said the second Alchemyst, Olivia. She sounded pitying, as if she knew his inner turmoil. "Can I come in?"

He shook his head stiffly. "What do you want?" It came out as a whisper, matching the thoughts in his head.

She raised her hand, fingers splayed lightly. His thoughts seemed to recoil, leaving him with silence for the first time since he could remember. Blinking slowly to shake off the stupor, he realized she was wearing the Night Key. "So, Sorsha gave it to you."

"I'm just borrowing it," she said, seeing where his gaze rested.

A few moments later, a whisper returned. *She stole it. Why would she have it?*

Olivia's brow furrowed as she flicked her fingers. "Why isn't it working? Are you...hearing things?"

"Things," he echoed.

"Whispers?"

"That's my guilty conscious, dear," he said, taking a step back and reaching for the door. "If that will be all?"

"No, wait," she blurted, moving forward too. Her hand started to waver, but she still held it out like asking for him to take the ring from her finger.

Do it. Make her leave us alone.

Take it. Crush it. Make its power yours.

He swallowed thickly, tempted, though he knew a person's body could only contain so much magic, and he already had power over manipulating shadows.

"I'd like you to come with me and see the fae. They're going to try something that I think you'd be interested in," she said. He struggled to look at her instead of the ring.

Not like you're interested in anything.

Worthless. The whispers laughed.

Olivia grimaced. "Please, Adrius. Come with me." She turned her hand over, offering her palm. "I think you should see it."

"Leave me be, Alchemyst. It's bad enough you have her eyes," he muttered.

"I'm not Nyah."

And that's entirely the problem.

"And that's entirely the problem," he echoed his thoughts. Her beautiful eyes narrowed.

"What if I told you the fae are trying to scry into the Fell Lands?" she asked.

He imagined what he'd seen before—dunes of sand as far as the eye could see. Refugee camps of noncombatant Fell starving while cut off from their food source. "What do they expect to find? Sand? Bones?" he scoffed.

"No. They mean to find Nyah." Her words flipped a switch within him. His hands balled into fists, ready to fight those very words.

Leaning into her face with fangs bared, he snarled, "Nyah's *dead,* you charlatan. How dare you make a mockery of her memory."

"But—"

He knocked her hand away, feeling his thoughts return, flooding in, telling him exactly what to say. "But nothing. Get out of my sight."

"There's always a possibility—" She nursed her hand close to her chest, eyes rounding like saucers. "Your face. Adrius, you have to calm down."

Calm down? His thoughts were nearly gleeful, in counterbalance to the rage flowing through his veins.

"Calm down?" he echoed. "Calm down? You come to my door saying you want to talk to my *dead wife,* and now you fail to see what a mockery that is!"

How dare she?

Make an example of her!

She backed away, breathing shallowly, and he followed her into the hall. His rage was a living, burning thing. "H-help. Help!" Olivia turned from him with a terror-laced scream, taking a running start.

Pain pricked his palms. He looked down at claws piercing his skin, growing longer as he trembled with his fury.

You should run, little girl.

See how far you get before I tear you apart!

She was taking the stairs downward at a rapid clip, shrieking her head off. He cleared the whole flight in a leap. Landing in front of her, he turned and hissed. She backed to the wall.

This is what you get for messing with things beyond your control!

She let off a terrified breath. "Adrius, this isn't you! Stop listening to it."

The sharp edge of a blade pressed to his neck. "Not a step closer," rumbled Korin. He turned to see a few of the mansion's residents were out, staring at him with openmouthed shock. And behind him, Korin stood somberly, ready to end his life.

He will kill you. He's done it before.

Adrius had lost control before, and the one to put his sword through him to stop him was always Korin. Sirius could never bring himself to kill his brother, even if he knew the Shield Key would always bring him back. One of his closest friends had returned to the mansion just in time to continue carrying out the distasteful duty.

Not this time.

Run. He cannot catch you.

Embrace your gift.

Adrius smiled with all his sharpened teeth and dispersed into a cloud of shadow, slamming his way out of the mansion and into freedom on the city streets.

Chapter 30
Olivia

Olivia's knees collapsed from under her. Korin sheathed his blade and went to her first, tilting her chin up. "Are you all right?" he demanded.

"Yes. I'm sorry. I didn't realize." She was still breathing so hard it was difficult to get out a complete sentence. She didn't think the whispers had wormed so far into his brain that he would start repeating what they said and erupt in a rage so black it stained his features and veins with Fell Madness.

Her heart felt fit to burst from her chest with how close she'd brushed death. "It's not your fault," Korin said, standing and panning until he pointed at Violet. "I need Sirius. Now."

She nodded and turned to Alex before summoning a portal. He headed through and came back with Sirius and Julian. The former went to Korin, and it took them about two moments of conferring before they were running out the door in hot pursuit of Adrius.

Julian took one look at Olivia and went to scoop her up in his arms, bridal style. "What happened?" he asked, starting to carry her back up the stairs.

"Adrius. The whispers. Fell Mad," she said, taking a deep breath to steady herself. "It was like they took him over."

His jaw tightened as he nodded and pinned his gaze on the fae trio at the top of the stairs. "And who helped you?" he asked.

"Korin put his sword to Adrius's throat," she said.

He stopped a few feet from Sorsha, placing Olivia on her feet with an arm around her hip to steady her. His gaze was a frosty blue, glowing with his magic as it rested on the open doorway Adrius had vacated. "And where were you three during all of this?" His breath misted in the air as his aura sucked the warmth from the area.

"I was prepping a spell. We heard a scuffle, and it was over that quickly," Sorsha said.

Olivia could feel a chilly tide of anger building in Julian, something bottled up and shaken, just ready to burst free. "Julian, it's okay," she said, tugging the back of his shirt in warning. The very last thing they needed was him picking a fight when she was sure the three of them could turn him to a pile of ashes in a blink.

"No, it's really not." He was smart enough not to go an inch closer as Keegan gripped the hilt of his sword, reading the aggressive line of Julian's body. "This woman here is the most important person in my whole life. She nearly died a few yards from your room." He pointed out their corner suite with an accusatory jab.

"I apologize. I didn't expect—" The words caught in Sorsha's throat and she coughed like she'd swallowed them back.

"Now you're trying to lie to me?" Frost crept up from his fingers with a crackle. "You *did* expect Adrius would lose control of himself. But you let Olivia walk right into danger's grasp without being there to help her. What use are you?"

"Julian," Olivia said more insistently, feeling a nervous sweat down her back. Ash shifted her balance, her eyes narrowing at his tone.

"What use are any of you? Refusing to separate, barely doing anything to help us with the Fell Mad." It was like the floodgates were open. No word of caution would stop him, nor the baleful looks from two experienced fae fighters.

Sorsha held up a hand, possibly for everyone's benefit. "I'm sorry."

"Sorry doesn't—"

"You're right," she continued over him. "We haven't been as

present as we could be. I have no excuses to offer you, just a promise to do better."

Julian's mouth snapped shut with the click of colliding teeth.

"With anything that involves the Fell Mad, we have to exercise the utmost caution, to the point of hiding. If we sustain a bite, we would turn into a full Fell. And a Fell with the power that even one of us possesses..." She rubs her arms, chilled. "The carnage would be instant and irreparable."

"So, it's not that you won't help us. It's that you can't?" Olivia supplied. She could sympathize with that, even though it still troubled her that they hadn't warned her that Adrius could snap right in front of her.

Sorsha nodded. "That is accurate. I apologize to you as well. Did you mention Nyah? I should've warned that a spike of intense emotion was just the trigger the whispers could use."

"That was what set him off," she confirmed, bowing her head. "I mean, he was right. Unless you can reach her, suggesting we were going to was like a spit in the face..." She glanced up at Julian, whose brows were drawn together. "We're going to try scrying into the Fell Lands."

"It's ready, if you would like to join us," Sorsha offered, her voice hushed. Though she couldn't pick up her emotions with the other fae present, Olivia knew this was a tender moment for her and Keegan for a different person they might see.

"Give me five minutes," she said.

Nodding, Sorsha headed there first. The other two fae finally relaxed as the tension left with her. They spared Julian a warning glance apiece as they followed.

"I don't know what's scarier, Adrius turning Fell Mad or watching you challenge all three fae at the same time." She sighed once their door was closed. He tilted her chin up, capturing her lips in a fierce kiss of teeth and tongue, his hand fisted in her thick curls.

"I'd face so much worse to keep you safe," he said against her lips, his forehead to hers.

For once, she had nothing to say, not when she could sense

what he was feeling, and the magnitude of it took her breath away.

He met her eyes. "I understand now why Alex doesn't leave Violet's side," he said, cupping her nape. "I'm sorry I wasn't there to protect you."

For a split second, she imagined how horrible it'd be to watch Julian challenge a rage-addled Adrius. She knew who'd win that fight. "It's okay. You don't have to worry about me," she promised. "I was dumb this time. But it turned out all right."

"And next time, I'll be by your side. I don't want anything to happen to you," he promised. "I love you. I know I'm not the best at showing it—"

She cut him off with a kiss in playful protest. "Implying you're anything but the best thing to happen to me," she said, smiling against his lips. "I love you too."

"This spell Sorsha invited you to see—is it dangerous?" he asked. She felt him take a deep breath.

She knew he'd be there if she said yes, but as far as she knew, scrying was just looking at something far away through a window. "It shouldn't be. But I don't think they want to see you again right now." His expression filled with turmoil to part with her just as he'd said he wouldn't leave her side. "I'll be fine, and it won't take long," she added.

"Then I'll see you in my room later?" He started to part from her reluctantly. An idea seemed to gleam in his emotions, something he would try in her absence.

Knock yourself out, she thought, hoping it was something pleasant to round out her frazzled nerves. "Of course," she said, waving as they parted and she headed to the fae's room. The door was unlocked, so she let herself in to see they'd set up a full-length mirror to face their couch. It was an antique made of solid wood, resting on a stand of two carved nubs for feet. Its face was cloudy, smeared with a thick layer of some unknown substance.

Sorsha stood before it and, upon turning to see Olivia there, said, "Have a seat. This is a two-way spell, meaning I need to search for someone to connect with on the other side."

The couch had a place for her to sit. Keegan flashed her a

quick smile as she gingerly rested on the cushion next to him. His gaze was a little unfocused, and he returned to watching Sorsha after that acknowledgement.

"Don't say a word," Sorsha warned. She snapped her fingers before the mirror, sending up purple sparks of magic.

Snap. Snap.

The glass glowed from within with a hint of the lilac color her magic manifested as.

Snap. Snap.

Other than the outline of magic, the surface turned black as night. Sorsha began to speak in a foreign language, a jumble of syllables as she swiped her hands. The darkness shifted, as if she searched within it. Ash nudged Keegan, her brows raised as she nodded.

"She's made it through to the Fell Lands. Don't hold your breath yet," Keegan told Olivia privately.

She nodded too, feeling her anticipation build as Sorsha started swiping more rapidly in search of someone else to connect with. If there was any life at all on the other side, she should find it...

The line of the Archfae's body grew more rigid as she searched and searched. Minutes stretched out until Olivia started wondering if there really was anything left. They'd warned her that the Fell Lands were a desolate place. Life wouldn't naturally sustain anyone there, not even the first Alchemyst with two Fell Keys on her fingers or Sorsha's legendary mentor.

So, when the mirror suddenly showed the visage of another person who greeted them with a shout, she nearly fell off the couch in shock. "Who's spying on me this time? Get your Fell face out of my bathroom mirror!" called the woman in the reflection, glowering at them as Sorsha took a few steps back to give them all a better view of her.

She was a fae too but so different from Sorsha. Her skin was fully gold, sparkling like star shine. Maybe Sorsha would be as glittery if she was even older. Muting her radiance was a leather breastplate pulled up just enough to cover her assets, and the image of her stopped somewhere mid-abdomen. Her eyes were equally striking, a pure and swirling white like a nebula seen from a great distance. Wings like fine stardust flickered behind her. And sticking out from a thick coronet of white hair was a pair of sharply pointed ears.

"Wait—you're not Fell," she said a moment later.

Sorsha's face split into a wide smile, practically radiant herself despite her human glamor. "Hi, Izell. Do you remember me?"

Izell smiled too, baring pearly teeth. She had extra sharpened canines, showing eight exaggerated teeth like the bite of some predatory animal. Olivia felt herself recoil as it fractured her view of the gorgeous fae façade. "It took you long enough, kid. You didn't give up on me, did you?"

"I couldn't reach you through the veil," Sorsha admitted.

"Ah, no matter. You're here now. You, my great...how many greats is it, grandson? I've forgotten." She turned her attention to Keegan.

"Five," he responded.

"Great-great-great-great-great grandson, and your little Unseelie friend too. The gang's all here." Izell kept that disconcerting grin, and it felt like her flat gaze turned Olivia's way. "But who's this?"

"This is Olivia, grandmother," Keegan responded. "A newly turned Alchemyst."

Izell lifted a finger and walked away from the mirror, leaving them looking at a blank wall. The fae exchanged a glance. "It's like we last saw her yesterday," Ash remarked.

Olivia was wondering just who or what this person was, because she'd noticed the scales drifting down Izell's forearm, a shade of sandstone just lighter than her skin. The back of her arm was lined with inch-long spines and her fingers tipped with hooked claws. But the fae were acting like nothing was amiss, so she didn't question it yet. "Time means different things when you get that old," Sorsha said. "I bet she didn't miss us. But I missed her." She put a hand to her chest, still smiling more openly than Olivia had ever seen.

They heard Izell before she reappeared, though her voice was muddled. Someone else spoke too, her voice high and sweet by comparison. Izell came back into the mirror's reflection alongside someone who nearly made Olivia's heart stop. She didn't recognize her, but she *knew* who she was.

As Olivia's mouth hung open, Izell gestured to the newcomer. "Look! I have an Alchemyst too!"

"Queen Nyah?" Olivia breathed.

The woman appeared completely human, with the stately features she'd expect of a queen. A heart-shaped face and laugh lines didn't hide the noble lift of her chin or the confidence she carried, even when dragged to view four people in a mirror. A butterfly rested on her shoulder and another atop the delicate crown on her head. Eyes of molten gold, the same that Olivia looked into every morning in the mirror, flashed to her. "Yes, that is I, at your service."

Chapter 31
Olivia

Olivia was glad she was already sitting down. "You... you're alive."

"I am. Well, last I checked. Pinch me?" She offered her arm to Izell, who tweezed it between two claws. "Ow. Consider filing those things down."

"So sorry. I'll keep them blunt on the off chance you want to make this joke again." Izell's grin was completely unrepentant.

Olivia exchanged an incredulous glance with Keegan, who seemed just as surprised as her. Ash was chuckling to herself, while Sorsha had her hands clasped, waiting patiently. "But how are you alive?" Olivia asked.

"I'm sorry, dear. It seems you all have me at a disadvantage," Nyah said.

Sorsha jumped in to make introductions with herself first, and Izell filled in, "She's Caladorn's daughter." This drew a gasp from Nyah.

"Oh, your father loves you very much," Nyah said with a sweet smile. "Will you be here long? I can go get him."

"Maybe after we catch up," Izell said before Sorsha could get a word in edgewise. The Archfae's face was still lit up like a kid's at a surprise birthday party, nodding along eagerly.

"Back here is Keegan, my Blade," Sorsha continued.

"You two left the Fell Lands together. I wish I had family you could say hello to," Nyah said to him, drawing a shrug from the stoic fae.

"Izell is plenty for me." His tone implied that he considered her more than enough.

"Isn't it Dragon Blade now, boy?" Izell asked, raising a brow.

He glanced to Olivia, who took a keen interest the moment anything dragon-related was mentioned. "Yes."

"Yet you're still acting like a common Blade?"

"This is my place, as it has been for centuries," he said, sighing. Privately, he told Olivia, *"It's a fae thing. Maybe I'll show you later."*

"I'd love to see it!" She wished she knew more about the secretive trio. Especially if there were dragons involved.

"Anyway, and this is Ash," Sorsha said like there wasn't anything more to her than that.

Izell propped her head on her chin as Nyah and Ash made small talk. "Were you going to mention the part about her being your Spellbreaker? And what of her family?"

"I don't have any family," Ash said flatly.

It seemed for a moment that Izell was going to say something more, something Ash didn't want acknowledged, but Nyah read the situation and put her hand on the other woman's arm. "Izell, please. I'm dying to meet this other Alchemyst."

Olivia waited for Sorsha to introduce her before blurting out, "I have so many questions for you! I'm only the second Alchemyst *ever*. And things are going wrong so fast around here. Maybe you can help us? Maybe...you both can?"

She thought of Adrius and his sudden surge of Fell Madness. Maybe the lost queen could give her some insight into the problem. She pulled back from that idea almost as soon as it formed in her mind. It seemed cruel to bring up the woman's husband just to tell her that he'd fallen prey to his vampire hunger. Especially when she was a world away, unable to help more personally.

Nyah's brows rose. "Things going wrong? That sounds like a more interesting story than my survivor's tale."

"It sounds like we all have our stories to tell." Sorsha drew up a chair at last, sitting with a sigh. "Do you wish for us to go first?"

"Your woes are guaranteed to be more topical than ours," Izell chuckled, waving her onward with those sharp claws.

"Where to even start?" Sorsha tapped her fingertips together. "Nyixa rose from the ocean. That's probably the start of our newest problems. Lucia protected herself and a handful of survivors who woke from long comas with no knowledge of how much time had passed, except for Lucia. She immediately tampered with the Dark Eye to prevent a proper midsummer crossing for the Seelie and caused the turning of a new vampire Sorceress."

Olivia watched the faces in the mirror. Nyah's sunny smile faded at the mention of Lucia, though Izell seemed much more interested in news of the Dark Eye. "Lucia attempted to make a portal to the Fell Lands to usher in a second Fell invasion. The second Sorceress stopped her, but we paid a bitter price for it—only the three of us made the crossing the split second after the Dark Eye destroyed itself."

"But there aren't any more Fell..." Nyah trailed off. Olivia felt her eyes nearly pop out of her head at that news. The fae exchanged glances of shock.

Izell tapped her claws against her jaw. "We can talk about that in a minute. Is that precise language you were using? It destroyed itself?"

Sorsha wrung her hands, her expression shading to worry. "Yes. When given the command to stop, it interpreted it in such a way that it exploded to abort the portal's creation."

"Mmm. So that's what we felt a while ago," she remarked to Nyah. "You are aware of what a catastrophe losing the Dark Eye is?"

"We are collecting the Fell Keys," Sorsha said.

"How could you possibly recreate an Eye of Worlds without these?" Izell grasped one of Nyah's hands, turning it to show a ruby and an emerald ring on her fingers.

"We're still working on that," she admitted, ducking her head like a chastised girl.

"Hmph." The elder fae crossed her arms. "Well, that's not the end of it, obviously. Continue."

"No, it gets worse. Lucia is a vector for a new infection, which turns vampires Fell Mad, transferred by a bite. It's cured the same way, though." She gestured to Olivia, who waved. "Combine that with Olivia being able to sense a shadowy...something lingering by the side of a few of the Ancient vampires, whispering negatively in their ears."

Izell pinched her brow. "What a disaster."

Nyah pushed her partway out of the frame, leaning in. "How can we help you? What did you need from me?"

Now it was Olivia's turn to talk, and she felt her thoughts swirl into a hundred questions for the first Alchemyst. "Gwendolyn speaks so highly of you. I was just hoping you could teach me how to be like you," she said earnestly. She saw shock register over Nyah's face at the mention of her mother, followed by her putting her hand over her heart. "I'm not that good at making magic blood yet. I need hundreds of potions to make anyone take me seriously about saving the vampires Lucia turned into Fell Mad. Is there a trick? Some sort of secret?"

A warm smile returned to her features as she listened, nodding along. "I can share with you what I've learned about myself over the years. As an Alchemyst, you are a force of change for all things magical. Your blood not only can cure the incurable, it can also turn a spell in motion into something else. To create magic blood, you have to have a desire to help others in your heart. It cannot be selfish. You cannot force it." Olivia had learned the hard way that she couldn't force it but nodded in fascination with the rest.

"The most important lesson I've learned is that we all share a spark of creation in us. It is part of our legacy, carried in our blood," Nyah continued. "One drop of gold from myself will activate that spark in the blood of others. If you need volume—there you have it. Turn the charitable donation of another into vials of gold. That's how I saved a race of people."

"No way," Olivia breathed. She felt her hope soar. She just couldn't do it alone—and there was something poetic about that, that the strength of her magic lay in the contributions of others as well as herself. "Can I ask you one more question?"

"Of course."

"Do you know how to make a potion that will release a vampire from a blood oath?" She felt the fae eyeing her curiously, but Nyah supplied the recipe off the top of her head once Olivia retrieved a pen and paper to write it down. She'd need help figuring out some of the ingredients, but this saved her hours of searching and squinting.

"Thank you. Thank you so much," Olivia said, sharing the hope etched across her face with Nyah, who winked, before Izell took over the frame.

Olivia whispered the truth to Keegan and Ash just so she didn't have to carry the burden of this knowledge alone. "It's for Elandros. He was going to work out a deal with Adrius to join us. But now that Adrius..." she drifted off, and they nodded in understanding. "Maybe he'll still come. He needs this potion to tell us what he can."

"I'll see about getting in contact with him," Keegan promised.

"Olivia, it's about time we invited Gwendolyn to this conversation," Sorsha said, flashing her an apologetic look. "Us older folk have some reunions to make. And some stories to be told, such as how the Fell are gone."

She stood, completely understanding. Sorsha wanted to talk to her father, and Nyah, her mother. She was the odd one out, with a lot of work on her plate tomorrow when she'd return to the hospital. "It's been three thousand years here. Don't you have any faith in your old mentor?" Izell scoffed. Olivia kept her ears perked as she left the room slowly.

"But, we thought you all were dead...that everyone was dead..." Sorsha's voice trailed to quiet until Olivia had to close the door behind her.

"Wow," she murmured to herself, wondering what this said about Lucia, who'd destroyed the Dark Eye for...nothing, apparently.

She wondered where to even find Gwendolyn as she shook off her introspection. The woman's voice drifted up from the stairs, giving her something to follow. She bounded down them to approach the Ancient, only stopping short when she realized she was in conference with Neala and Jaromir in the plush seats right off from the foyer.

Gwendolyn looked up at her and smiled. A genuine smile, perhaps the first she'd seen aimed her way from the particularly demanding woman. "You're in good spirits," she said.

"I have a nice surprise for you. Come with me?" Olivia offered. Her empathy untied itself from its close proximity to the fae. Despite what had happened earlier with Adrius, Gwendolyn was happier than Olivia's empathy had ever felt.

The whispering shadow was gone.

Chapter 32
Julian

Julian vowed to himself that he would not feel this way again. Alex had retrieved him from war planning by saying Olivia was nearly attacked. The thought that she could be in danger without him knowing...

Well, he planned on changing that tonight. He knew he had time while Olivia finished her business, so he gave his room yet another makeover. She'd taken such joy in his surprise at walking in to a "European spa" that he wanted to return the favor. But he also wasn't so creative, so he spent time making a list of possibilities on the kitchenette table with his knees tucked uncomfortably high in a chair built for a smaller person.

He settled on something he could do with a quick trip to the supermarket, so he enlisted Violet's help to get him there and back faster and changed up the room at record speed.

By the time Olivia walked in, muffling a yawn, he'd lit candles for ambiance and had the traditional music of his homeland playing. He left a pan to simmer as he turned to her, dressed smartly in his best suit. "*Ciao, signorina.* Table for one?"

Her jaw dropped as she glanced around. "Oh my gosh. This is amazing. You did this for me?"

He broke character with a proud smile. "Let me show you to your table." He offered her his arm for the short walk to the kitchenette, where he'd set the table with a checkered tablecloth and wineglasses for them both.

"Oh, thank you, waiter. Is that dinner I smell?" She sat facing the stove, where he quickly went to stir the seafood risotto he'd made.

"As long as you're not allergic to seafood." He hadn't thought to ask until it was already made and ready.

"Nope. It smells divine," she said eagerly.

"Well, here you are, *signorina*. Already prepared for you." He plated it up and placed it before her.

"Now this is service. Thank you." She blew on a steaming spoonful as he poured wine for them both and had a seat opposite of her. He waited for her to take that first bite and enjoyed the bliss across her face as she savored it. A warm feeling coiled in his chest to know she liked his first attempt at her kind of surprise. "I'm going to give this restaurant a five-star review. What's its name?"

He swirled his wine as he considered. "Julian's Italian Kitchen."

"That is far too literal, sir. You are Julian, and that's your kitchen." She pointed with her spoon.

He shrugged. "I'm a simple man. The name tells you exactly what you get."

"Well, I appreciate it." Her face softened. "This is really special. Especially after the day I've had."

"You can tell this waiter your woes, if it pleases you." He downed a swallow of wine. It'd be better with the seafood pairing for her. He just wanted the warmth to help chase away a lingering chill starting to form from him saving up his Winter Key-borne powers.

"Well, I have good news for the waiter. I just watched Sorsha reach the Fell Lands and had a chat with her mentor...and Queen Nyah. They say it's been three thousand years and there's no more Fell."

He nearly choked on his wine, shooting her an incredulous look. "Like, Adrius's wife?"

"Yeah. Just in time for him to not see her." Her lips quirked.

"But she taught me some important things, and I think I'll have a lot more purification potions ready to go tomorrow. Enough to cleanse the Fell Mad rather than kill them."

"You're sure?" he asked. If she could pull that off, they might still be able to change tactics to get cleansing potions to the infected, one way or another.

"I'm sure. I can do it. I'll be a potion-making machine," she promised.

She savored her meal while he rested his chin in his hand, just admiring her. "You're incredible, you know that? This is supposed to be our darkest hour. The moments of greatest uncertainty. You will be the one to lead us back to the light, just like you did for me. And if there are no more Fell...well, we don't have to live in fear of the shadows anymore."

Olivia set her plate aside, finished, giving him the opening to take her hands in his. She was blushing, a sparkle in her eyes. "Do you really think so?"

"I know so," he said, leaning in to kiss her fingertips. "And along the way, you're going to need a protector. Something I wholeheartedly volunteer for."

"I couldn't imagine anyone else in that role. Do you want to get more comfortable?" she asked. He followed her to the couch, where she fit perfectly under the crook of his arm, her hands idly unbuttoning his suit.

He gathered his nerve, something difficult when she could so easily distract him. "What I'm saying is, I want to ensure your safety. To always have a sense of if you're well or not and know where you are if you need help."

"You want my blood? For your tracking ability?" she asked, flicking a layer of curls off her shoulder. A stream of liquid gold lay just under the surface of her skin, just waiting to be tapped like the precious resource it was.

His mouth watered, fangs coming unsheathed behind his closed lips. He forced them back for the moment so he didn't give her the wrong idea of his intentions. "I meant what I said earlier. You're the most important person in my life. You're charming, you're silly, and you're my opposite in many ways. I'm glad I made that promise to Rosa so long ago, because you are worth every moment of the wait. My lifemate, my heart."

He sealed his words with a kiss, feeling her wrap her arms around him. Her soft curves against his hard muscle. Opposite, but made for one another.

"I love you too," she murmured. "Ever since you rescued me from Haven, I've found my purpose. I'm useful. My skills are helpful. You finding me was the best thing that's happened to me."

He stroked her cheek, admiring the eyes shining like precious metal back at him. "Be my mate," he implored. The process was sacred and permanent for vampires, a melding of the soul. Mates could sense each other's thoughts and feelings in an intimate bond. That they were lifemates proved that they were perfect together, and the time they'd had only proved that to him. He hoped she agreed.

"You don't think it's too soon?" She looked torn between desires, but to see that she wanted it made his spirits soar.

"I believe that the heart knows what it wants. And what mine wants...is you," he said earnestly. "When this all blows over, we can go off into the sunset together, just you and me. See the world. I want to show you everything."

"I..." She bit her lip to stop a too-quick answer. An excited smile took over her expression, as eager as he felt to take this next step together. "Yes. I think you make me better. Let's be even better together."

He swept her from the couch, feeling air hit his bare chest. She'd undone most of his shirt and jacket while he'd confessed. After he took her to bed, he finished the job. She presented herself like an offering atop his sheets. While he didn't know the steps, he knew the dance that would tie them as mates. Together, they figured out the way.

Chapter 33
Olivia

Olivia was satisfied down to her toes as she went back to work. Good or bad, she could handle it. *Bring it on,* she thought.

Julian was her rock now, an anchor of steady emotion that she knew was somewhere in the building, waiting outside of the cramped back room as she was presented with blood from the hospital's donations. Melanie had identified older blood that was less likely to be used, but that didn't assuage a hint of guilt when presented with the life-saving packages. Gwendolyn poured only one into a beaker.

One chance to fulfill what Nyah had told her was possible. The three fae and Gwendolyn were all there to watch, each in higher spirits. There was no return of the whispers, which had seemingly abandoned Gwendolyn in the knowledge that Olivia would banish them anyway with the Night Key.

Olivia pierced her thumb with a clean scalpel, watching a bead of blood as it formed golden. She wanted this so badly, and she felt Julian echo the desire like a silent cheerleader. It dropped into the beaker, bobbing on the top like a soap bubble. She leaned in with bated breath.

The blood dissolved as they watched, spreading out in a metallic ripple until it filled the whole beaker. In moments, it was more magic-laced blood than she'd ever hope to produce on her own. All of it pure and precious.

"It's a miracle," Gwendolyn breathed.

"*It worked?*" Julian asked, making an effortless mental connection with her.

"*It worked!*" She held up the beaker with both hands. Each drop, the salvation of a life.

He came in as an extra pair of hands as Sorsha started distributing medical equipment and the crushed herb mixture the magical blood activated. "I have fifteen different teams waiting for these. How many do you think we can make?" he asked.

"As many as needed," Sorsha replied. Her nimble fingers made short work of the simple task of packing syringes while Gwendolyn filled fat vials with double the usual dose.

Their strategy, as Olivia understood it, was as straightforward as the situation could merit. They were weaponizing the purification potion. A mindless pack of Fell Mad would hurt each other to get to the potion if one of the larger vials hit the ground and shattered. If Lucia retained more control over their base instincts, they were supplying darts and syringes. There would still be loss of life, but she was sure her efforts were not in vain.

Once they'd boxed up their first load of potions, Sorsha made a portal for Julian to deliver it to one of the groups awaiting their supply. They had a blown-up image of the New York City underground tacked to the wall, with coordinates and team numbers at fifteen different entry points. Julian sat next to her and caught her studying it. "It's the best we could do on short notice. Each are mixed coven groups that've had some time to prep together. I hope it's enough."

"It looks like you've done a lot to make this a success," she assured him. There were red stickers throughout, locations he'd identified as having pockets of Fell Mad. There were many—their locations changed and roved like a seething horde. It was their luck that they hadn't come to the surface yet, waiting for their dark mistress to let them off their leashes instead.

She felt something was niggling at him as he looked over the map. "What's wrong?" she murmured.

"What if it's a trap?" His eyes were dark with memories and worry alike.

"That does seem like her style, huh?" Her fingers faltered as she was forced to consider the possibility. "Holding something back to surprise us with. Where do you think she'll be in all this?"

He pointed to the only odd pop of color, a neon green dot down a warren of tunnels at a seeming dead end. "Right there. Haven's vampire headquarters. You know, I've never found it for myself. Haven guards it with all the security you can fathom, making it impossible to approach on your own."

"So, how do you know where it is?" she asked.

"An honest drug dealer." Though he spoke with a scoff, there was a hint of humor under the surface. "The only kind of delivery Haven accepts right at the front door. The dealer described the headquarters like the mixture of a bank vault and a bunker. That's where she'd be—as safe as possible. We'll have to defeat her army to get to her."

"Figures," she muttered.

He stole a quick kiss as he went on another delivery run before returning with Charlotte and Armando to help their output. Armando's face lit up after Keegan showed him the simple task they needed him to do.

"When I was small, I wanted to be an apothecary," he said to no one in particular as he got to work.

Sorsha glanced up. "What stopped you?"

"See these hands?" Armando held them up. "They're much better for punching things."

Julian rolled his eyes with a good-natured smile. Despite that, Olivia felt his affection toward his nephew.

"Hopefully, those hands are good for mixing ingredients too, or we're going to be replaced," Charlotte remarked. She held up a dart, her face lighting up as she shook it and the potion within activated and glowed back at her.

As they continued to mix and pack, Olivia passed a fistful of filled darts and syringes under the table to her friend. Charlotte's brow pinched as she took them. "Shh. Just some insurance," Olivia whispered.

"Girl, I'm gonna be fine." She still secured them into a bundle to pocket later.

"Just making sure," she said. "I know you're going to scream the Fell Mad into submission, but...can't I worry about you?"

"I'll be fine. I got that guy on my team." She jerked her chin toward Armando. "Plus a bunch of other full-blood vamps. They won't know what hit 'em."

Olivia sure hoped so. She wanted to pass more under the table to her, but she knew Charlotte's pride would get in the way of that. If she wanted to prove she was just as tough as a full-blooded vampire, she needed to fight like one.

"What about blood? It's been a while..." Her friend needed to feed rarely, but it seemed about time for it.

"I've already got some." Charlotte dropped her voice to keep from being overheard. "And a new blood donor."

"No way. Who?" she whispered. That meant her friend was bound to protect a new person for at least a month, or at least until the hunger returned. For a wrenching moment, she worried that Charlotte had returned to her old master or someone else who would take advantage of her dhampir nature.

In response, Charlotte gestured to Armando again. "My new partner. I have to protect his silly self anyway," she confided.

"Wow. Does that mean...?"

Her friend's skin darkened. "It doesn't mean anything. He offered, I took it, that's that."

Olivia smiled to herself, returning to packing potions. It was an awfully quick denial, before she could even ask her question. She suspected she'd missed something between the two of them. When things settled down, she would ask for the details.

More boxes of potions left, and they squeezed in one more person to help their productivity. The room was starting to over-heat with the proximity of too many bodies. Yet spirits were high, except for Olivia's when she felt someone trying to get her atten-tion mentally. *"Olivia?"*

"Hi, Elandros." Oh, he had the worst timing. Sirius had reported to Gwendolyn that they'd chased Adrius all night, only catching up to him when they spent the daylight hours sheltering

in the same warehouse on the city outskirts. Apparently, they were all hurt badly. In Adrius's case, she feared it'd turned out worse than that, but she didn't know for sure.

"Do you have the potion for me? I cannot seem to get a hold of Adrius, but I have what he asked for. This other man keeps insisting I work with him, but he won't tell me who he is." He still spoke like an aristocrat, like she was lucky to be graced by his presence and attention.

What had Adrius asked of him, though? He'd never said. Then again, they'd both kept the possibility of this deal close. Now he was gone, and she was left holding the envelope. She glanced to Keegan and caught his eye. "What did Adrius ask for?" she asked him.

"I'm unsure," he responded. "However, I told him to bring it to the hospital."

"Adrius is...indisposed," she said carefully. *"Bring it to the hospital my acquaintance told you to bring it to. We did make your potion."*

"It. Great. He's not there, and you don't know what he wanted." Elandros sighed. *"Why'd I go through all this work for nothing?"*

"Well...what is it?" She couldn't help being cross when it sounded like he wouldn't have upheld his side of the deal if he'd known Adrius wasn't waiting for him at the end.

"Blood Prince Taryn, trussed up all nice in the only pair of nephilim chains I could find. I nearly got my face punched in for my efforts," he scoffed.

Another Blood Prince? Just how many were there? She relayed who was coming, and who he was bringing out loud, just to feel Julian, Gwendolyn, and the fae stare at her in shock. "He's coming here now?" Gwendolyn said. She put a hand on Sorsha's shoulders. "Quick. We need to make up a cure. We can spare a drop for this."

Both of them started looting through Sorsha's sack of rare ingredients. "A cure for what?" Olivia asked curiously. She craned her neck to watch them.

"A long time ago, Nyah and I brewed a batch of the strongest love potion. Stage three," Gwendolyn explained as she laid out a few canisters and another beaker. "We found that it was too strong to be legal. Drinking it induced such powerful love for another person that it was an obsession. The victim became so enamored they fell prey to their own devotion.

"Taryn is an excellent example for why we don't brew stage three love potions under any circumstances," Gwendolyn continued. "He's been love-struck by Lucia for so long that I fear there may not be any of him left inside. And if he's still aware, he will be fearsomely angry at losing so much of his life in service to someone who's used his emotions."

"Elandros said he'd be in nephilim chains?" She didn't know the significance, but it made Gwendolyn relax.

"And thus, he will stay in them. We should prepare a tranquilizer as well," she said, taking out more herbs for that purpose.

"I think we should move to a larger area so we can invite everyone who should hear what Elandros has to say for himself," Sorsha said, gesturing to the cramped room. "And potion production should not stop."

"We can show some folks what to do," Charlotte volunteered.

Under Sorsha's control, they got an assembly line of new vampires working, including a man with wolf-like, amber eyes and ruddy skin by the name of Luke. Olivia got the impression that Julian trusted him greatly to take over in their stead. They headed into the hospital's main waiting area, where she hoped they had someone who could wipe the cameras if anything unexplainable happened. So much could go wrong.

Julian put a hand on her shoulder, flashing a reassuring smile. "This is why we can erase memories," he said like he'd picked up on her thoughts. "We'll be careful."

"How are you going to avoid picking a fight with this guy?" she asked, sensing the turmoil in him to see Elandros again.

"If he truly means to help us...I can put it aside. We have a bigger enemy to face tonight." He cracked his knuckles, though, as if that didn't completely satisfy his urge for revenge.

They helped clear a circle of chairs, sitting in a semi-circle as they waited. Gwendolyn helped portal in Alex, Violet, Neala, and Jaromir, the latter of whom carried a bulging suitcase with him. He opened it to reveal rows of medical equipment and a pile of metal. He withdrew a set of shackles glowing with magic and offered them to Gwendolyn wordlessly. She twirled them on her finger like the metal cuffs weren't swinging inches from her face.

When Elandros arrived at last, he was carrying another man over his shoulders as effortlessly as holding an empty sack. It was a testament to just how strong he was as an Ancient, because the other person easily doubled him in muscle mass. On second look, Elandros's immaculate appearance was ruined. Red stained his cravat, and his coat was torn. His styled hair drooped around his face in greasy strands. His maroon eyes tracked to the shackles first, his pace cutting back to a solemn march as he saw the lineup of Lucia's enemies waiting for him.

He stopped a few yards away, stooping to roll the other man from his shoulder. *So this is Taryn,* Olivia thought. He reminded her of Korin in bulk, though she'd have to wait and see if he, too, had a gentle giant's personality.

She also wondered how they were going to free him of Lucia's influence when he was out cold. A pair of magic shackles were around his wrists, presumably there to keep them safe should he fly into a Fell Mad rage upon becoming aware of himself and what was done to him.

Gwendolyn stood, the potion for breaking oaths in her free hand. "So, you wish to join us." Despite the hunch stealing her height, she managed to look down her nose at him.

"Adrius has already punched my sternum for my crimes. I imagine you all wish to do so much worse." Elandros bowed his head, his hands clasped before him. "Know that I regret my decisions and offer you the penance Adrius asked of me."

"And how do we know this isn't a trap?" she asked.

The question weighed on Olivia heavily. He served someone who wasn't below using him for traps and the like. He'd told her the truth of Lucia when he'd held her captive: *nothing is as it seems.*

"I would swear a blood oath to you, but I need that potion to break a much older one." He breathed a heavy sigh, his shoulders drawing in. "I act of my own accord, at great personal cost. I've brought you Taryn, who will wake any moment from the tap I gave him."

Gwendolyn thrust the potion at him. "Drink it. Then swear to tell us the truth of all that we ask."

He snatched it and drank, a shudder passing over him the moment the last drop hit his tongue. "Oh, that burns." Seizing his middle, he dropped to one knee, and not one person moved to help him as he clutched the carpeting with white knuckles.

Olivia shifted uncomfortably as she felt Julian wanting it to hurt him worse. She shot him a look. *"Can't help my opinion. He should honestly be dead for what he's done, but this is a good compromise,"* he said privately.

"I suppose." She just didn't want to wish harm upon someone like that. Even Elandros. She wondered what he'd done that was so dire to have him swear an oath to Lucia to avoid it coming to light.

He wasn't recovered by the time Taryn started to rouse, his bloodshot maroon eyes swiftly opening. Neala and Jaromir flanked him, putting pressure on his shoulders to keep him on his back. He was snarling like an animal the moment he realized what was going on, thrashing and kicking to upset their balance.

"He needs that cure now," Jaromir called, holding Taryn's jaw to fend off a bite as the other man's teeth clacked.

Gwendolyn turned to keep both Ancients in her sight. It was Sorsha who produced the cure for a stage three love potion. Her magic paralyzed Taryn's muscles long enough for them to force it down his throat, and Jaromir used his fingers to coax him into swallowing.

Olivia clutched Julian's forearm as they watched Taryn for any signs of it working. Jaromir palmed a syringe, waiting for the worst.

Taryn started to murmur under his breath, his head whipping back and forth as if in the midst of a nightmare. "No, she wouldn't..." He gasped. "She didn't..."

"I'm sorry, old friend," Gwendolyn said.

His hands balled into fists. "Where is she?" Olivia knew her hope he'd make the transition without a hint of Fell Madness was like hoping a weed would thrive in the desert, but it still shocked her to see just how fast the transformation took him. Veins darker than his skin riddled his face and arms as he struggled anew against Jaromir and Neala. "How dare she use and *discard* me like some plaything!"

Jaromir glanced to Gwendolyn, who nodded the go-ahead to give him the injection. Not a purification potion, just something to knock him out. "We can't afford for either of you to be injured," she said, her expression creasing with sorrow as the anesthesia kicked in and Taryn went limp with a *thud*. "We need to get him to the infirmary with the others. Jaromir, please stay with me." Gwendolyn indicated Elandros, whose breathing was starting to even out.

"Of course," he said.

Julian stood, volunteering to help move Taryn through a portal Sorsha summoned. Neala shot him an annoyed look, like he'd insulted her capabilities, but they still took him through together.

Olivia felt a shift in the air. She rubbed a chill from her arms as she wondered if they'd already caught Lucia's attention and ire.

Chapter 34
Julian

"I just wanted to see them," Julian told Neala as soon as they were through the portal. The infirmary had three occupants already. Three of their best fighters, neutralized together on the eve of a battle they were desperately needed in. If that didn't stink of Lucia's influence, he didn't know what would.

"Look at how we're tearing ourselves apart," Neala said, tisking aloud. They placed Taryn on the fourth bed, with her stringing his chains up on a newly added hook above his head. Half of the beds had this attachment now, hastily hammered in with Adrius in the first bed, showing their necessity. As Julian had suspected—he wasn't breathing.

Korin was sleeping off a Gifted healing beside Adrius, looking the least injured of the three. What drew Julian's attention and concern was Sirius, nearly mummified in bandages in the third bed. His bloodshot eyes were open, blinking slowly to focus. His dry lips moved.

"Save your strength," Julian murmured. He had to wonder what kind of catastrophic injury would merit so many bandages when Sirius had both the most Gifted of Ancient healers to tend to him and incredible preternatural healing on top of that.

"He...didn't..." Sirius persisted in a rasp. "It wasn't him."

Neala joined him by Sirius's bedside, tilting her head curiously. *"I saw him turn with my own two eyes, Sirius."*

"It wasn't...*just* him." His eyelids started to droop, like he couldn't fight off healing sleep for much longer. "He's turned before...he's never fought...like this. Like a man possessed."

"*Something dark's at work here. I promise to end it in your stead. Sleep, brother.*"

Sirius seemed to smile as he drifted off with a sigh. "Brother?" Julian asked.

"*In the loosest sense of the word. By my adoption and his brother's marriage.*" She turned to him with a frown. "*I will not miss what Elandros has to say. Nor will I be the next Blood Prince in this line. Does it seem like my peers are being targeted?*"

He nodded, finding it hard to make eye contact when he knew she had just recently been under attack by the same whispers that'd claimed Adrius. "Clearly. Since Qin has run, there are only two of you standing and ready."

She didn't move, and her bulk was in his way of getting back to the portal and the hospital room where the others waited. "*What do you know that I don't?*" Her red eyes were heated. "*Do not think I haven't noticed you and the young Alchemyst acting strangely in my presence.*"

He felt all the moisture in his mouth dry up in one moment. If he told her too much, he might trigger her, but she seemed ready to shake him for some answers. However, she kept talking before he had a chance to answer. "*Know what I think? This bed is for me.*" Her hand landed in the middle of the next empty one with a *whump*. "*Whatever insanity took Adrius thought I was as easy a target. Isn't that right?*" She stared him down, definitely requiring an answer.

"I...believe so, yes," he said, wishing he had Olivia's sense of empathy so he could get a better read on her.

"*Thank god. Finally, a straight answer.*" She shook her head. "*I wondered if I was going mad. Every time I looked at you, I would think...of him.*" Julian tensed, watching her closely for any sign of Fell Madness. "*Remembering moments when we were married. The things we would do together for fun.*"

"You remember him?" he asked in a hush, realizing that nothing about her was changing. She remembered Marcus and her marriage to him? That was the line he'd been told not to cross, yet here she was, stepping over it instead.

"No. But Lucia thinking she can torment me with him is rich." She snorted, lifting her chin. She spoke the Sorceress's name purposefully, daring her to see this moment with her future sight. *"I know I have a massive hole in my memories, and it is shaped like Marcus Hartson. Sorsha tried to give me those memories back, and I nearly infected her and Keegan with the Madness for her efforts. Ever since then, everyone's walked on eggshells about him, like I'll somehow magically snap again, but I know. I know what Lucia did."*

"So, you don't miss him or want those memories back?" The more she talked, the more he relaxed, realizing he'd joined her tiptoeing friends when he was the walking heir to her former husband, the undeniable reminder of him.

She glanced down at her hands, tugging at her ring finger. *"How can I miss what I don't remember? And why would I want to remember someone I'll only miss? And yet... the whispers were oddly comforting. It was nice to remember someone I loved. Perhaps your dream walker friend can assist me in remembering him in a safe way, over time."* A smile stretched the scar by her mouth. *"But that's not why I'm comforted. Even after all these years, Lucia fails to understand me. And that is why tonight, I am a warrior rather than a victim."*

"I'm glad for you," he said honestly, following as she headed toward the portal with a new certainty to her step.

She stopped before the hole in reality for a moment, laying a hand on his shoulder. *"You are a good man, much like what I remember of him."*

With that, she was gone. He stared into the rippling portal, mastering his expression before heading through. Neala had given him such a shock of hope that it rendered him breathless. She'd proven that, for all her power, Lucia still made errors in full faith of her flawed abilities, mistakes they would exploit.

Once he was on the other side, he saw that they'd put Elandros in nephilim chains. He knelt before the half-circle, face red and brow trickling with sweat while he panted like he'd just finished a sprint.

Julian felt unease steal over him as he went back to his seat next to Olivia. He didn't know if the feeling came from him or her, but as soon as they were touching, he knew they were picking up on some undercurrent of malicious intent in the air around them. "Did I miss much?" he asked her quietly.

"He's just gotten started," she whispered back.

He listened in on what Elandros was saying. Someone had retrieved a paper cup of water for him, which he sipped from awkwardly. "Her main plan was to switch bodies with Violet and re-open the portal to the Fell Lands. She believed wholeheartedly that she would have complete control over this second invasion and that she could dispose of any governments that opposed her complete rule by feeding civilians to her pet Fell."

Yet there were no more Fell, he thought. Her plan was doomed from the start, but Lucia hadn't seemed to know it. What had caused such a huge oversight in her planning?

Alex in particular looked down at Elandros with undisguised disgust. "I recall at the time, you were more disgruntled that she hadn't picked you as a mate rather than that she was about to bring back those monsters."

Elandros scoffed. "All signs indicated that she would sit on the Nyixan throne as the world's ruler. She'd manipulated events perfectly to get her way. What did you want me to do, be the first one fed to her Fell?"

Alex leaned in, his inner beast coming to the surface as his expression curled into a snarl. "I would've expected you to speak up somewhere around the time she asked you for help *stealing someone else's body!*"

"She didn't succeed." He shrugged, his manacles clinking with the motion.

"Enough, Alexander. We don't have time to rehash the past," said Gwendolyn when it looked like he was about to get up and strangle Elandros himself. He growled but sat back, glaring sharply at the Blood Prince.

"Anyway, after she failed with that, she took the defeat

surprisingly well. No screaming, no throwing priceless objects. She's gotten the loyalty of enough vampires to have a stronghold here, close to her greatest enemies." His gaze rested meaningfully on Gwendolyn and then over to Julian. "She no longer spoke of how her body had been ruined. It was almost like she'd forgotten she wanted to be younger and less...Fell-like. Her new obsession was Julian. Julian, Julian, *Julian*. Gag me. It's been worse than Marcus. He at least returned her affection for a time."

Julian felt himself flush ice cold. "Affection," he deadpanned.

"You were supposed to be hers forever." He rolled his eyes. "Except she didn't foresee that Adrius would have a purification potion for you."

"That is...insanity. Complete utter insanity," Julian sputtered.

"She's lost her mind, I agree. You haven't had to watch her talking to her own shadow every time she steps out of her room or the things she's been doing to our allies..." He shuddered in remembrance.

Olivia rubbed Julian's shoulder. "She can't take you from me now," she whispered. A sick feeling gripped him, because Lucia had broken a mating bond before. But what use would she have in Julian anyway? He hated her too viciously for her to get what she wanted unless he was forced by the darkest of magic.

"What has she been saying to her shadow? And why, specifically, her shadow?" Sorsha spoke up, looking troubled.

"She turns back to look at it. Sometimes she laughs, but it's never a friendly one." He shuddered again. "It was hard to get close to her when she talked to it. I would feel uncomfortable or be reminded of something terrible from the past, so I would just avoid her when she started talking to herself."

There was movement behind him, his dim shadow warping. Keegan was on his feet first, his sword out in a flash. Elandros paled. "What? What is it?"

"Demon," Sorsha hissed, summoning two fistfuls of purple flame.

Elandros looked behind himself, where his shadow grew and darkened into a humanoid shape with the outline of razor claws and a whipping tail. *"Are you the finest Earth has to offer? What a joke."* Its voice was like a chorus of whispers to Julian's mind, and Violet was the first of them to recoil upon hearing it.

Julian stood, drawing his blade. *It's foolish of this creature to reveal itself,* he thought. Between the three fae, Neala, Alex, Violet, and himself, it faced steel, magic, and menace immediately. It retreated with an echo of cackles as Gwendolyn hurled a Latin-sounding phrase after its shadowy form.

With Julian watching it, he was a split second too late to realize what its gambit was. Until Gwendolyn released a cry of dismay, cut off quickly. At the back of the group chasing the demon, he turned to see a portal close where Gwendolyn was standing. Another ate up Elandros, his gaze stricken with panic as he fell into the hole beneath him.

He turned to Olivia, who was on her feet. Her heart pattered to the same thunderous beat as his own as she rushed to him. Her gaze was on the ground between them. He fully expected another would open to swallow him, his muscles bunching to leap.

But a portal appeared under Olivia's foot instead, causing her to stumble. She slipped downward as if someone grabbed her ankle on the other side and pulled. "Julian!" she screamed. Her extended hand disappeared last. By the time he dove for her, he hit solid carpeting.

He remained on his knees, scraping at the spot where she'd disappeared. "Where'd it go?" he heard Alex shout.

"It disappeared," Sorsha confirmed.

Julian could still sense Olivia somewhere below the city, miles away. Her panic and terror were like needles in his heart. He tore at his hair. It'd been so fast. So *easy* to snatch her away from him.

"What happened? Where's...?" Violet's voice drifted over to him, stifling when she saw his expression. "Oh, Julian."

"She's gone," he said from numb lips. His fingers trembled with extreme cold as his magic coiled.

Throwing back his head, he roared. The whole hospital shook with the first wave of wind. Violet took a step back as he stood. His eyes glowed with icy magic, bathing the world in blue.

A final portal opened in the midst of his friends and allies.

Though Sorsha swiped it closed, out erupted a single Fell Mad, leaping straight for her with fangs bared. Julian held his breath in the split second before impact. The Archfae's mouth opened in an "o" of surprise, and then she was on the ground.

In her place stood Jaromir, his bicep bleeding as the creature's fangs sank deep. He shook off the attacker, who died from a quick stab of Keegan's blade. Jaromir stumbled backward, holding a hand over the wound, which leaked black poison that leached through his skin with incredible speed.

He held his other hand out, his medical case flying to him from a burst of telekinetic energy. As the fae backed away from his quickly turning features, he flashed a multi-fanged smile and plunged a needle full of sedative into his neck.

"W-we need a geas," Sorsha stammered, peering out from behind Keegan. She produced a syringe of golden purification potion from a portal and handed it to him to administer.

As Julian's cold wake passed by them, she snapped up a hand to intercept him. "Can you sense where she is?"

"Down below," he gritted. "I will get her back."

"No, keep your head. I'm talking about Lucia," she said.

He forced himself to look away from Olivia with his blood tracking, long enough to realize their more immediate problem. "She has us surrounded," he reported. The two ground-floor entrances opened a few moments later, spilling out several men and women sprinting for them.

"We'll take care of it!" Sorsha exclaimed. She lunged for Keegan's hand, who held Ash's. Both fae women beckoned to a fourth person, Violet. "It takes four to cast a geas! Get over here." That was all the explanation the young Sorceress received before she was hauled into their circle of linked hands.

Julian felt a lurch of magic in his gut, like the four of them joining their magic was a shockwave. A circle of multicolored magic surrounded their feet. Yards away, the fastest of the Fell Mad was frozen in place with an expression of hunger and dismay at being caught. The rest were similarly stuck like grotesque statues, magic swirling underneath them. *"We need someone to go cure the Fell Mad before the geas wears off. They will be frozen,"* Sorsha projected.

"I'll do it." Alex was off running toward their usual laboratory back room.

Julian felt the cold in him start to mount. *"Julian, for you. We delivered potions to this location."* Sorsha opened a portal close by. Her head was bowed, eyes closed. A quiet murmur of another language came from her.

He plunged in without a second thought.

The team clearing this tunnel had already left. Olivia lay somewhere in the middle of the warren of tunnels, close but not close enough. Behind him, the portal rippled, revealing Neala, the last person standing who could help him now.

Wind howled down the tunnel ahead with all the fury of a winter storm. He wanted Lucia to know he was coming.

Chapter 35
Olivia

OLIVIA FELL INTO A HEAP ATOP A FADED CARPET. THE FIRST thing she saw was a pattern of crosses and the swing of a black-jack that knocked Gwendolyn unconscious next to her with a crack. She crab-walked away, looking up into the vacant stare of a Fell Mad man who regarded her terror with a tilt of his head.

They were in some sort of bedroom. Other corrupted vampires dragged Gwendolyn's body and Elandros's helplessly thrashing form out the door. Olivia pressed herself to the wall, expecting to be the next victim of the baton this man carried. Instead, he offered his clawed hand.

"Will you go willingly, or must he get rough with you?" The whispers were back, shadows curling around her shoulders and arms like an intimate caress. She yelped and tried to shake them off. When they moved with her, she used the Night Key to try dispelling them, drawing a chorus of laughter. *"That trinket will not save you here. Take his hand, Olivia. You need not die tonight if you cooperate."*

She put her hand in that of the corrupted man's, letting him pull her to her weak knees and lead her from the room. She stum-bled along behind him, feeling near sick with how her belly contorted. Pulling her shoulders in, she focused on her bond with Julian, clinging to any embers of rage he could spare. It didn't fill her with heat but instead with the kiss of icy promise that was unique to her mate.

"So you're a demon, huh?" Now she was the one talking to shadows, her eyes roving over plain stone walls as she sought to keep it occupied while she found a way out. There was an engraving at the end of the hall, a lighthouse. A beacon in the dark. *How ironic,* she thought.

"Isn't the irony delicious?" it whispered instead, haloing the lighthouse symbol in its darkness. *"Vampires who think they're vampire slayers. A cult of the religious as damned as those they hunt."*

Really, she'd asked a stupid question. Of course the whispering darkness was a demon. *"Of course,"* it agreed a moment later.

"Are you reading my thoughts?" she asked nervously.

"Try as you like, feigning enthusiasm and interest won't get you out of this."

So it was in her head. She kept looking over her shoulder, expecting to see a person whispering behind her. "All right. What do you want from me?" she demanded with as much force as she could muster. She was led to a stairwell, where they started to descend. An errant thought occurred to her, that they were going to where this demon had come from, down and down...

"You shall see, little Alchemyst."

"Why are you offering to keep me alive now when you made Adrius try tearing me apart?" she asked, not needing to feign the nervous swallow at the reminder of that moment.

"You were never in danger. You're much too valuable for that."

"Yeah?"

"Yeah." It sounded mocking.

"For being made of shadows and voices, you're not very talkative," she remarked. It was, perhaps, the safest-seeming manifestation of a demon she could imagine. But safety was a relative term. This creature was insidious; she'd seen it when it'd pushed Adrius too far right before her eyes.

"You would not dare to say such things if you knew who I was."

She stifled an eye roll, feeling some of her confidence return. "Why don't you enlighten me?"

The corrupted vampire stopped abruptly on the stairs and stepped aside. The darkness swirled into the shape of a humanoid figure that towered over her. It was as hot as standing before a bonfire, flames flickering within its hollow depth to light its face like a jack-o'-lantern of sharp teeth and hate-filled eyes.

But what terrified her into hunkering down before it was the sheer malice it gave off. Just like when she'd scared it off from Neala, it felt like the type of creature that would laugh if she died right before it. It *wanted* her to suffer.

"*I am Jazrach, greater demon of corruption. Your continued survival lies in the palm of my hand.*" It flexed both of its hands into shadowy fists, for all the care it had for her. "*Now come, before I lose my patience with you.*"

"U-uh-huh." She picked herself up, glancing to the corrupted vampire and expecting some solidarity there, some acknowledgement from him that he'd had to deal with this thing for a long time. Instead, he started marching after Jazrach's shadowy form without a hint of recognition.

She didn't say a word for the rest of the descent, her tongue glued to the roof of her mouth after that display. Her every pore screamed that she needed to turn around and find some escape, but she knew she wouldn't get far before she was swarmed by Fell Mad. As she watched the one leading her into the gloom, she wondered if they'd gotten it all wrong. Maybe Jazrach was controlling these corrupted vampires, not Lucia. He was obviously the one they were warned about—the wicked soul that was working with her.

It chilled her further to know that Lucia was trying to ingratiate herself with a demon. She only knew the woman through hearsay and wished it would stay that way. If she was lucky, the corrupted Sorceress wouldn't be at their destination.

At the end of the stairs, they entered a low-ceilinged room shaped like a bulb. It might've been a pantry. Several shelves were stacked to one side in a haphazard tower of metal and random dry goods. A bag of flour had fallen and been smashed below an errant boot. Cockroaches scurried from the powder in the wake of the demon.

There were chairs against the wall. In one, struggled Elandros, who'd been gagged. His eyes widened, and he fought harder when he saw Jazrach. Bound next to him was Gwendolyn, lolling to one side with a terrible welt on her temple. Beside her, a woman wearing a silvery gown was seated primly. What was instantly recognizable about her was her thick veil, atop which perched a crown of silver and moonstones.

Olivia went shock still, recognizing every description she'd heard of Lucia. "I was just keeping it warm for you." The woman stood, and an occultarus orbited from behind her shoulder as she gestured for Olivia to sit.

She didn't move. "I like standing, if you don't mind."

"Oh, I mind." Lucia gestured lazily. Something hit the back of Olivia's knees with bruising force, sending her down hard. Rough hands seized her wrists and bound them before she was shoved into the seat next to Gwendolyn.

At this vantage, at least, she could see that there were dozens of Fell Mad waiting for instruction with limp hands. At odds to this was a pair of normal-looking vampires standing at the edge of a circle inked into the dusty ground. The ginger-haired man was in his Sunday best, complete with a tie with crosses on it. His expression was as vacant as the Fell Mad, his hands frozen in a clasp before him. While by his side was a woman in a form-fitting black dress cut just right to reveal more than it hid. She had the face of a supermodel, though she was panting and blotting at her face with a kerchief. Dark veins marked her shoulder, slowly but inexorably spreading corruption through her.

"We've succeeded, Jazrach," Lucia said. "The Alchemyst, the Portal Key, and the Traitor, all in one."

"*Did you doubt?*" The whispers were back to a shadowy caress, but the demon was still coalesced in all his fiery glory beside her.

"This isn't how I saw it coming to be." Her tone held a frown.

"*Your solo attempt failed.*" Olivia heard the echo of its chorus: *failed, failed, failed.*

She shook her head like she was dislodging the little voices. "We're missing a piece. We're missing...Julian."

"Oh, yes. Julian."

And the mocking laughter as it repeated: *Julian, Julian, Julian.*

Gwendolyn gasped as she awoke, startling Olivia. Her heart felt like it was about to burst with its continued racing. "Shh," she hissed as the Ancient woman's gaze darted around to take in the scene.

"Oh, you are a creature of my own design, aren't you, Lucia?" Jazrach purred. *"Don't worry. He's coming. Do you hear the wind whistle? So comes the heir to his father's legacy."*

Lucia put a hand to her head. "I don't see us succeeding if we wait much longer. If we wait for Julian..."

"Don't worry. We'll get started."

Olivia felt herself sweat. It was sweltering down here, so close to the inferno inside the demon. She glanced to Gwendolyn in despair. They were conspiring to take Julian away from her, and she'd be forced to watch if they didn't do something.

Gwendolyn was muttering under her breath, shifting against the ropes binding her. *Praying,* Olivia realized.

Their gazes met. "Use the Key, girl. Untie me," she whispered before going back to prayer. Olivia closed her eyes, focusing on the Night Key still on her finger. She imagined its shadows reaching out, taking the ropes binding Gwendolyn and plucking them loose.

Cracking open an eye, she glanced over to see her shadows splashing uselessly on the back of the old woman's chair.

Maybe I am useless, she thought with a sigh.

Gwendolyn ground her foot atop Olivia's, waking her from the beginnings of a stupor with a shock of pain. "Let me tell you something," she muttered. "If you don't free us, it's more than likely that demon will consume our souls. It's been smart enough not to get the attention of the High Heavens yet, and it may continue to do so if we don't escape."

Well, that was certainly a wakeup call. Olivia focused harder until the Night Key's shadows started bending to her will, into the shape of a vice grip. This, she could use.

She glanced up in time to see Lucia gesture to one of the corrupted vampires in the room. His head whipped to the side with a sick crack, drawing a cry from Olivia as he fell to the ground. Jazrach moved its hand next, its shadows catching something bright from midair and drawing it to the middle of the circle.

"Is that a soul?" she whispered to Gwendolyn.

The older woman nodded grimly. "Hurry."

Olivia's shadows plucked and jimmied at the knot holding her hands apart and incapable of making them a portal to safety.

Another corrupted vampire offered Lucia a broom. She took it and a dagger from her waist, heading over to the unfortunate she'd just killed and slitting his jugular. She wetted the broom bristles in the resulting puddle of blood.

C'mon, c'mon, Olivia thought, her own hands trembling as she struggled to budge the knot holding Gwendolyn bit by bit. Lucia swept patterns of blood into the dirt like some infernal maid.

"The soul of a victim," she intoned as she finished a pattern around the circle.

"*The blood of a traitor,*" Jazrach whispered.

Lucia turned to Elandros, flicking her bloodied dagger. He made muffled noises against the gag as he struggled. Oliva held very still as the silver-cloaked woman drifted over to them just to feel cold steel press to her cheek. "I know what you're doing. Stop." She reached behind the chair to pluck the Night Key from her finger. She turned it over with a hum.

"Think obsidian suits me, Gwendolyn?" Her voice was deceptively mild as she stripped off a glove. Underneath, her hand was gnarled and clawed with a network of black veins coursing through every digit. She placed her new ring on one of those fingers, tilting her hand to admire its shiny surface.

"It's not too late to stop this," Gwendolyn said. "You are at a crossroads. Can you not see that you are working with an incarnation of evil?"

"When is it too late, hmm?" Those deadly claws drifted up to her veil. "Wasn't it too late for me when you damned me to this existence?"

She threw the cloth covering to the side, revealing a Fell Mad's face. Two dark pools for eyes, sharp rows of teeth made to rend flesh. The only thing different about her from the other corrupted vampires was her fanatical expression and the hatred pulsing off her, soaking into every crevice of Olivia's empathy.

"Wow, you're uglier than I expected," she said just to get that hatred turned away from her mentor, even if for a moment. She felt its full blast as Lucia's head panned her way.

The Sorceress hissed. "What did you say?"

Olivia leaned in despite a warning look from both Gwendolyn and Elandros. "You heard me. You're ugly. Both inside and out."

The angry flush that overtook Lucia's face stained it darker. She held her dagger in a clenched fist, upraised and trembling. "You're lucky you're useful, you mouthy brat." She snarled with all those teeth on clear display.

Just as she'd suspected, Lucia wouldn't do anything to harm her. Yet. There was only one reason she was here—they needed her blood, so they needed her intact. And that gave her a shot of adrenaline in the face of this...creature. "I have a breath mint in my back pocket too."

Lucia drew herself up, her nostrils flared. *If looks could kill,* she thought, quailing back as it appeared she was getting stabbed, Alchemyst or no.

"The blood, Lucia," Jazrach reminded, its many voices growing impatient.

She turned away from Olivia with obvious distaste, taking the pair of strides that would bring her in front of Elandros. "I know you're sorry. I don't need to remove this gag and hear your blabbering," Lucia remarked, opening up a pair of cuts on his upper arms. Shadows coiled around her, funneling his blood toward the center of the circle, where the glimmering soul bobbed. She cupped his cheek as he choked on a sound of pain. "It's all right, dear Elandros. You can swear yourself back into my service after this. We'll forget it ever happened."

Gwendolyn spoke up as Lucia turned away from them. "I would pray for your soul if I thought there was anything left of it."

Lucia lifted her hand in a dismissive gesture over her shoulder. "Don't bother."

"What do we do?" Olivia whispered, watching Lucia walk away with their only advantage on her finger.

The Ancient turned not to Olivia, but to Elandros. "Are you still on our side?" He nodded rapidly in reply. "The nephilim chains have a secret release. While they're distracted, I will speak the phrase to release you. Then, you'll release Olivia and me. We'll escape."

Elandros's face went slack with relief. At first, Olivia wondered why they hadn't started with that plan. But she didn't put much stock in Elandros's loyalty either.

Lucia was drawing a new set of symbols this time, making a ring inside of the circle and leaving a foot-long space under the mixture of soul, blood, and shadows untouched. She turned to the couple once her task was done, flicking aside her dagger with a careless clatter. "*Now the heart of the stubborn. You are sure this one will suffice?*" Jazrach asked, swirling around to linger behind the ginger-haired man and his scantily clad companion.

"She was amongst the first I bit, yet she has not turned. Look at her fighting it." Lucia petted the woman's neck covetously while Olivia wanted to vomit witnessing the intimate touch.

"*Then it's time to relieve her of her condition, don't you think?*"

Lucia smiled like a ravening shark. She snapped her fingers before the man's face, drawing his attention and releasing the thrall laid upon him. "Hold still, my dear," she told the woman, her claws lengthening. Olivia glanced away.

She heard the wet sound of tearing flesh. The man's cry of anguish.

And a whispered phrase in a language long forgotten, dropping the nephilim chains from Elandros's wrists with a *click*.

Chapter 36
Julian

Without Olivia, there was no warmth in Julian's heart. His magic made an impenetrable wall of wind and ice with him and Neala in the eye of the storm. Walls iced over, fixtures groaned, and water froze in place.

A team of vampires rushed them just to stop short in the face of a blizzard underground. "Get behind me or get out of my way," Julian yelled, slowing the brutal winds long enough for them to join in his wake at a safe distance. He'd memorized the map of the underground but didn't need it, navigating twists and corridors based off his gut alone. They started passing by the bodies of unconscious men and women—former Fell Mad. By his mate's compassion, these people would see another day.

They overtook another fighting force, but the creatures they'd been fighting were already gone. "They're retreating!" one vampire called.

There was movement between shadows, Fell Mad seeing him coming and running for their lives. Lucia, the invisible puppeteer, knew it would require more than a few people to take him down in his full rage.

So instead, she tormented him through Olivia. He felt his mate's every twist of emotion and the modulation of her terror, but whenever he tried to reach her mentally, he felt like his awareness skidded away like it slid on a dark mirror. No matter.

He'd come straight to her instead, and there was nothing that would stop him.

"Make way for the Winter Key!" Neala bellowed mentally, heard by all even with the howling of Julian's storm by how vampires of all covens moved aside to let him pass. He was their general now, their battering ram to hammer on Haven's front door with gale-force winds.

They entered a corridor he recognized, one full of traps. It was the farthest he'd ever gone on his own. His winds activated numerous traps, both seen and not. Muffled explosions and thuds followed. He kept his gaze roving, freezing the inner workings of anything still active. The Fell Mad must've re-activated these traps, showing either they still retained some intelligence or Lucia knew the inner workings of Haven's lair like her own.

Following a bend in the tunnel, he came to a halt upon seeing a large chamber filled with black-eyed Fell Mad all poised to strike at once. *"I will not strike to kill if you wish it."* Neala turned to him, her sword at the ready.

He let the winds amplify his voice so everyone would know his intent. "Strike to maim. If you have cures, use them! These people aren't our enemies!"

To think he would say such things of Haveners, who had to be in the mix of these people. Enemies who'd sworn to Lucia. But they hadn't asked for this fate, and he'd given Olivia a promise. He slashed a hand, throwing a gale to toss the first line of these corrupted vampires back into their fellows.

And then he walked forward like the unstoppable incarnation he was. Snow and ice pelted the unnatural creatures struggling to regain their footing. When one leapt at him, wind carried that person over his head and in a long arc toward the waiting army. He watched a single dart hit its chest and throw the corrupted vampire into fits as it began the painful process of shaking off the darkness in its veins.

He pushed the Fell Mad into two sections, repeatedly flinging them around like ragdolls. Neala jumped into action, her solid form disappearing into the flurries of his blizzard.

"Tell your mistress I'm coming," he snarled, throwing icicles like daggers toward the older Fell Mad who were strong enough to put up a fight despite the raging storm around them. "Tell her she's tormented the wrong man long enough!"

The cavern shuddered with his roar, wind dashing away the hint of falling rock. They moved on, leaving Lucia's thralls decimated as they endured the agony of transforming back.

Only to find that she'd saved another group waiting for them on the ceiling of the next section of tunnel. Julian batted them out of the sky the moment they tried to leap down. After this group, there were more Fell Mad. And more even still.

His storm started to lose its sharp edge, blunting on the sheer mass of bodies Lucia threw at him. There were far more of her thralls than he'd expected. Even after saving his Winter Key magic for days, the cold pits of his gut were warming.

Every storm came to an end eventually. He drew in his strength until his wake was a simple snowfall, drawing his daggers like anyone else.

"Julian, we're out of the cure," reported Luke Tsosie's clear voice. He'd taken over coordinating the covens' united army in Julian's absence, but now, he was clearly waiting for orders.

"Then we cannot spare any more mercy." He quashed a hint of regret as he leapt into combat. Lucia knew what she was doing —and he couldn't play by the rules of a monster. He was in a full battle trance now, just as his old man had taught him. Closing off the screams of the wounded or dying, he met the dangers coming at him and the allies closest to him.

He ended up back-to-back with Neala, her blade soaked in black. *"Like old times,"* she said with relish. Amidst the chaos of countless bodies, she was in her element. Nothing got within a sword's reach of her. He imagined her on a battlefield of old, her leather armor replaced with shining plates of steel. It didn't matter that her face was scarred and her body too muscular to be pretty—in motion, she was perfection of form. The true lifemate to his father, a warrior until the end of his days.

Together, they pressed on, unstoppable even without his magic as an active force. *"Lucia's buying time from us,"* he told her, feeling a trembling in his lifemate bond. Something terrible was mounting, something he could only feel from Olivia.

"These creatures are desperate." Neala surveyed the battle-field. They were inching forward at a crawl. *"They may be the last of her army."*

"We need to push harder." He could sense that they were close. Olivia's blood called to his ability, just like he called to her once more over their bond. Nothing echoed back to him.

His head started to ache with exertion as he stopped his magical storm, saving what remained of it for the confrontation to come. They had an opening to see what lay ahead. A domed bunker squatted at the end of the tunnel. It was the same color as the surrounding stone and sealed with a heavy metal door. It truly was the end of the line unless more traps lay within.

Seeing where he was looking, Neala said, *"Go. We can handle this."*

He spared her a glance, shaking his head. *"Come with me."*

"What?" she said incredulously.

"Lucia expected me to come alone. Come with me." He tore off toward the bunker.

After a few moments' thought, Neala followed. They took on the thick door together between his freezing magic and her great strength. Creating a gap where metal met metal was the hardest part, but once Neala had a good hand hold, she started breaking its internal mechanisms with sheer force. The door buckled in on itself in the shape of her hands, leaving a gap wide enough for them to slip through.

Once he'd stepped foot inside of Haven's headquarters, he sent another scream for Olivia down their mating bond. He breathed a brief sigh when her voice echoed back. *"Julian? Julian! The whispers really are a demon! It's controlling the Fell Mad too!"*

"Are you all right?" he demanded. *"Where are you?"*

"A basement somewhere!" His instincts tugged him straight downward, so he moved his feet to get to her. *"Wait. Julian, wait. They know you're here."*

"*Good.*" The bunker was oddly silent as he charged through and found a stairwell, taking the steps two at a time. He summoned a blast of wind, listening to it howl and echo wildly in this enclosed space.

"*No, you don't understand. She's going to give you to the demon!*"

Chapter 37
Olivia

Olivia looked up to see Lucia's bloodied hand wipe the man's face as he fell to his knees in anguish. "And to finish us off, the tears of a widower." She tossed her macabre trophies toward the center of the circle. They combined and flattened into a blood-red disc, reminiscent of a portal. Lucia flashed a toothy smirk Jazrach's way. "What would you do without me? Haven't I proven myself in this moment?"

The shadows making up its terrible face canted to one side. *"Your service is admirable. But I need a portal and a vessel, of which I have neither."*

Her smile faded immediately. Elandros was only just starting to move when she placed a hand on her occultarus, the other reaching out. Gwendolyn was torn from her chair with such force her rope bindings broke, leaving bloody lashes on her body. She struggled against an unseen hand as she floated closer. "Only one vampire in this world has the power to make portals." Lucia looked her over in disgust. "Take her power, so graciously offered by myself."

Gwendolyn looked the demon in the eye and muttered a phrase that had it hissing and cringing away from her. It laughed in a chorus of voices. *"What a surprise! You really were a nephilim."*

Olivia turned to Elandros, her eyes wide with panic. "Do something," she snapped.

He, too, seemed to be seized by his own fright. "W-what would you have me do?" he whimpered. "I can't kill her or I'll take on her curse."

"Then punch her in the face, knock her out. *Something*," she said, wishing she could throw her arms up in exasperation.

"*I love the taste of nephilim*," Jazrach continued. It tossed shadows at Gwendolyn, which wormed their way into her wounds. "*Too bad you're sullied with vampire blood. But this power in you. Delicious. We may not need the Alchemyst after all.*"

Its shadows exited the same way they'd come, circling the disc and making it ripple like a true portal. But its red depths seemed to intensify as it grew, turning to flames and smoke.

The ropes holding Olivia went slack, Elandros finally reaching over to free her. "Run. If they need you—you have to escape," he whispered before jackknifing to his feet. He ran at Lucia with a scream, drawing her attention in a snap. She tossed Gwendolyn like a ragdoll, and she landed against the wall with a hard *crack*. Sliding as gravity took over, the old woman clutched her hip and groaned. Darkness was trying to worm its way in her veins around the closing wounds the demon had violated.

Lucia turned to grab Elandros next with magic, tisking her disappointment. "You never announce yourself. That's a rookie mistake."

As she spoke, Olivia told herself, *You are silent, you are sneaky. Don't look at them, and they may not notice you leaving.*

She felt like a coward as she tiptoed away. *The demon wants my blood to make the portal work*, she reminded herself. It looked like a portal straight to Hell, too. The thought of more creatures as malicious as Jazrach coming to their world chilled her to the bone. But it still needed her to willingly offer up her magic, which she would never do.

The whole bunker shuddered like a bomb had gone off nearby. Wind whistled down to them, an eerie sound born out of nowhere in the musty underground of the bunker. Unfortunately, that also meant that both Jazrach and Lucia glanced at the stair-well and thus toward Olivia halfway there. With an exasperated sound, Lucia snapped her fingers and pointed, causing two of the Fell Mad to grab Olivia as she started to run.

"Pathetic," she said, shaking her head.

Struggling in vain, Olivia took heart in another blast of wind shrieking its way down. She thought of Julian and gentle snow-falls, smiling despite it feeling like her arms were being wrenched out of their sockets from rough treatment. When it was apparent she'd only damage herself trying to escape from the two cursed vampires holding her, she turned a glare at Lucia's grinning face.

"Points for effort." Lucia's clapping managed to sound sarcastic. "Do you hear that? Your mate is coming and with him, a doomed army. Behold...the doorway to our true fighting force." The portal Olivia was dragged toward practically boiled with heat as smoke started to pour through it.

"We're making contact," Jazrach said, steepling its fingers with a pleased hiss, many voices sighing in relish.

So, they *didn't* need Olivia after all. She sweated and watched the portal, wondering with trepidation what they'd do with her now.

The demon laughed, reading her thoughts. *"Don't worry, little one. We will find a different way for you to serve."*

"Julian's coming. It's happening," Lucia repeated to herself in elation.

Olivia shook her head in denial. There was a way they were still using her. Just by being here, Julian would come for her in time for them to steal him away more permanently.

Jazrach caressed Julian's name as its voices echoed it back again.

As if it summoned his presence, she felt a twinge of aware-ness along her mating bond. *"Olivia!"* Julian sounded desperate as he shouted for her.

She spoke in a flurry, trying to warn him. Trying to stop him. *"No, you don't understand,"* she found herself saying. *"She's going to give you to the demon!"*

"At last, I will have everything I wanted," Lucia crowed, throwing her head back in a laugh.

Olivia glanced over her shoulder, wondering if she should scream for him to turn back. They were defeated, and he was about to be the next victim.

"I've done everything you've asked, demon. Now you can return—" A wet gurgle cut her off. Olivia whipped around to see the ginger-haired man behind her, her forgotten dagger embedded in her chest. It was too far up to hit her heart, her chest sucking as she took a surprised breath.

Just a few inches more, she thought with a sigh.

He withdrew to stab her again. "You killed my wife! You don't deserve anything, you *bitch!*"

She released her hold on Elandros to send the other man sprawling off her, the dagger flipping to clatter to the ground harmlessly. Lucia released a cry of rage as lightning crackled over her fingertips, arcing to punish him.

Olivia felt the pressure on her arms release as both men holding her fell at the same time. A front of cold blew in, battling back the heat of Jazrach and its portal.

"Julian," she breathed, turning to see him and Neala's figures partially obscured by a swirling blizzard of energy. He looked like a wraith with glowing blue eyes, arm extended to fire more icicles like the ones that'd struck her captors.

"Julian, *no!*" she cried a moment later as Jazrach turned and laughed at his presence. She moved back to shield him, as if she could chase the shadows away with just her body.

"Your obsession is here," it whispered to Lucia. *"Too bad I hate the cold."*

The demon dissipated into a black mist, flowing not for Julian, but for Elandros still trying to catch his breath from the vice grip of Lucia's magic. He breathed in a deadly dose of Jazrach, grabbing his throat as the shadows forced their way into his mouth like a funnel.

Olivia screamed as his body started to seize, bending at unnatural angles.

Lucia shrieked in impotent rage and whirled on Julian, her hands sparking with electricity. "If he will not have you, then I will be rid of you at last. You killed my lifemate. Prepare to die!"

Chapter 38
Julian

Julian pulled Olivia behind him. "Take shelter," he whispered to her in the eye of his storm before turning to Lucia. She was flushed, two tears marking black rivulets upon her ruined face.

Neala slipped off to dispatch the remaining Fell Mad in the room, leaving him to face the Sorceress alone. "My father was not your lifemate," he said, summoning every last shred of winter within him for the fight to come.

"Liar!" she roared, throwing lightning. He sidestepped, her magic leaving a black mark where he'd been standing. "Charlatan! Wearing your father's face to mock me!" She hurled more bolts with ease, keeping him moving.

"You took him from the woman he belonged with. You ruined him!" He threw a wave of ice back at her, watching the sharpened tips melt as they encountered the ambient heat in this enclosed space. Cursing to himself, he knew he was at the disadvantage here. Neala was fighting other people, Olivia was hunkering down behind him, and Gwendolyn and Elandros were both disabled. He caught a glimpse of Gwendolyn dragging herself by her arms toward the writhing man.

How could he win this fight without help? Lucia had taken a wound to her chest at some point, but it'd already healed up to a glossy rip of black on the otherwise immaculate color of her dress.

She continued hurling lightning, and he realized what he needed to do. He advanced like the unstoppable wall of a storm. His blizzard melted to unpleasant humidity as it encountered the molten-hot disc behind her. He paid it little mind because he had no other choice. Lucia was using fire now, melting through his magic until it was just the wind and the dampness of rain soaking through her hair and clothes. He kept his storm going, using cold rain despite it evaporating.

Olivia flashed by his line of sight, distracting him for the split second Lucia needed to throw a fireball straight into his chest. The cold in him crackled as his skin seared, his shirt melting from the intense heat. "Let it be known that I was the one who melted the heir to the Winter Key!" she roared. Another fireball formed between her palms as she gestured, flicking the heat up higher and higher.

What was his lifemate doing? He'd told her to take shelter, not to run back into the room. His hands clenched to fists as he felt his magic sputtering its last gasps of chill. As long as he was numb, he couldn't feel his flesh screaming alongside the smell of its burn.

He had one good push left within him. The longer they stalled, the less he felt he could call upon. Rain fell around them with the forceful droplets of a tropical storm, fizzling off the fireball she sent flying at him. It tested his footwork as it exploded into smaller, white-hot missiles. One sizzled into his thigh, burning through wet material.

Lucia laughed as she watched him scrape the magic from his skin. "Stop struggling! It'd hurt less to give up." She lashed out with a line of flames, scorching his side as he rushed forward. He felt the heat this time, the pain nearly debilitating. His chest hurt; his lungs seized with a spasm of agony. All the same, he forced himself to dash for her, grabbing her mid-cast of another fireball. It seared already burning skin in a flash of white-hot pain, so bright he thought he might white out.

No. He couldn't let her win. He'd come all this way to save his lifemate, and that was what he was going to do. No Fell Mad, no demon, no Lucia could stop him. Lifting her over his head, he threw her with a grunt as charred skin pulled from the effort. She sailed away from the oppressive heat of the portal, back toward the stairwell.

He gathered up every shred of magic, the last whisper of cold left within him, and exhaled on a cloud of vapor as the water soaking Lucia turned to ice. She became a living statue of frozen menace, only her open mouth free of ice but stuck in a grotesque snarl.

Heat rushed in all at once. He was hot all over, burning up with seared, damaged skin and muscle that itched as his body struggled to repair itself before he overexerted and caused another serious injury.

"Julian!" Olivia hollered. She threw the heavy manacles of a pair of nephilim chains in his direction. As he rushed to grab them, the ice encasing Lucia startled to crackle and split. He cursed his fatigue as he scooped up the chains, but he could already tell he wouldn't reach her in time.

Of course, he wasn't alone. Not truly. Neala got to Lucia before him, grasping her wrist right before she could reach her occultarus and command another spell. *"Let it be known that Julian Fairfax was the one to freeze your machinations in their place."* She gave the woman's wrist a brutal twist and caught the edge of the occultarus as Lucia attempted to call it to her other hand.

He rushed to clap her broken wrist in the magical chains, watching with relief as her magical tool went unresponsive and thumped to the ground. Lucia turned a hate-filled glare his way as he finished the job with her other wrist. "Cheap trick," she spat before rounding on Neala. "And you! You weren't even supposed to be here."

"Guess you'll have to keep my infirmary bed warm for me." Neala punctuated that with a hilt strike to the back of her skull, sending Lucia unconscious in a heap of broken ice.

Julian clutched his knees, breathing in ragged gasps now that it was done. "We did it," he said, resisting the urge to kick her while she was out. He'd save it for when she was wide awake and spitting like a cobra. Now that they'd caught her, she would need to go on trial for her crimes against vampire kind. They couldn't have an execution, not with her curse, but maybe Gwendolyn could lock her away where she took all vampires too possessed by the legacy of the Fell.

"*Not yet,*" Neala said solemnly, pointing. Across the room, Elandros still writhed and cursed. Gwendolyn knelt by his side, crossing the air and praying over him. Attempting to hold him down was Olivia, though her gaze was fixed upon the red-hot portal still growing in the center of the room.

Dark magic was still afoot. They might've cut off the source, but there was the demon that was Lucia's partner and whatever unholy magic they'd been casting before he arrived.

Worst of all, Julian didn't think he could help. His magic was burned up, and exhaustion pressed in on a tail of bloodlust leaving a needling spike in his middle. Burned flesh tore as he fell, trembling, to one knee.

Olivia's attention flashed to him. "*Will you be okay?*" she asked, horrified as she took in his terrible wounds.

"*I will be, bella,*" he assured, though he wasn't so sure as he felt the heat pulsing from the portal.

"*We'll get through this. Promise,*" she said.

Chapter 39
Olivia

Olivia promised her wounded mate something she wasn't so sure about. Jazrach was laughing in its chilling chorus of voices as Gwendolyn continued to mutter above its victim with her hands clasped.

"You're not a nephilim anymore. What makes you think you can exorcise anyone?" it mocked.

While it struggled for control of Elandros's body, the portal continued to grow in strength. Some part of her had hoped that an unconscious Lucia would mean that it would stop, but it was a vain thought. She couldn't interrupt Gwendolyn, not when a life hung in the balance.

"He's mine. Why bother slowing the inevitable?"

Olivia left the two of them to turn to the portal. Shadows and smoke moved on the other side, creatures presumably noticing the weakening hole between worlds and preparing to clamber through. The worst possible thing for their world would be an invasion of demons. It'd only taken meeting one demon for her to realize that.

In their brief interaction, Nyah had taught her a lot. She'd been the one to give her hope, to show her that there was a way to share her golden blood more easily.

You are a force of change for all things magical.

The portal to Hell was magical. It might've needed her to

come to fruition if the Portal Key within Gwendolyn wasn't so potent. She spared one last glance back at the Ancient deep in prayer.

"Don't you know what he took from you?" Jazrach hissed. *"Don't you know what he did?"*

"She doesn't care. Stop wasting your breath," Olivia muttered.

The demon laughed in a chorus of voices. A furrow appeared between Gwendolyn's brows as its mocking seemed to echo. *"You mean to tell me she doesn't care about the fate of her husband, the great Gabriel Legion? How Elandros, his most trusted pupil, was the one to murder him?"*

Gwendolyn's eyes snapped with a gasp. As her litany of prayer ceased, Elandros's body went slack.

Gazing down at him with numb shock, Olivia realized he was dead. His chest was still, his eyes glazed over. "Oh. Oh no. No," she said, tears streaking her face. All her worries spilled over in that moment. That a demon could end the life of one of the most powerful Ancients just like that...

"It...it is in the past," Gwendolyn said with heavy effort, her expression stricken. "I...I forgive you. Elandros, I forgive you." She shook his shoulder. "Wake up. Quit your foolishness. You did everything Adrius asked and more. You're one of us now."

Her hands shook, just like her voice as it broke. "No. No...I couldn't have failed. The heavens have always listened before. No demon has succeeded under my watch." Olivia caught sight of the band of darkness around Gwendolyn's arms fading rapidly as she spoke. Magic haloed her, something new and bright.

Below her, Elandros opened his eyes. But it wasn't him anymore. Darkness swam across his sclera, eating up the white to leave the maroon pupils swimming in a sea of black. "It's not your fault. Heaven doesn't shine upon vampires. They would turn to ash," the demon said with Elandros's voice as he drew breath once more.

Olivia jumped away with a cry of alarm as he started to flex his new muscles. The glow around Gwendolyn heated, nearly burning the air. When she opened her mouth, her fangs were receding into blunt, human teeth. She seemed to grow as change rapidly seized her, casting a long shadow. "I've had enough of you, foul creature," she cried, summoning light to her palm.

She looked at it with undisguised awe. And then she turned it on Jazrach in an explosion of radiance. "*Back, demon!*" her voice called from the center of the blast.

Olivia felt the sizzle of magic as it hit her skin. Like standing next to the sun—beautiful, but deadly. She flung herself forward only to be caught, swung around, and sheltered behind the bulk of Neala. "*Incredible. Impossible,*" the other woman whispered.

When the light faded, leaving spots over her vision, Olivia grasped at Neala's tunic. "Do you have something sharp? Something...clean?" she asked, having seen the smear of black on her sword and Julian's daggers.

Producing an unused blade for her from her boot, Neala cocked an eyebrow as Olivia took it. "There's something I have to do," was all she said as she approached the burning portal that'd gone unchecked for too long. She looked over to see Gwendolyn unconscious.

A badly burned Elandros clutched at his face, screaming wordlessly. The demon inside him couldn't stop her now. But she would stop his plan cold...if this worked.

You are a force of change for all things magical, she reminded herself with a grounding swallow.

This was a mess. A disaster. Olivia thought of the one person she wanted more than anything to be here with them. Someone with poise and calm. Taking a deep breath, she cut herself fingertip to elbow, biting down on her lip to muffle a scream. The blood welling from the wound was pure gold. She clenched her fist to keep the precious substance from leaking to the floor.

"You're not a portal to Hell. Not anymore," she told the floating disk as it belched sulfur stink. Something on the other side brushed claws over the surface, trying to reach her. If she lingered too long, it'd be able to pass through, just as Jazrach intended.

Olivia couldn't let that happen. Before she could second

guess or let her wound close, she plunged her arm into the portal up to the elbow. *Either I lose my arm or...*

She made her wishes known to her magic with a fierce grit of her teeth. She wanted to change the portal's location. No longer did it reach into the depths of Hell—the heat left it with a sputter. Holding her breath, she felt her elbow rotating, but not the rest of her arm. She was afraid to pull back, worried only a stump would remain.

That was, until someone else's fingers wrapped around hers. She pulled back inch by inch, revealing her arm, unhurt, and a portal shimmering with darkness. Pale fingers followed hers into the humid cellar, followed by an elegant wrist...a smooth arm clasped in leather.

Stumbling the rest of the way after her came Queen Nyah, her delicate face peeled back in a snarl. "What is the meaning of —oh." Her golden eyes rounded in shock as she took in their surroundings.

Where her shoes touched, the ground rippled with a wave of new life. Grass and budding flowers surrounded Nyah. A butterfly fluttered down to perch on the first pink blossom.

"No time to explain—demon!" Olivia pointed a shaky finger toward...nothing. Elandros's body was gone, leaving only wisps of darkness behind.

"There was...he was right there." He must've run when he saw that his portal was neutralized.

Nyah's nostrils flared, and her expression hardened further. "You're right—I can smell something lingering." She took a few steps away from the portal to survey where she was, her gaze landing on Gwendolyn. Her hand flew to her lips to muffle her shock. "Mother?" She rushed over to kneel by her side.

"Nyah?" Neala met her by her mother's side. The two of them embraced and clung to one another. *"You're alive. After all this time."* She sounded choked up, even mentally.

Meanwhile, from the portal came someone else's head, a cross expression across her cloudy eyes. "What is this strange portal in the middle of my living room?" Izell growled.

"Thank God you're here," Olivia said, feeling herself relax at last. The moment her shoulders fell, it felt like she was hit with a wave of exhaustion so potent she swayed on her feet. She may have changed the portal with her blood, but it had its consequences.

Strong hands caught her before she could start to tip backward. Julian put his arms around her middle, resting her carefully against his wounded chest. She winced as she felt the twinge of pain from even that slight touch. But both of them needed the comfort of each other after what they'd been through. "I told you I would come for you," he murmured against her hair, laying a kiss at her crown.

"You did it—you beat Lucia," she whispered back, feeling a flush of pride for him in the middle of her muddled emotional state. With so much going on, her empathy had tapped out, leaving her with only her own tangled feelings.

He echoed that feeling back to her, their mating bond alive and well so close to each other. "And you stopped the demon's plans. How...?" He was looking at the portal and the strange fae climbing out of it. Now that she saw Izell in the flesh, she realized the fae had a long, whip-like tail that flicked behind her like an irritated snake as she circled the portal, making the occasional motion toward it with her impressively long claws.

"My blood changes magic. And...I really thought we could use some help," she admitted. "We already talked to these two, so I knew they were out there."

"Alchemyst!" Izell was pointing one of those claws straight at her now. "You owe me an explanation!"

She put up her hands defensively at her sharp tone. "I'll explain, I promise. It's just...we've been through a lot..."

Izell marched toward her with the lithe stride of a predator. "Indeed. I smell the magic in the air. And you are injured, large vampire." She seemed to eye Julian, as difficult as it was to track the motion when she had no pupils. Despite her comment on his size, she scraped six feet tall herself. "Nyah!" she called.

The queen looked up mid-sentence to Neala. "Yes?" She glanced to Julian when Izell gestured, gasping as her gaze roved his burnt clothing. She bustled over to him. "So sorry. I can't believe I didn't see...hold on."

She snapped her fingers, making a flower appear in her palm. She offered it to Julian. "Eat this, would you? Great curative for burns. The magic in it will be like you rubbed a nice, cool salve on yourself. Doesn't that feel better?" She asked this as he took the flower and gingerly put it in his mouth, chewing while holding down an obvious gag reflex.

"Oh yeah, much better," he muttered as he crunched on the stem.

"You're not supposed to—whoops. The stem is the really bitter part," Nyah said, giggling as he pulled a face.

Despite that, the heat radiating from his burns was already fading, coming down from an angry lobster red as he sighed with relief. Nyah and Izell were the first of them to look up as boots sounded down the stairwell. A group of vampires with Luke at their helm stepped into the cellar, glancing around. One whistled low at the carnage.

Julian signaled Luke over with a wave. "Status?" he asked.

Luke flashed a tired smile. "We won."

Chapter 40
Julian

Julian insisted on carrying Olivia out of that literal hell hole despite being the more injured of the two of them. Some scars lingered below the surface, and he could tell that Olivia had seen things that would stay with her forever. He was so proud and thankful for her as he emerged from Haven's headquarters with Nyah and Izell bringing up the rear. The fae was carrying Gwendolyn with cradled care, while behind her, buoyed by magic, bobbed the bodies of two people he didn't trust himself—or anyone else—to remove from there without doing harm to them.

One was Lucia, haphazardly veiled to hide her monstrous features. The other, a surprise to him, was an unconscious and badly injured Bryant Collins, leader of Haven. Alex would be keenly interested in hearing how they'd acquired him despite Olivia's tale of his bravery in the face of Kim Cox's gruesome death. The man still had a lot to answer for when he allied with Lucia in the first place, not even including his centuries-long grudge against Coven Rehnquist.

He kept Olivia talking so her attention wouldn't turn to the battleground they passed through. Once she started telling the story of what'd happened and the demonic ritual she'd been forced to watch, it was like she couldn't stop. Izell listened keenly behind him but didn't interrupt or question, instead murmuring to Nyah.

"Where is everyone?" he asked after a while, realizing most of the multi-coven army was missing.

"One of our allies opened a portal to safety. The able-bodied are transporting those we could save," Luke said from the front of their group. He led them straight to that portal, where many of the brave men and women who'd fought were passing unconscious victims through. Julian felt the attention of several turn to him, respectful nods rippling toward him like a wave.

He didn't think too much of it until they were on the other side, where Charlotte and Armando were amongst those waiting to help. They were in Coven Rehnquist's mansion, and a few portals on the other side of the foyer were funneling victims to a safe place. "You got her!" Armando exclaimed.

"He did. He saved me again," Olivia smiled, resting a hand gently on Julian's chest. The remnants of a burn twinged under her palm, feeling more like a sunburn than the burnt flesh from a magical attack.

Armando's smile faded to a look of wonder. "And who is that?"

Julian fully expected to turn around and see beautiful Nyah with her crown of gold and butterflies, but the woman who had his nephew going slack-jawed was Izell, shielding her overlarge eyes from the sudden influx of ambient light. She had not glamored over her fae features, leaving several people to stop and stare as the recovery effort ground to a halt.

"What? Never see a lady before?" Izell grumped, realizing the attention her appearance had earned.

Sorsha leaned out from behind one of the portals, her expression shading to childish wonder. "By the stars," she gasped. "Izell...you can't just...how...?" She bustled over to take her elbow and guide her to the infirmary. "Sorry, everyone. Carry on!" Behind Izell bobbed their two prisoners. Julian was only half tempted to follow, figuring they were in good hands.

"So, Bloodhound. Some of us are trying to figure how to combine your old name with your new one. Any suggestions?" Charlotte asked.

He blinked in confusion. "I have a new name?"

"Well, yeah. You can't just turn into a gigantic storm and assume no one was gonna name you after it." She shrugged with both hands. "My money's on Hurricane Bloodhound. It's got a ring to it."

He eyed her askance and shook his head, pivoting to head upstairs as Olivia laughed heartily at his expense.

Julian did his reporting to Alex mentally, sharing events for both him and his mate. *"You're a living legend now, you know?"* his coven master said dryly. *"Word gets around fast when you take on Lucia and win."*

"Violet did it before," he pointed out.

"Yes, but no one who gossips was there that day. Except me. And how was I going to explain that my mate prevented an other-worldly invasion of monsters that no one had heard of before our Fell Mad incident? Especially when I'm hearing rumors that there were no monsters all along."

Julian glanced to the closed shower door, where Olivia was probably deep-scrubbing herself. *"Olivia prevented the demon invasion. I just did what I had to."*

There was a pause on Alex's end. *"Good job. Take some time off, Hurricane Bloodhound. You deserve it."* He cut the mental connection as Julian spluttered. Now he just had to hope that silly nickname didn't stick.

Once he had his turn in the shower, he found Olivia in bed, a pillow over her head. "I'm not sure I'll be able to sleep," she admitted when he laid out with her. She shifted to peel back the covers over his bare chest, which was improving by the hour. A good rest and no one would know he'd nearly been incinerated.

"Me neither." The early hours of morning brought back everything he'd suppressed in the midst of battle. The screams especially. "It helps to think about something else."

Olivia, usually a font of random thoughts, stared at him blankly. "I nearly lost you. I saw the demon consider taking you instead of Elandros." She pressed herself close, holding him tightly.

He'd meant for her to dwell on happier thoughts but stroked her back as they sank into one another's embrace. "I know. I saw it too. If I were a cat, I'd have one life left. And I know who I'd want to live it with."

A smile tugged at her lips. "Yeah, well, it's dangerous to dwell on 'what if's' right?"

"It is. And I would go through worse to get you back from danger," he said with all his heart and soul. Even if the demon had tried to possess him, he knew he'd give it the fight of its life for the attempt. "I love you, and I will *always* come for you."

Her golden eyes sparkled of their own accord. "I love you too. I'm so lucky you're mine."

"No, I'm lucky to have you." He flashed her a tender smile. "You made it possible for us to save countless lives. In the long run, that's more important than any showy magic from me. What remains of two covens is now in your debt. But...that's not important right now."

She hummed curiously as he unplugged the clock radio by their bedside. "I've earned some time off. We don't need an alarm." Without it, the only way to know the passage of time would be when the shutters closed to block out sunshine right before dawn.

"Let's play a game," he said. "Ask me anything."

"Only my favorite kind of game." Their conversation veered away from the horrors of the night as they discussed things they'd seen and done. Julian kept her talking until her lids were heavy and she drifted to sleep safe in his arms.

Chapter 41
Nyah

Nyah no longer considered the passage of time in days and nights. Three thousand years in the Fell Lands, a place of eternal darkness, had thrown off her rhythm. Her old friends spoke of a thousand years of distance between them, and she didn't have the heart to remind them again that time passed much more slowly in the land of punishment she'd been banished to.

The young Alchemyst had defied all odds in bringing her back to Earth and opening the way for a permanent portal to help others escape. It'd originated of demon magic, but Olivia had twisted it into something good to help countless souls with the misfortune to be born in or banished to the wrong place.

A handful of her most trusted healers had already crossed over to assist the recovery effort. Coven Rehnquist's infirmary was where she stayed, attending to a mix of old faces and new. Most got up within a day of being admitted, waking from the stupor of going from full Fell Mad back to their senses.

Eventually, all she had left was the familiar. She started at the back of the infirmary, heart in her throat. It'd been ages since she'd been so excited to see another person, the one still resting in the first bed. She stayed away so she didn't constantly check on someone who deserved some privacy.

Her mother lay at the end of a row, her hands crossed peacefully over her chest. "Why hasn't she awakened?" she asked Izell as they both leaned over her for a routine check.

Gwendolyn was one of the last people she'd expected to see still alive, though it felt like her hold on her mortal form was fading. The two Keys on her hand flared to life when she held Gwendolyn's frail hand in her own. Used in tandem for ages, the Spring and Autumn Keys were capable of incredible feats together.

She poured pure life magic into her mother as Izell considered, tapping a claw against her chin. "Fell Mad to vampire is just the lifting of a curse. Vampire to nephilim? Who's heard of such a thing?"

"Not that vampire to human should even be possible," Nyah pointed out. She gave Gwendolyn as much life magic as she could hold, smoothing out wrinkles and adding definition to weakened muscles. Not even magic like hers could keep a mortal alive forever—but for her mother, she could try to buy as much time as possible.

"Jazrach only confirmed my hypothesis," Izell said. Her tail flicked behind her as they moved to the next person, his arms strung up with nephilim chains. Jaromir insisted on them as a precaution. Despite several rounds of potions, his affliction was slow to clear. Black veins still dominated his skin.

He came in and out of awareness during his treatment. For the moment, he was awake. "What hypothesis was that?" he asked curiously. Darkness tinged his eyes, but his teeth were receded back to two vampire fangs.

"Fell, and by extension your race, are the result of demonic influence," Izell said, touching his nose gently with the tip of a claw. Nyah's lips quirked in quiet amusement. Very few men caught her attention. At some point, she figured Izell was too old and quirky to seek such base pleasures as those found in another's arms. That she'd choose to flirt with gentle Jaromir was something she completely encouraged.

"What a delightful thought." His voice was free of bite, just a sigh like he expected something else to kick him while he was down.

"Isn't it just?" She chuckled dryly. "Don't you worry. We've figured out a permanent cure for all things Fell-related. If you don't improve, we can put you through it too."

He gazed at her hopefully as Nyah prepared a purification potion for him to try. It was easy for her with a mortar and pestle, as she created all the ingredients she needed with a flick of her wrist and a glimmer of her Keys. "You can go through a companionship trial like all good little fae do in school," Izell explained. "We've...modified the trial some." She stroked her scaly forearm meaningfully.

Jaromir's brow creased with confusion. "Animal spirits are completely immune to Fell corruption," Nyah supplied as Izell put on a teasing smile. "So, a merging of spirit and man is also immune. Corruption gets expelled, but the results can vary."

"We call the combination shifters," Izell said. "You and your spirit jockey for control and decide if you'll be a man, an animal, or something in between. My dragon and I decided to be in between."

"I'm sorry, madam. I thought you just said dragon," he said politely.

Izell grinned to show off her fangs. "You don't see chompers like this on just anyone, do you?"

Nyah nudged her to the side, offering Jaromir a freshly mixed potion. He opened his mouth to receive it, used to the routine. "I'm a shifter, too," she confided as he finished, causing him to choke on the last swallow. She patted his back as he coughed. "Sorry, old friend. It was a necessary decision."

"What animal?" he asked after he'd gained his breath back. His lids were starting to lower as the medicine did its work within him.

"A wolf. Someday, I'll show you," she promised as he drifted off to sleep.

While Izell wore her shifter status out in the open, she did it because she was proud of what she was and the creature she was bound with. Her dragon spirit had been her companion nearly since she'd learned to walk—making him one of the oldest beings in this land and the next.

On the other hand, Nyah preferred the human form she was born with. Her wolf spirit, Night's Howl, rested within her when she was not fulfilling her most taxing duty as a trial guide.

As they moved to the next bed, she saw someone she was sure would need a trial. Taryn had stopped conversing or responding at all. His glassy black eyes were fixed to the ceiling. Nyah's empathy told her that she was looking at someone made whole only at the thought of revenge. He was one of several reasons why Lucia was locked away in a more secure location.

"Going to talk to us today?" Izell asked, poking his shoulder.

As expected, he didn't say a word. Several injections of purification potion had not broken a moment of his Fell Madness. And frankly, Nyah couldn't blame him. He would have to forget the greater part of his life at this point to let go of the vendetta searing in his veins. Unfortunately for all involved, his rage would lead him to kill innocents, as the Madness would induce hallucinations of the person he wanted most to strangle.

They left him with another injection, just in case it would help. Nyah could only take him back to her kingdom when the dust settled on the last battle. Eventually, she would set him down the path of self-control with a spirit trial, but until then, the potion would have to suffice.

Izell walked ahead of her as Nyah pushed her supply cart into a corner and drew the privacy curtains around her friends and mother as they rested. She busied her hands with growing nerves until the fae beckoned her over. Nyah felt her shoulders tense up as Izell said, "He's awake."

Her heart leapt to her throat. They'd waited for this moment for days, feeling the molten-hot Shield Key attempting to return Adrius to life. His last death was clean—but Sirius had haltingly told her not to expect much from this reunion when he was dismissed from the infirmary with a clean bill of health.

Which was nonsense, really. Nyah had waited three thousand years with the hope in her heart to see her mate and husband once more. They were the starriest of star-crossed lovers, and in his absence, none but duty had filled the void in her heart.

She hurried to Adrius's bedside as Izell stepped back and drew the curtain to give them a moment alone.

Adrius was paler and thinner than she remembered, dark bruises under his eyes as he stared down at the manacles in his lap. A Fell Mad precaution he didn't seem to need on first glance.

She'd imagined this moment so many times. How he would smile like sunshine to see her again. She had so much to tell him, so many wonders and horrors that she'd seen in their long separation. "Adrius?" she said with a hopeful smile. "Adrius, it's been so long, and I've missed you dreadfully. The nights were long and cold, but now fate shines upon me to be at your side once more."

His gaze lifted to hers slowly, his brow crinkling in confusion. There was no recognition there, nor any sign of the smile she'd waited three thousand years for. Instead, he asked, "Who are you?"

**Will Adrius gain his memories back? Find out in...
Queen's Return: Blood Legacy Series Book 3**

Also by Elise Hennessy
Altare World

Are you ready for a high-flying adventure on gryphon-back? Join Sivana as she becomes the first female cadet at the highly competitive Gryphon Rider Academy after the blind gryphon Arimus chooses her as his new rider.

Dragon Riders of Pern meets Song of the Lioness in this YA fantasy series in which a pair of underdogs rewrite what's possible in a formerly all-boys military academy.

- See Gryphon Rider Academy on Amazon -

About the Author

Elise Hennessy is an author of young adult fantasy full of adventure and found family. She holds a master's degree in journalism and enjoys crafting unique stories. When Elise is not busy writing, she's trying to reduce her prodigious TBR list. She lives in Texas with her family and is owned by two cats.

Find out more about her books at: www.elisehennessy.com

Glossary

Alchemyst: An incredibly rare sub-distinction of vampire with golden blood. They can create powerful tonics and potions with one drop of their life essence. They are immortal, but lack the superhuman aspects of vampirism and the bloodlust.

Blade: A fae skilled with martial magic and a weapon of choice, usually a sword. Traditionally they serve as bodyguards to Sorcerers.

Blood Prince: A title given to the few Fell Hunters that survived the Fell Crisis. They are the first vampires and each started their own unique bloodlines.

Coven: A group of three or more vampires, assembled for the protection of its members. Large covens establish territory where they can hunt with reasonable assurance that they are safe. Coven members are sheltered by their coven master, the oldest and strongest vampire in the group. A vampire without a coven is considered a rogue and often live short lives due to vampires' natural territorial tendencies.

The Crossing: Seelie fae can cross The Veil and travel between Earth and Faerie or vice versa during midsummer in a magical process called The Crossing. The only way to otherwise cross between the two worlds is through one of a handful of well-hidden portals.

Deveaux Accords: A set of laws created by the major covens of New York City and enforced by Ancient vampiress Cossette Deveaux. Covens are required to police their members to keep mortals safe.

Dhampir: A half-human, half-vampire by birth.

Eyes of Worlds: A pair of giant tools that anchor The Veil into place. One was created by the willing sacrifice of an Archangel—it is the Light Eye located in Faerie. The other was created from an unwilling greater demon and became its prison—it was destroyed during the events of *Dream Walker*.

Faerie: A separate world magically linked to Earth. The place of origin for all magic and mythical creatures.

Fell: A fae afflicted with a curse of eternal hunger. The curse was spread from Fell to fae via a bite and was considered incurable. Fell are twisted creatures known for squat, frog-like legs, sharp and interconnected teeth like a bear trap, black veins, and pitch-black eyes. All Fell were banished from Faerie to The Fell Lands. The Fell Crisis or Fell War occurred when the Fell learned they could create portals to Earth during the Dark Ages and began consuming man and beast alike like a black tide of locusts. After their defeat, all records of the Fell were expunged from mortal record to hide the existence of vampires.

Fell Hunter: The first vampires. Soldiers exposed to Fell blood became strong and fast enough to fight Fell in the service to humanity. Though the first Fell Hunters were turned by accident, many were turned on purpose after the phenomenon was studied. In those days, being a vampire was considered a sacrifice for the greater good. Most Fell Hunters died fighting monsters.

Glossary

Fell Keys: Thirteen in total, referring to a set of rings with gemstones of pure magic. Each one represents one of the schools of fae magic and grants the wearer great power.

Fell Madness: The boogeyman of vampirism. First manifested in Fell Hunters when they consumed too much Fell blood. Fell Madness gives vampires black veins, a mouthful of sharp teeth, and endless hunger for blood. Very little is known about the affliction because those that manifested it were swiftly executed. In modern day, the affliction can be cured by an Alchemyst's potion.

The Gift: Some vampires manifest the Gift rather than the abilities of their bloodline. They are capable of healing others from even the worst of mortal wounds. The Gift leaves if a vampire uses it to harm or kill others.

Lifemate: A perfect match to a vampire. It is possible to identify a lifemate on sight and many vampires describe the sensation as being as subtle as a punch to the gut. A lifemate is usually a vampire's perfect opposite. It is possible for a vampire to have more than one lifemate, but the phenomenon is exceedingly rare as most vampires don't survive to an advanced age if they lose their first lifemate.

Nephilim: A person with angel parentage, who is capable of wielding light magic. Nephilim are considered extinct in modern day due to The Veil and the Heaven-Hell Accords.

Nyixa Island: A chunk of The Fell Lands that the Fell managed to drag to Earth. It is a relatively large island with the Dark Eye at its center. After the Fell were defeated, vampires made it their seat of power before it was sunk to the bottom of the ocean in a bid to eradicate Fell Madness. It has only resurfaced recently in modern times and is considered inhabitable.

Occultarus: A tool used by Sorcerers to concentrate their magic. Instead of using complicated gestures to summon magic, a Sorcerer can hold an occultarus and cast spells more quickly. An occultarus is a sphere of glass forged by dragon fire and contains concentrated magic within. The Eyes of Worlds were modeled after occultari and are giant versions of them.

Seelie Fae: Greater fae who aligned with angels before The Veil separated Faerie from Heaven and Hell. Their tongues are cursed to utter only the truth. While Faerie is at peace now, Seelie and Unseelie have historically been at war along the same lines as their patrons. Their sub-races are terran fae (earth), solar fae (fire), astral fae (water), and aether fae (wind).

Spellbreaker: A fae skilled in reflecting or mitigating magic. A highly trained Spellbreaker can render a Sorcerer's magic useless.

Sorcerer: Originally a distinction for the rare fae who can control all thirteen schools of magic, this title is also awarded to the sub-class of vampire that has silver blood and the ability to control every school of fae magic. Sorcerers are highly trained and often manifest extra rare abilities called virtues. The five virtues are: true sight, future sight, empathy, druidism, and mediumship.

Unseelie Fae: Greater fae who aligned with demons before The Veil separated Faerie from Heaven and Hell. Their tongues are cursed to utter only lies. While Faerie is at peace now, Seelie and Unseelie have historically been at war along the same lines as their patrons. Their sub-races are curse fae (earth), destruction fae (fire), death fae (water), and blight fae (wind).

Vampire: Descendants of the original Fell Hunters, spread by their cursed blood. The existence of vampires has become a myth to modern mortals as the purpose of vampires has tarnished from war heroes into former mortals trying to avoid their mortal coil. Contrary to popular myth, vampires are not walking corpses; they eat, breathe, and reproduce, though the chance of conception narrows as a vampire ages. Young vampires act a lot like humans with a taste for blood, though as they age they grow more powerful and inhuman. Vampires manifest an aura, which communicate to each other how old and powerful they are.

The Veil: A magical barrier that separates Earth and Faerie from the realms of Heaven and Hell. Anchored in place by the Eyes of Worlds, it's been in place for over a thousand Earth years and prevented the worlds from coming to ruin by being battle-grounds for angels and demons.

Cast of Characters

Modern Day Vampires
Residents of New York City's covens.

Alexander Rehnquist

A vampire nearing his five hundredth year. Master of Coven Rehnquist and skilled shapeshifter. He is bitter rivals with Bryant Collins and lost his first lifemate due to the conflict between their covens. Fate crossed him one night and he ended up partnered with a second lifemate, Violet Reynolds.

Violet Reynolds

Formerly a mortal zookeeper, Violet was exposed to vampirism after Lucia secretly turned her into a kind of vampire that hadn't been seen in a thousand years. She became a silver-blooded Sorceress, learned how to master her magic, and captured Alex's love.

Julian Fairfax

One of the officers of Coven Rehnquist. The only vampire who mysteriously manifests an icy cold aura. He searched for his life-mate for hundreds of years until they were united via Lucia's machinations. He was viciously hunted by Lucia due to him killing her obsession.

Cast of Characters

Olivia Cooper

A struggling mortal actress who was kidnapped to New York. She knows of the vampire world due to her best friend, Charlotte, but was quickly over her head after turning into a vampire.

Charlotte Smith

Olivia's best friend and the only dhampir around. She is loyal and protective of her friend, joining Coven Rehnquist when Olivia did.

Armando Nizzola

Julian's cousin and a member of the supernatural police.

Bryant Collins

A bitter rival to Alex and Coven Rehnquist. He owns the telecommunications company Haven and thus members of his coven are referred to as Haveners. He is an Ancient a religious zealot, and one of Lucia's allies.

Kim Cox

Bryant Collins's wife, known for her sadistic personality and enjoyment of torturing others.

Cossette Deveaux

The Ancient leader of the most powerful coven in New York City. She is an albino and a rare vampire who possesses future sight. She is stuck in the body of a little girl due to the twisted ideals of her vampire master. Due to her unique circumstances, her mind is damaged. She usually acts like a cheerful and sweet girl, but sometimes shows hints of her age as she delivers prophecies of the future.

Ancients

Surviving Fell Hunters whose bloodlines have shaped the vampire world in their absence.

Cast of Characters

Adrius

King of Vampires
Strongest Fell Hunter and owner of the Shield Key. He fell into a deep pit of depression to be separated from his lifemate, Nyah. Possesses every vampiric ability.

Lucia

The first vampire Sorceress and briefly Queen of Vampires in *Blood Curse* while struggling with the titular curse. Nyixa was sunk partially to contain her evil.

Gwendolyn Firetree

A nephilim who represents the grace of duty. Conspired to sink Nyixa in *Blood Curse* to contain Fell Madness and Lucia. She has committed her immortal existence to curbing the damage of old vampires on the brink of Fell Madness by making them mysteriously "disappear."

Sirius

Blood Prince Sirius, the Dawn
Adrius's second-in-command and brother. Was once a kind and giving man, but emerged from his thousand-year rest bitter, angry, and unable to fully control the whims of his inner beast. He is a shapeshifter and possesses the ability to walk in daylight without harm.

Korin

Blood Prince Korin, the Bane
The gentle giant of the Ancients, a steady and quiet personality. He is a blood tracker.

Neala

Blood Princess Neala, the Wraith
A mute orphan raised by Gabriel and Gwendolyn. She defied the odds and survived the Fell Crisis, though she sustained several terrible wounds that scarred her face and chest. Despite being an illusionist, she refuses to hide her scars or make herself more

269

attractive and feminine. Loved and lost her first mate, Marcus Hartson, to Lucia's machinations.

Elandros

Blood Prince Elandros, the Legion
Possesses the ability to make minor illnesses and blights. Lucia is blackmailing him for a crime unknown, commanding his unwavering loyalty.

Jaromir

Blood Prince Jaromir, the Mender
The doctor of the surviving Ancients. He is in possession of the Gift.

Qin

Blood Prince Qin, the Ascended
He is considered a greedy coward by his peers, as he took a payment from Lucia and went into hiding, never to be seen again.

Taryn

Blood Prince Taryn, the Blade
Lucia's bodyguard due to taking a stage three love potion and being enslaved by his emotions.

Marcus Hartson

A close friend to the Ancients and Neala's former mate. After his mating bond was severed by Lucia, he was poisoned by her cursed blood and grew increasingly insane as the years passed. Died in an honorable duel with his son Julian after he drove the family to the brink of ruin from countless wars with other vampires. Deceased as of *Blood Curse*.

Other

Nyah

Queen of Vampires
Banished to the Fell Lands in *Blood Curse* due to Lucia's machi-

nations for her throne. The first Alchemyst and Adrius's lost mate.

Izell Firebrand

Considered to be the oldest fae alive. She's been through a lot and has learned to keep her true thoughts hidden under a thick layer of cynicism. She's a distant ancestor to Keegan Firetree, much to his chagrin.

Sorsha Shadestone

An astral fae Sorceress with the true sight ability. She was born in the Fell Lands, but her father gave her to Neala to raise, who adopted her alongside her brother-by-circumstance, Keegan. She is petite, sweet, and still sometimes acts like a teenager when she lets her guard down.

Keegan Firetree

An astral fae Blade who comes off tight-lipped and reserved. He was adopted by Neala alongside Sorsha and took on his adoptive mother's warrior persona.

Ashaela Dread

A cagy and sarcastic Unseelie fae who accompanies Sorsha and Keegan. She is a Spellbreaker and trained assassin who relies heavily on her shadow magic.